BLOOD
REFLECTION

RONN READ

OakTara

WATERFORD, VIRGINIA

Blood Reflection

Published in the U.S. by:
OakTara Publishers
P.O. Box 8
Waterford, VA 20197

Visit OakTara
at **www.oaktara.com**

Cover design by Muses9 Design
Cover image man in hallway © iStockphoto.com
Back cover image, blood © Jon Fife, j/f/photos

ISBN: 978-1-60290-193-3

TO MY WIFE, JANIE,
AND TO OUR FIVE KIDS

There is simply no way
to say thank you
for the "push" you guys gave
to get this book written.

Acknowledgments

I would like to thank OakTara Publishers, and especially Jeff Nesbit and Ramona Tucker, for taking the chance on a first-time author. May your commitment to give people like me an opportunity be greatly rewarded.

Prologue

"You've got blood on you."

He looked down at the bloody uniform. Of course he had blood on him. He always had blood on him after one of these things. Usually neither he nor she took that much notice.

But this time was different. Not only in the amount of blood, caused by a spear thrust to the side to make sure the prisoner was truly dead, but because the man himself had been different. No screaming for mercy. No cursing of those who had falsely accused him, or even of the duty detail that carried out the execution. Not even an effort to stop the inevitable by fighting against the soldiers when they began the painful process of nailing his hands and feet. No—something was way out of the ordinary about this whole thing.

"I don't think there's any way I can do anything to…"

"Just throw it away!" He never wanted to see it again anyway.

"Throw it away? Throw it away? Do you know how much work it's going to take me to make you another before…"

"Throw it away! You won't need to make me another. I'm never going back there. I'm never doing that again. I've served way beyond my commission. I can give my notice tomorrow and be done with the whole thing. And that's what I'm going to do. Throw it away."

She backed down. She'd seen him like this a few times before. He had always hated his job, but it seemed he had gotten much worse about it lately, which had only made him meaner. She had to admit, though, this time he didn't seem mean.

But what she did see in him made her even more afraid. She saw fear.

"Throw it away," he mumbled again.

"That's the place—that's where he went in."

The two men crouched behind a low wall on the narrow street. Though it was late and there was little possibility of being seen, they weren't supposed to be out this late on a holy night. They would be stopped if they were seen, and there would certainly be questions as to their purpose.

"Are you sure?" Malchion knew his young friend was sure, but he asked anyway. He knew the importance and had volunteered to follow the officer from the crucifixion to let Malchion know if he had ever stopped to remove his cloak. They both knew the importance of the cloak—or, more importantly, the blood on that cloak: the blood of the Master Himself. Juday had made sure that they knew, and had given them both plenty of incentive to make sure they somehow retrieved the Teacher's blood, no matter what it took.

"He hasn't left my sight since he finished up and left the hill. I followed him directly here. I'm sure."

"I don't know how this will do us much good—just knowing where he lives. I have no intention of breaking into the home of a Roman centurion to try to steal his cloak out from under his nose!"

"But we must. You saw The Hill," his young friend said. "There were too many people tramping all over to give us opportunity to get anything from there. And you saw the centurion! He was covered in blood. We'll never get the robe those soldiers gambled over. This is our only chance."

"Chance." Malchion snorted. "That's a good call. We might as well have tried to join in that game of chance with those soldiers as to try to break in there and get this one's uniform! There's just no way. And I'm not sure that I'm willing to chance my own life for this strange request of Simeon, no matter how much he pays."

Malchion looked at the young man beside him. Like himself, the young man had abandoned much to follow the Teacher; yet, like himself, he was an outsider from the group that had been with Jesus for several years. They had not been there to witness many of the miracles, and they certainly had not heard many of his teachings firsthand.

Simeon, the leader of their small band, had never been accepted into the circle of disciples, though he had followed the Master for quite some time. He *had* heard the sermons, or at least many of them—whenever Jesus had spoken publicly. And he had passed them on to those who, like him, were outsiders. He had told them of Jesus' teachings and had taught them especially about the importance of His blood. They didn't know before this day if all these things were true. But when they heard from His disciples what Jesus had said as he served the Passover meal to them, just the night before, it all made sense. Now they knew. They both knew. He was the One. His blood was their hope. So they had followed.

They knew Jesus was dead. Though for safety's sake they had stayed far removed from most of what had happened this day, they had seen enough. They had heard the cries of intense pain when his hands had been nailed, and together they had watched as he agonized through the labor of death by crucifixion. They stayed far enough away, yet ventured as close as possible in hopes of seeing something—anything—that would help them to remember this Man whom they had given themselves to. As sundown approached they and the others had watched the soldiers break the legs of the two on either side of the Teacher—and they had watched in disbelief as the head of the crucifixion detail had thrust his spear through the Man's side. A bloody gush had poured from the wound, spilling onto the soldier, covering his cloak in blood.

That's when Juday, another one of the more distant disciples, had approached them, Simeon himself at his side. "We need the cloak."

Malchion and his young friend were to follow this centurion to his house, wait until he was asleep, break in, and steal the cloak. "What a treasure that would be!" they agreed. "What a way to always remember and continually worship the Teacher," Malchion ventured.

No, Simeon had told them. It was not the cloak—it was the blood. There was no other way to atone for their shame, than with His blood. The plan was simple. Follow the cloak, for on it was their salvation in blood.

It had seemed like a good idea...then. Now, as Malchion waited, it seemed like a foolish death wish. But maybe death would be okay.

What did he have to live for now anyway?

Malchion leaned against the small wall. As he thought about all that had happened on this horrible day, he prayed. How had all this happened, and what could ever replace what he had felt over these months?

"What is that?" whispered his young friend. Stirring himself from his thoughts, Malchion peered over the wall toward the dwelling of the soldier. "She's carrying something out like it is *cursed*." They stared at her, then turned and looked in amazement at each other.

It was the cloak. And she was throwing it away.

One

"**Y**ou're weird, kid." John had heard that many, many times—usually just before he hit the person who said it. He was weird.

This time, though, it was the new kid. And this time he didn't get angry. What he did do was probably worse. He threw up on the guy.

What John did that led to the upchuck *was* weird. He had just tried to swallow a live cicada.

There was no way John Turner belonged at Batterson College. On their own his parents never could have afforded the pricey tuition, and he did not fit the Batterson profile. Most of these guys would go on to graduate school at Harvard or Princeton, then on to some outstanding career in law or even politics. Even if he wanted, John wouldn't likely make it anywhere for a post-graduate degree. His family didn't have the pedigree—or the money that went with it. He was only at Batterson for two reasons: his parents were missionaries, so he had been given reduced tuition, and he could play football. The Batterson Bears needed a strong left guard to defend their star quarterback, and John Turner was their man.

Always the biggest kid in school, without really having an athletic build, he was simply large. On more than one occasion he had been called "The Hulk" as he grew up, in reference to the comic book character. He wasn't really fat—just big. Too big for the regular uniform of Batterson—the gray pants and the maroon blazer—he was forced to wear gray sweats, making him look strange and feel very uncomfortable. The tight jacket certainly didn't help. Plus, it seemed no matter how short he cut his thick, black hair, it usually ended up growing out too fast and too wild to be combed into civility. Perpetually looking like he needed a shave, the five o'clock shadow didn't have the sexy *Miami Vice* look; rather, it was looked more like that of a binge drinker. Since there was no way he could button the top button around his too-big neck, wearing the school tie "according to regs" was out of the question. It always seemed to hang way too low from his neck, yet it was never quite long enough to cover his belly. The fact he had always been taller than most classmates and now taller than most people, led him to walk a bit hunched over, as though needing to be at eye level with those he came into contact. That combination, plus the fact he was never afraid to speak his mind, no matter the audience, caused many people to think him a bit strange. Most voiced their opinion one way or the other. Weird was, in fact, the most common word. His normal reaction was to simply come at the accuser with fists flying. His anger had taken on legendary status, and few people who knew him challenged him.

Even though John was there on scholarship, spending money was tight—and John *needed* his nightly pizza. So, to get money from all these rich snobs, he had taken to challenging them that he could eat just about anything. It had started one day in Physiology and Anatomy class when they were dissecting a cow's eye.

"Please take the eye out of the specimen jar and place it on the Petri dish at your table. I will return with scalpels and study guides in a few moments." Dr. Tyler went into his office just off the lab. As soon as Tyler was gone one of the snobs taunted, "Hey, Turner—this thing looks like your midnight snack last night!" Though his first reaction was, as usual, anger, he had to admit that it did indeed look somewhat like the lump of marshmallow crème and chocolate he had inhaled the night before.

"Maybe you should take one of these back to the dorm for tonight's snack!"

In the midst of the stifled laughter that ensued from the comment, John fumed. Taking a step toward his antagonists, he was suddenly struck with a thought. "What's the matter—you don't think I could eat one of these?"

The laughter stopped.

"No way, dude. That thing's been soaking in formaldehyde for who knows how long. You'd be sicker than a dog if you ate that!"

"How much?"

"Money? Dude, I'd give five bucks to see you eat that thing—and throw up!"

The laughter started up again, but John wasn't biting. "Five—is that all? Like you said, man—this is gonna make me sicker than a dog. That ought to be worth a lot more than five bucks!"

The first snob stepped forward. "I'll give ten—and I'll even provide some further pickling juice to help you get it down." He pulled a flask from his blazer.

Several more students stepped forward with cash—mostly ones, but a couple more fives. John looked at the bulbous glob sitting in the Petri dish before him.

"Do it! Do it!" the students mouthed in mock cheer. They didn't want to make so much noise that Dr. Tyler would come out of his study and stop the proceedings. Wondering how he got himself into messes like this, John tried to hold off the actual deed without looking like he chickened out. Maybe Dr. Tyler would hear their ruckus and stop him before he had to down it. Picking it up cautiously, he held the eye in his fingers and, with the glazed pupil facing out, held it up to his own eye and "glared" at the young men surrounding him with the dripping eyeball.

"Nobody knows the trouble I've seen!" he mimicked. This got a stifled laughter from the group, two or three of them having to hold their sleeves over their mouth to keep from laughing right out loud and bringing Tyler out.

"Come on, wimp." It was the chump with the flask. The guy who had made fun of him in the first place, Jason Collier. Talk about wimp! "Your money's on the table, so are you going to eat that thing? Or perhaps you really are just a great, big wimp."

In one quick motion, so quick that many of the guys would miss it, though they would never admit to it, telling even their children years later that they were "eye" witnesses of the fabled event, John popped the cow eye into his mouth. Swallowing it whole, he grabbed the money off the table and, with a fistful of dollars, punched Collier in the eye. While Collier yelped in pain, the others scattered to their seats as Dr. Tyler came charging out of his office. Though John would spend the rest of that day in detention, it was worth every minute and every penny. The extra large hand-tossed pepperoni pizza he had that night never tasted so good.

Since that day in the lab he had been challenged to eat many, many strange things—and eating them had kept pizza money in his pocket. So there was nothing unusual when someone picked a live locust off a tree on campus and challenged "Hey Cyclops!"—his new nickname since the eyeball episode—"Ten bucks says you can't eat this thing *live.*"

He took it from the kid. It was about four inches long and had veined, transparent wings, fly eyes that seemed to stare at him in defiance, and a row of claw-foot ending legs on its underside. It wasn't too big, but no way did John want to take it in bites; he had learned from the cow-eye episode that swallowing whole was the way to go.

"Ten bucks? No thank you. That's not enough to take on this monster!" He started to put it back on the tree trunk.

"Fifty bucks." Fifty bucks! John had never been given more than a handful of cash for the various oddities he had put in his stomach. He turned to see who was so generous—or stupid. It was the new kid.

"Fifty bucks," he repeated. This kid just screamed cool. He had the maroon Batterson blazer slung over his shoulder, his tie undone and his shirttail out, and he stood off to the side of the small crowd of boys, nonchalantly sipping a Coke and leaning against a tree. Though he was tall and thin—even somewhat gangly, he held himself with a posture that showed extreme confidence—but in a warm way, not at all cocky. John could tell he had class: the angular face, the neatly cropped hair, the manicured nails, even the perfect and somewhat exotic darker complexion, but he could also tell he knew how to have fun. He acted like spending fifty dollars to see someone eat a live locust was an everyday occurrence! Who knows? Maybe it was. With a broad smile revealing perfect and brilliantly white teeth, and his dark eyes dancing under the rounded eyebrows, he handed the Coke to John, took out his wallet, and waved a fifty-dollar bill in front of him.

"Fifty bucks. Let's see it, big boy."

Once again, as so many times before, the chant began. "Do it. Do it. Do it."

John looked at the fifty-dollar bill, then at the big bug once more. Closing his eyes, he put it "head-down" into his mouth and started swallowing. But unlike the cow eye and most other things he'd eaten for a price, this thing didn't want to be swallowed. He got it past his gullet, but then it started using its pincers to try to climb back up. John started gagging as he tried valiantly to swallow, but the creature's battle was choking him. He started doing everything he could think of. He stretched his neck up as high as he could and violently massaged it, trying physically to move the locust down. The guys gathered around him, howling in laughter at his antics. He could feel his eyes bugging out and his face turning red. Couldn't they tell he wasn't playing around? He was choking, and he could not swallow.

The Coke! He still had it in his hand! Tipping the can up and swallowing like mad, he finally washed the battling bug down his throat. Suddenly he was not feeling so good. Was that thing flying around in his stomach?

"You're weird, kid."

John looked up at the new kid, ready to agree—when it all came back up. Coke, cicada, and whatever mystery meat the cafeteria had served a few minutes before. All over the new kid's shoes.

And that's how John Turner met Brock Auzman.

Two

Batterson Academy was founded in 1844 by missionaries of The Haimaelien Brothers to train their young while they served in the field as well as to train the next generation "the faith." The Academy, which it was rarely called, did both with excellence. Eventually adding university level classes equivalent to two years of college, it became known as one of the best prep schools in the country, producing more Ivy League alum than any private academy in the nation and, as a result, more business, law, medical, and political leaders than any other school of its kind. Partly because of that fact and partly because of the rather palatial façade of the main administration building, complete with turrets, Batterson was known as "The Castle"— the place where kings were made.

For the past couple of decades, however, Batterson had been a castle with a problem. There was the cheating scandal of 1967 when eleven students were expelled, including the son of a prominent alumnus, causing Dr. Malcom Forrester, Headmaster, to lose his job. In spite of the heroic reputation-saving actions he had taken before the scandal broke as well as the ones afterward, one simply did not expel the son of the third highest donor to the school.

That was closely followed by the years of challenge under the new headmaster, Dr. Stanley Johns. He had come in with a progressive viewpoint, allowing students much more leeway, feeling that they should be allowed to voice their opinions regarding the Vietnam War, the draft, and even the possibility of allowing young women to matriculate at Batterson. Drawing the wrath of many supporters and alumni, the dress code had been relaxed where it concerned hair length and facial hair. Johns, too, found out that the board would only take so much complaining from donors, even if it meant firing a retired two-term United States Senator.

For the past ten years, therefore, the job of keeping students, faculty, staff, and alumni—especially alumni—happy, had fallen on the stooped shoulders of Dr. William Stoker. And so far he had done a decent, though not outstanding, job. While nothing great or progressive had happened over these years, nothing scandalous had either. For most of the board, that was good enough. A few complained Batterson had lost its standing as the premier proving ground for leaders—there hadn't been a Batterson grad on the front cover of *Time* for years. They were outvoiced, however, by those who recalled the last grad in national news had been photographed being led away in handcuffs down the front steps of the federal courthouse, having just been found guilty of insider trading. "Fraud! From a Batterson grad! Better *no* publicity than *that kind*" had been the typical reaction of most of the board and alumni. Dr. Stoker kept his head low, put in his hours, kept his staff and faculty in check, and pretty much "flew under the radar" year after boring year.

Most blamed football for the change. If Batterson was no longer going to be the birthplace of kings, perhaps it could at least be known as the birthplace of quarterbacks. Though many of the alumni might not have considered football to be a gentleman's sport, they certainly were impressed and pleased when Chad Melton led the team to the League Championship two straight years. And donations to Batterson greatly improved when another graduate, Douglas Westover, led them to the national championship game two years after that and was drafted in the first round. Many donors started giving to specific scholarship funds to help recruit more athletes who could never have entered Batterson on their academic prowess, but offered much athletically.

At the same time, though, there were still many who felt that football—or at least giving scholarships to football players—was leading Batterson down the same slippery slope the school had experienced years before. They blamed these "bull-necked behemoths" for most of the discipline problems that seemed to be troubling the school once again. This was especially true when the local news printed a security camera photo of three young men, who fortunately for the school could not be identified in the grainy photo, stealing a sign from the front of a closed store. Everyone knew the fact they were never publicly identified or disciplined had nothing to do with the dean's good graces but everything to do with that week's game against the rival Newman College Lions.

Though John was not one of the three culprits, he was guilty by association. Every generalization and insinuation leveled at those who had stolen the sign fit him and everyone knew it. Most people assumed he was only at Batterson because of a football scholarship. Not much of an academic, he was known to be a prankster, and to stretch the rules on more than one occasion. But he would never have done this. This was breaking the law, and if there was one thing John was a stickler for, it was doing the right thing.

So John Turner was mad. He heard the whispers, heard the stifled laughter that seemed to erupt every time he left a classroom or the cafeteria. And he definitely heard the warning Dr. Stoker gave in convocation about the fact such behavior would not be tolerated at Batterson, even if it meant losing a football game. If they were going to blame football players, why not go ahead and do the investigation and prove who had actually stolen the sign? Why allow all the players to be implicated?

Or maybe that was their plan. In fact, maybe they hoped that by the implication John would just go away quietly. He had certainly not been quiet over the administration's dealings on several occasions. More than once he had visited Dr. Stoker's office to voice opposition about how he was leading, or not. And when Stoker didn't listen, John had taken his opposition public, or at least to the Commons, where students were allowed to speak out on topics without reprimand (a carry-over from Dr. Johns' tenure). Maybe Stoker wanted him to duck tail and run by allowing his name to be muddied. John would not run. But he was angry.

Even though his anger boiled to the top during the game, John was able to play his usual focused game on the field, directing most of his ire at the middle linebacker whose reputation was bigger than his talent. But each time the offense ran off the field, no matter how much John tried to avoid it, he couldn't help but see Dr. Stoker sitting there at mid-field with the president, founder, and namesake of the Newman Lions, "Doctor" Lawrence Newman, the biggest hypocrite John had ever known. Here was a man who spoke of values and morals from his bully pulpit, yet lived a lavish lifestyle off of the donations of the many who ignorantly followed his teachings. Seemingly he was building his academy under the guise of "training young lions for leadership," but John was certain the man was more concerned about building his own legacy. His stomach curled to see Stoker up there "wining and dining" Dr. Newman, trying to impress him so he could get something from him, John figured.

In truth, Lawrence Newman's doctorate was honorary, not earned, though that never stopped Newman from using the title. He was someone who expected to be catered to. He carried his tall frame with dignity and he was…well, the only word that would come to someone's mind if he would attempt to describe him was *regal*. That is, if that person was trying to be kind. Behind his back people referred to him more as *pompous* than *regal*. Even as he arrived at his seat at the stadium he waited until some underling came with a towel to wipe it clean and place a cushion on it. His hand-tailored suit would not be defiled by sitting on a cold aluminum bench like some commoner. Like a cotton tuft, his full head of glorious white hair shone in the sunlight, and his perfect teeth seemed to glow in contrast to his perfect tan. Though he wasn't the physical specimen he had been twenty years prior, he still worked at making himself seem that way. Yes, Lawrence Newman *expected* to be wined and dined.

These thoughts were on John's mind as he watched the defense once again shut down the Lions on a three and out. So far the game was scoreless, though the Lions seemed to be wearing down the Batterson defense. Pulling on his helmet after Denton Frew returned the punt all the way to the forty-yard line, John turned to see the two bigwigs at that very moment looking right at him. His face turned as crimson as the Batterson Bears jersey he wore as he imagined that they must have been talking about him. Maybe about the stolen sign. Maybe accusing him. Maybe talking about how he'd never be at Batterson if he couldn't play football. Probably agreeing with each other that he would never amount to anything.

John ran out onto the field. First and ten at the forty-three yard line. Six minutes to go in the third quarter. Zero to zero score. John knew all of this but didn't care one bit about any of it. All he could think of was the conversation he was now imagining in his head between Newman and Stoker. He heard the play the Bear's quarterback called in the huddle, and knew it was a running play away from him. He would be responsible for blocking the linebacker. With the rest of the offensive team, he moved to the line. As the quarterback barked out the signal, John was at full boil. When he called "hike," John threw his opposing guard out of the way and went full bore after Farnsworth, the overhyped linebacker. He plowed him over, knocking him several yards backward, even knocking his helmet off.

Burns, the tailback, was tackled by the weak-side linebacker, but John didn't even see it. Farnsworth had jumped up immediately, grabbed his helmet, and came up swinging. He caught John square on the side of his helmet, nearly knocking him out in spite of the protective covering. Before John could even clear his head, both benches were emptying and the brawl was on. As the ringing in his head finally cleared, John could hear the teams fighting, mostly just yelling and pushing each other around, since they were all wearing full pads and helmets. He could hear the crowd yelling, some for the teams to stop, others egging the battle on.

But above it all, one booming baritone voice stood out: "Doctor" Lawrence Newman. "Boys! Boys! BOYS!" he yelled, with his hands held outward to them, pushing downward with each shout, as though he could squelch the fight through some sort of Moses-like power.

John stared in disbelief, then started walking toward the tall man, then sprinting—rage boiling in every fiber of his being.

Jumping up onto the protective chainlink fence, usually meant more to keep fans off the field rather than players from entering the stands, John began screaming at Newman: *"You slimy snake! You empty windbag! SHUT UP! You have NOTHING to say! You have NOTHING worth hearing! You SLIMY SNAKE!"*

As he watched Newman's face harden into flint and his eyes narrow to slits that could have shot lasers through him, John felt hands dragging him off the fence. Several of the Lions as well as his own coaches and players were pulling him away as he continued to scream at Lawrence, with the crowd screaming back at him. In the middle of the melee, standing on his seat with his always perfectly-in-place hairpiece flying backwards, mild-mannered, boring, fly-below-the-radar Dr. William Stoker was beet-red, screaming at the top of his lungs, "That's IT, Turner! YOU ARE OUT OF HERE!"

Finally, above all the noise, all the screaming, all the unbelievable happenings around him, one voice rose above the rest. John saw Brock standing there calmly, looking right at him, telling him, "John Turner, be the better man."

Three

"Hey, Wiz. Why did you come to Batterson instead of Newman? They've certainly had a lot more success lately with graduates getting elected to big offices."

John was doing anything to keep his mind off what was going to be happening at the Discipline Council in just a few hours. He had taken to calling Brock "Wiz," as in Wizard of Auzman. The nickname had started because of Brock's last name, but had stuck as many came to recognize that it was nearly impossible to truly know the man behind the public curtain.

"Not my choice, dude. I was a minor, remember? And besides, so what?" Brock was lying on his bunk tossing a basketball up in the air and catching it, working on the perfect release point for his jump shot. Like John, all he could think about was the Discipline Council. He knew that Stoker was not going to back down on his threat, and he probably had the backing of every single board member, if not most of the faculty and student body. John had crossed a lot of people in his time at Batterson, stepped on many, many toes, challenging just about everyone from Stoker and the board to various faculty all the way down to students, including Brock himself! He had firm convictions about lots of things, wasn't about to stay quiet about them, and would rather fight than compromise. But he was John! That's just the way he was. And now he was going to be kicked out.

"Don't give me that. Your parents would have sent you anywhere you wanted to go, and it's obvious that they want the same thing you want—a career in politics. So why not Newman? They've got the best poly-sci around, and Lawrence himself has got some kind of connections. You know that. So, I repeat, man: why not Newman?"

Brock stopped tossing the basketball. He sat up on the edge of his bed and stared—no, *he glared*—at his best friend in the whole world.

"*Hey, Clops!* Get this through your thick head. *I don't want a* career *in politics!* That's *not* me, man. That, and *all* this—" Brock waved his hand around the room but meant the whole school—"is *him*, man, not me. *He* chose this school. *He* chose my field of study. *He* chose my advisor. The only thing he didn't choose, yet somehow he's probably somewhere behind all of *this*, is having *you* as my roommate! But believe me, he'll be one of the happiest ones around when you move out today."

Silence. Brock realized he'd said too much. John probably had suspicions that his dad had troubles with him, but he'd kept it pretty much to himself that he actually did not want Brock hanging around John at all. And he wasn't being the greatest comfort to his friend by being so pessimistic about The Council, even though they both knew there wasn't much reason for optimism. Stoker was a man on a mission, and it seemed a foregone conclusion that he wanted John's head on a platter.

"Hey, man, I'm sorry. You just pushed a button, you know? I didn't choose Batterson—and really didn't choose to go away to school at all. I guess if I'd had a choice and had wanted to make one to leave home, I probably would have chosen Newman, but only because they got girls on campus. This *all male* stuff—present company included—is for the birds. That's the only reason I'd have chosen Lions over Bears."

"Wizman, you can pull that stuff on other people, but get off it. This is me. You can blame your dad for being here. That part might be true. I don't know and don't really care, but I do know you like what you're doing here. I watch you study that stuff and it's nothing like when you're studying anything else. You eat that poly-sci stuff up, and it likes you, too. You love to make things happen. You're a leader from the word *go*. People listen to you, and you make them follow you. Heck, you could probably walk in that Council and have them apologizing to *me!*"

Brock shot up off his bunk. "Clops, you're a genius! Why didn't I think of that? Of course I need to go in there. You're right. I can argue for you. They'll listen to me. They have to listen. They have to."

"Brock, get this through *your* thick head. They aren't going to listen, not even to you, 'the great and wonderful Wizard.' I blew it. I let them get to me, *and* I hit that kid—hard! I'm lucky he wasn't hurt. I could never have forgiven myself for that. But I can live without this place. I never fit in here anyway. Maybe *I* should transfer over to Newman," John finished with a sarcastic laugh.

"No, Clops, you don't get it. It's really true what I'm saying. They *have* to listen to me. I don't know what kind of strings my old man pulled to get me in here, but I do know that now that I'm here, they want me here. I mean they *want* me here. All I have to do is tell them that if they kick you out, I'm going too. Trust me. They *have* to listen."

They were interrupted by a knock on the door. It was Jason Collier, a graduate assistant for the Dean of Men, sent by The Council to summon John. "C'mon, Turner. Time to face the hangman." He was way too happy about the whole thing. Brock felt like punching him.

As John walked out, Brock stopped the escort. "I'm coming too, Collier. The law allows everyone to have legal representation, and I'm gonna be his."

"Suit yourself, Auzman. As if it's gonna do any good. What are you gonna do—call character witnesses that tell The Council what a warm fuzzy guy Turner really is? That his tirade against Lawrence was an aberration? 'No really, your Honor—he's everyone's best friend,'" he mocked in falsetto.

That was it. Brock no longer just felt like hitting him. He went ahead and simply hit him, knocking Collier onto the floor. Then he caught up to John.

"Trying to get kicked out with me? What are you thinking, man?"

"You kiddin' me? Not even Stoker likes that chump."

Four

"**M**r. Turner, please stand and face the Board."

John stood, and Brock stood up next to him, feeling very much like a defense lawyer. Though more nervous than John, he realized that he liked the feeling.

"Mr. Turner, you are a great disappointment to this board. You are one of the last mission scholarship students at Batterson, and it was the hope of this board that you might actually follow in the footsteps of your father. In our decision the board has taken into great account your father's longtime service, as well as some other factors. Since you are only five months from graduation, making it nearly impossible for you to get into any other school at this late of date, and, since young Mr. Auzman is willing to vouch for and hold you accountable for your behavior during these last five months, it is the majority decision of this board, a majority by only the slimmest of margins, to allow you to remain at Batterson. You will be on probation throughout your remaining time, which means you may not leave the campus without supervision or you will be immediately expelled without further hearing. The same applies should you violate any—and Mr. Turner, we do mean *any*—of the standards of behavior as presented in *The Batterson Handbook*. You will apologize to Dr. Stoker for your outburst as well as to Dr. Newman from Newman College. And you will apologize to the student body for embarrassing the name of Batterson at next week's convocation. Finally, you will pay restitution to the Star Coffee Shoppe for the sign stolen from their front entrance in the amount of eighty dollars. Do I make myself clear?"

Benjamin Foster, chairman of the board, looked up from the page he'd been reading from and peered at John over his reading glasses. His white hair was hanging down and he brushed it back with his free hand, finally removing his reading glasses. John had been listening very carefully as Foster read the board's statement and was drawn to the steely blue eyes of the man who was giving him the news of his second chance. He didn't see warmth in those eyes. He didn't see compassion. Yet he had just heard there would be mercy. What he deserved, punishment for his wrong-doing, had just been removed. He would not be expelled. Realizing he hadn't yet exhaled from holding his breath during the reading of the statement, he finally released a long, slow breath and looked over the rest of the board before he responded.

John could tell Dr. Stoker was certainly not one of what must have been a slim majority of board members to vote for his stay of execution. John's collar felt two sizes too small as he listened to the board's statement. His forehead was dripping with sweat, and he kept trying to mop it with his handkerchief as he awaited the end of the proceedings. Other board members had extremely hard looks on their faces as well, but he could almost tell the ones who had voted for him to stay and those who were not on his side at all. The main difference was how they held their posture. Some leaned back in their chairs with their arms crossed in angry defiance. Others leaned forward with elbows on the table, hands cupped in front of them, as though imploring the young man in front of them to take the probation and prove himself worthy by meeting the conditions set forth.

John had not had a chance to speak at all in his defense, as Brock had done a masterful job of explaining that John was, indeed, very sorry and would, indeed, apologize to the board—on and on and on. But the issue of the sign had not come up. Nor had one other subject.

"Perfectly clear, sir. I understand, and I gratefully acknowledge the opportunity to graduate from Batterson. Sir..."

"And do you understand..."

"Sir?" John interrupted.

What was he up to? "Don't do it," whispered Brock. "We won, man. Don't do this!" But he knew John and knew that if John had something to say, he was going to say it, no matter what.

"Yes, Mr. Turner?"

"Sir, I am very sorry that I embarrassed you and Batterson by my behavior at the game. It was not my intention to embarrass the school's reputation. But Sir—Sirs—I will not apologize for what I said to *Mister*

16

Newman. I do not hold him in high regard. In fact, I think I was a bit too kind in calling him a snake. And I did not take the aforementioned sign, nor had I any part in taking it. I will pay the coffee shop for a new sign if that will help the reputation of Batterson Academy, but I will not do so if it is taken as a sign of guilt. Dr. Stoker—I do apologize to you, again, for embarrassing you in front of people at the football game. And I will apologize to the student body at the next convocation. I will also abide by the remainder of the requirements, as long as the board and Dr. Stoker are aware that I will not be silent if and when I see wrong being done, whether by students, faculty, or administration."

Whatever restraint Dr. Stoker had been showing up to now hit the breaking point and he rose up out of his seat. "You pompous, arrogant, ungrateful snot. I told this board you were undeserving of their mercy, and you prove me right. You are so gone, so out of this school, you arrogant—"

"Doctor Stoker, sit down." Board chairman Benjamin Foster had now turned his steely eyes onto the headmaster. "It is not your call to decide if Mr. Turner is gone from this school. That is a board decision, and the board has voted."

Dr. Stoker did not sit down. He stood there with his mouth gaping open in disbelief. Had Foster not heard the arrogance and absolute rebellion against the board's conditions? He couldn't believe his ears.

"Mr. Turner, you border on insolence. However, since it has not been proven or even investigated but only assumed..." Clearing his throat for emphasis, Foster glanced at the still standing but slowly sitting headmaster. "Since it has only been assumed you were part of the theft of the coffee shop sign, we will accept your claim of innocence and your willingness to pay for the stolen property, with no assumption of guilt from such action. And, speaking only for myself and not for the board, I agree with your assessment of the dear *Mister* Newman, so will rescind the requirement of an apology to him. In the future, however, you might be more careful of publicly sharing your insights. Others might not be so understanding, and that mouth has and will get you in trouble. With no further action required, this session is dismissed."

Brock couldn't believe it. Neither could the stunned Dr. Stoker, or many of the other bloodthirsty board members or attending faculty.

Even Jason Collier, standing off to the side, having been ready to personally escort John to his dorm room to supervise his packing, stood there with his mouth hanging wide open—and his eye rapidly swelling closed.

John Turner simply stood there with a huge smile. Brock hadn't seen that smile in a long, long time. Instantly he thought of the last time he had seen it. When Brock's mom had brought out her famous "death by chocolate" triple layer cake and set it in front of John for his birthday. *That* was the smile and the look he now saw on John Turner's face. Sheer delight.

Five

They weren't two steps out of the "Castle" before Brock started in on John.

"You are either the luckiest man alive, or you're so stupid people think you can't make it if they don't give you a break! What the heck were you thinking? When you opened that fat mouth of yours— 'Sir?'—I was lookin' for a hole to climb into, 'cause I thought old man Stoker was gonna explode. Did you see the veins in his forehead? I didn't know someone could get that angry. Really, I thought he was going to explode."

"*Wiz,* shut up! I was there, remember? And, honestly, I'm a bit worried about Stoker. I think he *might* explode, as in stroke out, then I'll have *that* on my hands. I wasn't trying to make him mad. I'm just not going to sit there and be told I'm not allowed to speak out on things around here, or anywhere else…that's just not *right.* And Newman, the man and the institution, are not right. I don't know what it is, but I do know I don't like it, and I know that *I will not apologize.*"

"Okay, okay, I get it. You don't have to start in on me too. I think we all know you don't like—how did you put it? *'Mister* Newman'? That was classic. Just classic. I wish he could have been there, especially when Foster *agreed* with you. Man, oh, man, would I have loved to see his face."

As often happened when Brock and John walked and talked, especially when he was this pumped up, Brock ended up doing an awful lot of the talking while John seemed to drift off into another world. Brock could see it happening now. John was no longer in the same conversation.

"All right, Clops. What's going on in there?" He playfully rapped his knuckles on the side of his big friend's head.

"What *is* wrong with that place, Brock? I gotta be honest with you. There are some things about some of the guys from over there that I really, truly admire. And there are some things that come out of there that are right on. But they just don't jive. Not with him. Some things about him scare me to death. You say you'd like to have seen his face? Well, I *did* see his face. When I yelled those things at him, I saw evil. Pure, unadulterated evil. I thought the guy was just a big hypocrite, ya know? But hypocrisy is saying one thing and living another. He's no hypocrite, but I don't think I like what he lives. I don't know what it is—not yet. But whatever it is, it's evil. You know the phrase 'if looks could kill'? Look," he said, showing Brock his arm, "I've got chills thinking about it right now. And I'm sure he's not gonna be too thrilled to hear that not only am I still gonna be here, but that I refused to apologize to him."

"Clops, dude. Are you scared of him?"

"Him? No. Evil? Yes. And, my friend, he is evil. I don't know what's going to happen because of all this, but I can guarantee you, we have not heard the end of Doctor Newton Lawrence."

Brock looked up and saw the beginnings of that faraway look in his friend's eyes again. "And my guess is, he hasn't heard the end of John Turner."

And there, once more, was that smile.

Six

Lawrence Newman *was* angry. In fact, he was livid. He had gotten word through his well-established network of how the proceedings over at Batterson had gone, and what had been said. When he first got the news, he didn't react much, not to the messenger. He dismissed the young man, then went over to the hidden liquor cabinet and poured two fingers of single malt scotch, downing it in one drink. The liquid didn't do anything to stop the slow-building tension in the back of his neck, his "elevens" as he called them. And this kind of tension only built when he was downright angry. Which he was.

Newman prided himself on self-control. "Never let them see you sweat" had been his motto since entering public life, and he wasn't about to let some punk kid with an anger problem change that. But if the truth were told, he wasn't angry at John Turner. He didn't know the kid, and since the only time he had even seen him was when he was climbing up that fence, fully padded and still wearing his helmet, Newman didn't even think he'd know him if he saw him on the street. And he certainly had no intention of ever doing that. Turner was nothing. A nobody.

No. He wasn't angry at Turner. And he wasn't even angry that Turner would be staying at Batterson. Let them have him! Let them have one more graduate lowering their all-too-oft bragged about percentage of graduates going on to Ivy League schools. Let them have what his informant described as "the big lunk who walks around in those ridiculous sweat pants with his way-too-small Batterson blazer.'" What a fine example of their "cream of the crop" student body. Pouring another drink he took a long swallow, finally feeling its glow. The scotch mixed with the pleasant feeling of remembering that, after Turner was ejected from the game, the Lions had gone on to win the football game, their first victory over Batterson in several years.

In spite of the scotch and the tremendous sense of pride over the victory, he realized he was still angry. Not, though, he again confirmed to himself, at John Turner. He felt sure he knew who was truly behind those proceedings, and it sure wasn't that puppet board or its chairman, Benjamin Foster. He'd heard what Foster said when Turner—that punk—had insulted his character. He'd deal with Foster another time. He had ways to settle that score.

And Stoker? He was a joke. Stoker was like the stupid fufu dog his ex-wife used to pamper. She thought she was giving only the finest of organic health food to her stupid mutt, but Lawrence knew that, like any dog, it would come begging anytime it smelled whatever hash he threw together when the ex was gone. Stoker was just as eager to eat whatever Lawrence threw his way if he thought he was going to gain favor with any one of the politicians or corporate leaders Lawrence had in his power grip. Lawrence Newman had learned how to find what it was that people wanted, and he had ways to get those very things. All for a price, of course, though he didn't need their money nearly as much as the many other things he might get from them. Stoker thought he was gaining valuable face-time with some movers and shakers and thought he was going to be able to cash in someday. He had no idea what price he would have to pay on that "someday," when it would most benefit Newman or his namesake academy. *Stoker,* thought Newman out loud as he took another swallow, *what a putz.*

No, Lawrence only had to hear who had come to Turner's defense and he knew. As soon as he heard the name of Turner's defender, though he had no idea how Auzman had arranged it all, he knew. After all, it wasn't his first run in with the Auzman family.

Oh yes, Lawrence Newman *was* angry. He was angry at Mr. Michael B. Auzman. Or should he say *still* angry, even after all these years.

But this time, Auzman would pay.

Seven

Michael Auzman was not a popular man. Certainly not now, even though he had just been appointed—or was it anointed?—to carry out the plans of The Council. He knew, as did just about everyone in the group, that he would never have won a popular vote. But that wasn't how it was done. Popularity was not what mattered most for the leadership of this group.

Michael had never been popular. He wasn't what anyone would call good looking. His eyes, dark and hooded, were a bit too close together and always seemed to smolder with some sort of hidden anger. His nose was somewhat too long and pointy, and the tip of it would curiously bounce with each spoken word. Most people seemed to drift to that focal point if in conversation with Auzman, rather than look at the dark eyes. His hairline had started receding in his late teens, and he had never had much of a physique. His arms always seemed to be a bit too long and didn't even appear to swing correctly when he walked. It was like his whole body was somehow out of kilter. Nor was he athletic in any way. His shoulders were narrow, his legs were long and skinny, and he had virtually no chest. He would never win any kind of physical challenge, probably not even against a girl.

But he was smart. Intuitively so. He wouldn't win any contests for it; he wasn't that kind of smart. He just seemed to know the right thing to say or the right thing to do at the right time—that is, what was right for him. One other reason Michael was not very popular was because it seemed that he was always one step ahead of anyone else who might be trying to gain or do the same thing as he, yet it was like he stepped in from the sidelines just before another harder working runner was about to cross the finish line. That usually resulted in a lot of frustration, anger, and even revenge. Michael, however, was even good at knowing what type of revenge his opponents planned to exact, and even when, and somehow, even in that, he beat them to the punch.

His first experience of realizing that he didn't have to be stronger than others as long as he was smarter happened when he was a young man. He'd stumbled on his intuitive ability rather accidentally when he was invited to compete in a speech competition with the specific theme of euthanasia. His speech was mediocre. No wonder, as Michael himself was mediocre. But, somehow, when it came to points awarded, Michael won. It seems he was the only one who actually stayed true to the theme. While others had tried to prove or disprove the merits of mercy killing, Michael had simply given a speech on what it was, various methods of carrying it out, and why some societies did it. When he was awarded the content points, which weighed more heavily than delivery style points, he won. And those who had worked much harder on every aspect of their speech were angry. Over the years that had become the pattern, though Michael had no comprehension of such anger, for he was simply doing what came naturally—delivering valid facts in a mediocre way to make, not prove, his better point. Argue all you want, he would still be right. And you would be even angrier, because you knew, always, that he would never be more eloquent in his presentation than you. But you would never be more right than he.

That's what happened to Lawrence Newman. They were both on the fast-track to leadership and success, but in two very different ways. Michael just did his thing of showing facts, presenting absolutely correct points in his usual absolutely mundane way, absolutely impressing those over him time after time. When any topic of a moral or political nature arose, Michael—again, intuitively—presented the clearest, best, most factual arguments. He stuttered, stammered, and largely made his listeners want to pull the slow and painstakingly delivered words out of his mouth, but at the end of the day, he convinced.

Lawrence, on the other hand, was the classical silver-tongued orator. With his good looks, tall athletic build, and smooth communication skills, he could have been anything from a politician to a lawyer to a preacher, and many had encouraged him from each of those fields to pursue such a career. But Lawrence lacked something Michael possessed. Though Lawrence could present his arguments, even the very facts Michael presented, with much aplomb and emotion, something was missing. Conviction. He knew the facts, but they didn't move him. There was always a sense that he was just a little too polished, a little too fake. But he was just so good! So he, too, found himself on the leadership track. No—that's wrong. He pushed himself there, while Michael simply found himself there.

Whatever the source of their presence, everyone felt that presence. They were like two boxers who had risen to the top of their game, forcing all others into a second tier. It would always be Michael Auzman and Lawrence Newman who would be called up to present. It would always be their arguments to debate. It would always be one of them who would come out with the decision in hand. And that would almost always be Michael Auzman.

Not that Lawrence didn't try. He simply wasn't dazzling enough, or quick-witted enough, or even charming enough. Not to counterbalance the simple facts that Auzman laid out, no matter how painstakingly deliberate he was in doing so. One would think Auzman would be boring, but that halting, faltering, stammering delivery only seemed to captivate The Council even more, rather than causing them to fall asleep. In reality, Newman had to admit, he often found himself rapt with attention to hear the profound points his opponent laid out, even when he lost, which was most of the time.

None of those losses, however, hurt like that last one. All others paled in importance to it. And that time, unlike most others, Lawrence had been passionate. Not just eloquent, not just smooth, though he was both. He was simply himself. No, that time he had experienced the "missing ingredient" The Council always referred to: conviction. He *had* conviction on that one. He had argued, cajoled, eloquently presented his ideas, even broken down and cried. But he had lost. Only that time, he felt more than just a loss for himself and his pride. He felt a loss for mankind.

Mankind deserved better than what Michael B. Auzman could provide.

Eight

Michael was nervous, which was uncharacteristic for him. He had been called before The Council on numerous occasions and he simply came before them, presented facts—albeit dryly, boringly, and unceremoniously—then left. Their decision, what they did with those facts, was out of his hands and was, in all reality, none of his concern. If they listened to him, and made their decision in favor of what he was presenting, so be it. If not—if they chose to go in another direction from what he presented (which was rare)—so be it. Few if any of their decisions directly affected him, so he didn't really care one way or another.

But this time everything was different. Not only was he presenting something that would forever alter his life, but the whole world as well. Not given to theatrics or exaggerations, Michael would never have had such a bold thought—let alone ever make that bold of a statement—but he knew that this time the thought should be allowed to be in his heart, and shared. This time he needed passion, and he had it, for he stood on the brink of something that went way beyond simple facts. He stood where only a few men in history had ever stood, and that had been thousands of years before now. Those had been men who stood before kings and put them in their place; men who stood before priests and condemned them for their hypocrisy; men who stood before people who brought empty forms of worship and challenged them to know real faith. And now he stood with those men. He stood as the representative of God, poised to announce the coming Messiah...at least if The Council listened to his plan.

Of course they would not be hearing him only. Lawrence Newman would once again be his opponent, arguing against not only his plan, but his part in the plan. Perhaps that was the true motivation for Newman. Perhaps if he were presenting facts only, like he usually did,

Newman would simply fight against his facts and, as usual, lose. But he was fighting for himself this time. He was not just giving facts—he was giving himself and his future, not only before The Council, but, ultimately, before the world. He was sure Newman would not present his usual eloquent but empty opposition, for he knew Lawrence felt that he had as much vested interest in the outcome as Michael. For one of the only times that Michael could ever remember, both he and Lawrence would be extremely passionate about this outcome.

They would meet before The Council in the usual fashion. Each would spend time alone giving their points without interruption, then the two would meet together in a debate format to give counterpoint to their opponent. In reality, *opponent* was too strong of a word, for under usual argument, the two presenters would work together to make sure that all points were covered from every angle, so as to allow The Council opportunity to make their decision from a complete frame of reference. Though the two might have opposite viewpoints, their purpose was not to prove their point but, as stated, to give facts. The reason that Michael was held in such high esteem was because he had always fully understood his role up to this point. The reason that Newman had not found the same respect and recognition was because, quite simply, he had not.

Michael would go first. He had requested such, for he wanted The Council to know two things from the very beginning. One, that he was the one who had initiated the idea that led to the plan that would forever change the world, and two, that his plan included himself in a very hands-on way. He knew that both would hit The Council with a great amount of surprise. And he knew he would hit the trifecta when he did both with passion and a very well-rehearsed, even polished, presentation.

"Gentlemen. We can bring Him back...."

Nine

"John Turner, are you trying to lose weight? You're so much skinnier than the last time I saw you. Are you sick?" Brock's mother gave the big boy a hug, then stepped back to look at him again. "I'm going to make it my goal to put some weight back on you this week!"

"Hey, Mom, it's not his fault! Oh, wait...I guess it is. Ever since that little tiff he had with Dr. Stoker and the president over at Lawrence, he's on campus restriction. Meaning, no midnight runs for pizza. You should hear him beg. Every night it's, 'Wiz, dude, I'm dying. You've gotta go get me a pizza!' I'm ready to get a job as a delivery boy. Why's he so skinny? 'Cause I don't bring him a whole pizza every night."

Brock and John were going to make this one of the greatest spring breaks they'd experienced—by doing absolutely nothing. John's parents were too far away for him to visit, so Brock had asked his parents and they had agreed that John could spend the week with them. Quite honestly, they wanted to get to know this young man a bit better. Though he had visited them on several occasions over the past few years and he had always been a part of their visits to Brock, they didn't really know him all that well. Since he was their son's best friend and seemed to have a very strong influence on him, this was an opportunity to observe his character up close.

"Hi, Mrs. A. It won't take any time at all to put weight on around here. Thanks for inviting me, and I don't want you guys to worry. I'll try to stay out of Mr. Auzman's hair this week. No arguments. No challenges."

They both looked at him for a split second, then Brock burst out laughing. "Sure you will, buddy. Not a word, right? Especially when he's—oh, I don't know—watching *and commenting* on the news, listening *and commenting* about something on the radio, observing *and commenting* about the weather. Or, especially, when he makes some comment about *you.* Oh, I'm sure you'll keep very, very quiet. Right mom? We probably won't even know he's here."

"Brock Auzman, you be good. I know just what John's trying to say, and I appreciate the effort. But, John, you won't be any bother at all. And in spite of what *your friend*—" she feigned Brock a hard look— "says, you don't have to try to be quiet during any of those times. I happen to know for a fact that Michael always appreciates the mental challenge of debate, which is exactly why he does throw out many of those *comments* he makes." She threw another hard lock at Brock. *"Some people* just don't understand that. Now, John, what would you like to eat?"

"Thanks, Mrs. A. You always have a way of putting me at ease. I guess I'm just trying to say I'll *try* to not get things so heated around here, unlike times past. I don't know why, but I can't keep my mouth shut—especially around him. But I'll *try*...unless I'm eating! Anything you've prepared, I know it will be a great improvement over 'the caf.' What can I do to help?"

As they headed off toward the kitchen, Brock shouted out, playfully, "I guess I'll just get both our bags, then. Don't worry about me, Clops! You go get fattened up while I..."

"Brock. I thought I heard the car pull up. It's good to see you. I take it you had an uneventful trip? And how is John?"

Brock set the bags back down on the floor and crossed the room to shake his father's hand, simply because it was expected. "Good to see you, sir. Yes, we had an uneventful trip. John is fine, though Mom recognized immediately that he's hungry. They're in the kitchen. I'm taking our luggage upstairs."

Cold. Distant. Nothing but the facts. A typical "conversation" between the two. Brock grabbed the bags again and started up the stairs. Their relationship had been strained for several years but had reached the near breaking point a few years earlier when Michael had made the unilateral decision that Brock would be sent to Batterson that coming fall. Brock had argued—oh, how he argued—but he knew from the first salvo on that he'd never change the already-made-up mind of his father. He'd seen the man win too many arguments with his cold, factual, unbending style. Even then Brock had known it would do no good to try to get his mother on his side; to try to get her to change Michael's mind. She, too, had probably learned years before that it did no good. The man was a machine. Facts in; facts out. If you expected anything other than that—such as compassion, understanding, reasoning, or anything of the kind—you'd be sorely disappointed. Brock knew that from way too many frustrating experiences. So he no longer tried.

Michael watched his son manhandle two large duffel bags up the stairs. He stood in amazement to see how much the young man had grown—not just in stature, but in obvious maturity. No efforts at argument. No disrespect. Perhaps they would actually be civil to each other during this break.

Yet, Michael knew that he must begin a process during this break that would, potentially and most likely, further the rift between father and son. He had little hope that Brock had matured to the point that he could begin to understand Michael's reasons for his past actions. Or for his future plans. He hoped that Brock's friend John would be an ally, but he had little hope for that either. These thoughts ran through his mind as he watched Brock make it to the top of the stairway.

"Son. It's good to have you home. We'll talk later."

Ten

Later came all too soon. Supper that night was, as usual, mostly formal and distant. John did a great job of keeping the conversation going by telling all the right stories, by asking all the right questions of both Auzmans, and an equally great job of not asking the wrong questions—the ones guaranteed to set Michael off. Yet, to Brock, something was out of kilter. Normally it wouldn't have taken a question to set his father off—the man was just wired that way. But not tonight. He seemed preoccupied, but also somewhat glad to have the two boys at the table…probably a distraction to their normal, empty night. Several times Brock saw the older man looking at him, studying him, almost like he had something to say but wasn't sure how it would be received. Or, maybe he was sure—so he thought it best to not say anything at all. At least not tonight.

"So when you started running toward the fence, did you know what you were going to say? Or did you just say the first thing that came to your mind, calling him a snake?" his mother asked John.

They had been listening to him tell the story of his tirade against Lawrence Newman, but they couldn't see any humor behind the story at all. Brock expected no less from his father—facts in, facts out—but his mother usually had a great sense of humor about such things. She, too, seemed more concerned with digging for details of the story than picturing this big kid in full football gear hanging by his fingers and toes onto a chainlink fence, yelling at the distinguished founder and president of their rival school. As a result, the conversation was taking on more of an inquisition feel than the funny narrative John had intended. Someone needed to help Clops out of this before it got ugly, but Brock was afraid he might not be the right one.

There was no way he was prepared for what was said next, or who said it, that did turn the heat down on John.

"*Snake* might be too kind of a word for Lawrence Newman, John. I rather think you might owe the reptile world an apology."

Brock couldn't believe his ears. He'd been staring at his food, wondering how he could stop his parents grilling of John, but his head jerked up with an involuntary look of surprise at his father's words.

"What's wrong, Brock? You didn't think I could have an opinion? Or at least one that wasn't contradictory to you or John?"

Brock could tell his father was taking a lot of pleasure out of the very fact that he *was* surprised—and that he certainly didn't think his father could have a noncontradictory opinion. He certainly had never experienced anything conciliatory before.

"I guess I didn't even think you *knew* Newman," Brock said. "Why would you? You certainly never acted like you did, or cared anything about him or his school, when you sent me to Batterson. So, yeah, I'm surprised. I would have thought he'd be your kind of guy."

"He's most certainly *not* 'my kind of guy,' Brock. I've had dealings with Mr. Newman, and they have not been pleasant. I'm sure you thought I was being unkind or uncaring by sending you to Batterson rather than Newman. But there are many things that you are unaware of—or unprepared for—when it comes to how I've chosen to raise you. I know you don't see things my way, son, but I do know what's best for you. And…"

That's as far as he got.

"What's *best* for me? And what gives you the right to decide what's best for me when you don't even *know* me? You've never even talked *with* me about anything—what *I* want, what *my* plans are. You just make my plans for me, with no finding out if maybe, *just maybe*, I wanted to do something different. How *dare* you say you're only doing what's best for *me!*" Angrily pushing his chair back and jumping up from the table, Brock looked away from his father to his friend. "C'mon, John, let's get out of here."

For the second time in just a few minutes he was surprised.

"Nah, you go on and cool off, Wiz. I'm gonna stay here and talk with your parents and help clean up. You need to take a walk."

Brock had nothing to say. Again, he couldn't believe what was transpiring. Only a few minutes before he thought he needed to "save" his friend from the interrogation his parents were pouring on him, and now it was him who needed to get out? His deep brown eyes smoldered with anger, even though he realized his friend was right. He did need to get out. Grabbing his jacket at the door, he headed out into the chilly night. Alone.

John watched his best friend—heck, his *only* friend—walk out of the house and could sense the rejection he must be feeling. But he needed to talk with Brock's parents, and he couldn't do that with his friend sitting there. He'd promised to not argue with Mr. Auzman, but...good thing he had only promised to try. That was before the argument that had just happened took place. It was especially at times like this that he felt out of place—when he knew he could not stay quiet.

"Mr. Auzman. Mrs. Auzman. I truly respect you guys and believe that you probably have your son's best interests in mind when you do the things you do. But I don't think you understand how hurt, how lonely, how empty, how disconnected, he feels. I watch him many, many times as he drifts off by himself, even in a crowd. And almost every night, he's either lying there wide awake just staring at the ceiling, or he's up—over at his desk, walking the halls. He's even gone outside and risked breaking curfew. Always alone, just like right now. It's like he's lost—not only 'cause he doesn't know where he's headed. That's not so unusual. I don't know that either. But with Brock, it's like he doesn't even know where he's come from."

"You're very perceptive, John. Very insightful. We've noticed the same thing about Brock and hoped to talk to you about him."

"No, Michael, you'll talk later. Right now you and I are going to clear the table and clean up." Getting up from the table, she came over to John, touching his shoulder. "John, you've had a long day. You're going to be here all week, and you and Michael can talk one of these days when Brock and I run some errands. Go find him. You boys talk, but don't stay up too late. You've got a busy day of doing nothing tomorrow."

Eleven

Standing at the large window at the top of the landing, John watched as Brock and his mom drove away. It had been four days since they arrived, and Brock still hadn't spoken to his father since their argument that first night. John had tried to get him to but knew better than to push. He still hadn't talked with Mr. Auzman either, but figured this was the time. Brock would be gone for several hours, and he was hungry to find out what Auzman had to say.

Heading downstairs to grab some breakfast before he went looking for Mr. Auzman, he was intercepted at the doorway to the kitchen. Mr. Auzman's dark eyes pierced through John as he was just coming from the kitchen with a steaming cup of coffee in his hands. As usual, John was instantly uncomfortable in the man's presence. Not only the eyes, but his whole demeanor. John always felt like he was a gazelle being stalked by a hungry lion—a lion about to pounce. And now the lion was pouncing.

"Good morning, John. It seems we finally have some time to talk. Would you please join me in my study? Oh—unless you'd like to get something to eat first." John shook his head no. He knew better. This was a man who expected you to work on his time schedule, and they both knew it. Breakfast could wait. "No? Then come in, have a seat. We've got a lot to discuss."

John followed him in to the elaborate study. The Auzmans certainly had a much nicer home than the mission house he had grown up in, but John still wouldn't have considered them rich. So this study seemed completely out of place. The walls were lined with bookshelves from floor to ceiling with the exception of the wall directly behind Mr. Auzman's desk. That wall had what could only be described as a "shrine" to Brock: pictures of Brock as a kid all the way up to what had to be his most recent, his senior picture.

It seemed out of place. Here was this man who had sent his son far away to school rather than keep him in what had to be fairly good public schools, yet displayed picture after picture of this same kid where he could see them all the time. Though Mr. Auzman gestured to the leather side chair across from his desk, John didn't sit—not at first—as though he could delay the inevitable.

"Thanks, Mr. Auzman. I've had a great time this week and want to thank you for your hospitality."

"John, sit. You're always welcome. And I am the one who should thank you. You've been a great friend to Brock, and I know you've put up with a lot from him over these past few years. You're right about him. He seems to be lost. Makes him moody, argumentative. Distrustful. I'm sure you've heard more than you care to admit what a bad person I am—how much he hates me. Perhaps I can tell you a bit more about his past, and maybe that will help. Maybe both of us. Now please, sit."

John at last did so.

"John, I'm not Brock's real dad."

"I know that, sir."

"Yes, I'm sure you do. Again, you've probably heard numerous ugly stepfather stories. I have to admit, I've probably not been the best at being 'dad' for Brock. I'm sure he'd have preferred someone who would have done more *with* him. But I can tell you, I've always, *always*, had nothing but the very best for Brock in mind in anything, everything, that I've done *for* him. Things other men couldn't have done for him."

"You mean like his *real* dad?"

Michael looked at this young man sitting in front of him. The kid was naïve but passionate. On more than one occasion he'd been bothered by that passion as John had spoken out in the midst of various social gatherings. It was like the young man didn't understand how society worked—that people could have opposing views, or that maybe they just liked to talk and try to shape their views as they talked. John saw everything as black or white, right or wrong. Yet, Michael thought to himself, he could still be very useful in helping to fulfill the plans laid out for Brock. Perhaps this young man's strong convictions could be put to use after all. Michael knew that John had not yet heard, so was therefore nowhere near ready to hear, everything. No one was ready for that! Not yet. But he sensed that John could be very useful if he knew just enough.

"John. Your friend Brock is a very special young man. He's—how can I put this? He's *destined* for great things. Now I know that every father likes to think that of his son, and I'm no different in that regards. I *do* want what's best for Brock. Though he has never looked to me as his dad—and I can understand that and live with that—I have always looked at him as my son, my responsibility. No, that's not right—my privilege. I knew what I was getting into when I married his mother, and I was, and am, as anxious about the relationship because of him as I was because of her. Like I said, he's destined for great things, and I knew that from the beginning."

"Mr. Auzman, I couldn't agree more. I see real leadership in Wiz...uh, Brock, too. I watch kids jump to be with him, go where he goes, listen to what he says. Heck, I'm one of them. He's—well, he's special. I can agree with your word *privileged*. I'm privileged to be the kid's friend. I'm challenged to be better because I know people look at me a certain way because I *am* with him. We can be out for a pizza and, literally, people will stop eating and come up to talk to him. He's like some sort of rock star! He turns on that smile, and it's like hittin' a spotlight. Then he talks to them—and he really, really talks *to* them, to *me*—and it's like nothing else, you know? 'Cause most people talk *at* people like me, not *to* me. And when he talks—what's that commercial about that Hutton guy? *People listen!* And they listen because it's like they *know* he has something to say. Yeah, it is a privilege to be his friend."

John paused and looked a little nervous as he continued. "But, sir, I don't think you see the other side of Brock. Like I was saying the other night, it's like he's *lost*. He's *searching*. He's one way when he's with people—the way I just described. But he is somebody completely different when he's not 'on'—somebody a long way from greatness. And he's not going to hit that *greatness* if he doesn't even know who he is now. With all due respect, sir, I don't think you've been straight with him. I don't think you want him to know his past, because you're afraid it will keep him from being what *you* want him to be. You're afraid he'll be everything you aren't, so you're going to keep him from being what he can be. You say you want what's best for him, but I don't think that's true. You may think he's destined for greatness, but it seems you don't want him to get there."

Auzman had to smile at the young man's straightforwardness. He could appreciate an argument of facts—the arena where he best excelled. But he had learned he could also appreciate passion. And that's what he saw most in John Turner now. He knew he could not provide what John was fishing for, but he needed him on his side, so he played along.

"And exactly what do you think I should be straight with him about, John? His *real* dad? His mother? Myself? What is it that Brock is lacking that I could possibly provide for him by being straight with him?"

Though John hadn't had nearly as many deep conversations as Mr. Auzman, he recognized that he was being played. Those dark eyes had a twinkle that he'd never seen, and even his body language was way too relaxed.

John stood to his feet, ready to walk out of the conversation and the room itself. "You could tell him the truth, sir. You could tell him who his dad was, what he was, what happened to him. You could tell him where you came into the picture, and why. You could tell him what his mother saw in you that was ever going to be good for him. You could tell him why you sent him away from here to go to Batterson. Quite honestly, sir, if what you said is true—that you really do care about him, that you really do want to do what's best for him— you could tell him the *truth*."

"Sit down, young man. Both of you boys are going to have to learn that you can't always walk out of an argument after spouting off. If you want people to listen to you, you'd better start by listening to them. So sit down and listen.

"I have not told Brock any lies, John. But you're right: I have not told him much about his background. Maybe he has been searching.

Maybe he does feel empty without that knowledge. You have been closer to him for the past few years than I have, and we don't communicate very well when we are together these rare times. But he doesn't want to hear it from me, you can be sure of that. So here's what I'll do. I'll tell you. Yes, I'll tell *you* why Brock Auzman is who he is, and why I *do* think he's destined for greatness. Then you'll know, and *you* can tell him. Perhaps he'll listen to you—and then maybe the world will listen to him. Sit down, John."

John sat back down. He could tell he was about to hear something big.

"No, John, I am not Brock's father. He doesn't have one. And he never did."

Twelve

"*Clops!*" Brock tried once more to wake John without waking everyone else in the tent. Back from spring break, they were on the annual "Batterson Bivouac" and Brock had been trying to wake John up for the past three minutes. As usual, he was finding the task nearly impossible. Turner was one of the heaviest sleepers he'd ever known. *"CLOPS!"* he whispered loudly again, right in his ear, and finally got the reaction he expected. The big kid shot straight up—still in his sleeping bag—with eyes wide open, just about to yell "WHAT" when Brock clamped his hand over his friend's mouth.

"What!" he whispered when Brock removed his hand, assured that John was now awake and wasn't going to yell.

"Shut up and follow me." Brock silently crawled out of the tent with John closely behind him—not quite as quietly. Though a couple of other campers stirred, none woke up as the two moved stealthily away from the tent.

When they were safely away, John asked, "What's going on? This better be good! Do you know how much trouble I'm already in without breaking curfew?"

Normally John would have been in the same tent with Brock, but he was still on probation from the incident at the football game. As a result he had been forced to sleep in the head counselor's tent and therefore had not been able to bring his usual private stash of forbidden junk food. Even now Brock was afraid his friend's growling stomach might wake up the other campers.

"Don't worry—you'll be back in the tent before anyone gets up. I just gotta show you something."

Even though they were walking through a thick stand of trees there seemed to be enough moonlight to see their way through. When they came out into a clearing, John suddenly realized why he could see—and what Brock wanted him to see. The sky was alive with the strangest, yet most beautiful "light" show he had ever seen—the northern lights!

"Oh man! How did you know? Did you know this was going to happen tonight?"

"No way. I couldn't sleep so I went for a walk...and saw this. I wanted you to see it, too."

They stood there for several minutes absolutely awestruck. It was one more of those unbelievable bonding moments that the two shared in private. They could have awakened the other campers. No counselor would be upset about this. But they didn't. This was theirs to see...and to remember. For the past several years their friendship had been forged by experiences like this—things they did together, tricks they played on others together, and times they simply spent talking. They talked about dreams, girls, and what they were going to do with their lives. They only had a few months before graduation from Batterson, then it was off to Harvard for Brock and—well, John was still waiting to find out what he'd be doing. One thing for sure, though; he wouldn't be joining Brock at Harvard. Not even football would get him in that place.

"Couldn't sleep again, huh?" As they watched nature's light show, John stole a glance at his friend. He had seen this look on Brock's face so many times, and knew there was a lot more on his mind than the sky. "Same stuff?"

"Same stuff. It's like there's something missing, man. Lots of 'somethings,' in fact. It's like my life is a jigsaw puzzle and not only do I not have the picture on the box, I can't even find any edge pieces to know what pieces go where, or where to start."

It was rare that John had nothing to say, but every time Brock got like this he found himself speechless, and frustrated. What could he say? Better than anyone else he knew of Brock's quest in attempting to "find himself"—a quest that only led to more questions, with few answers. And, better than anyone else, he knew the main question Brock fought.

"You know they sent you here to make you a better man. That doesn't mean he doesn't love you. Brock, I spent some time talking to

40

your dad, and he let me know some things about your past that really did show me how much he does care—how much he believes in you, how much he knows you have a real purpose."

"Yeah, right. He sent me here to get rid of me. But I think you're right. I think I've got some of this figured out. He did send me here for a purpose. His purpose. If I become what he wants me to be, then he'll feel like he's someone, instead of the nothing that he is."

"Brock! Enough. You know how much I hate that. *I'm* a nobody...much worse than your dad is. If it wasn't for you. I'd have been long gone from here—a nothing doing nothing. It's not about him; it's not about me. You may not know the answers yet. But one thing I know is this. There's something special about you. Look at that sky, man. *Look at it!"*

Brock turned to look again at the shimmering light show glowing off in the distance as John passionately continued. "Look at all that, and know this. You're like that sky, man. People stand and watch you just like we were looking at this show. I look at this thing and have no idea how it happens, what makes the colors, why it dances like that. I don't know, and I don't care. All I know is that I like what I see. I could watch it for hours, no matter how cold it is out here, no matter what else I'm missing—even sleep. And that's you, man. I don't get you all the time, and I certainly can't explain what makes you special. But I know you are. And I want to be around you because of it. I want you to be all that you're gonna be—and you are gonna be it—'cause that will make me better. So lay off your dad, 'cause he's doing exactly what I would do if I were him. And like him, I need you."

"Geez, Clops, I didn't know you cared."

"Hey! I'm not jokin' here. This is serious. I know you, and I know you'll try to blow me off. Brock, I need you because without you, I am nothing. Got it? Nothing! But with you, by helping you with whatever it is you're going to be, I just might be something. So you listen to me. Whatever is buggin' you, get over it. 'Cause you're carrying a lot of people on those shoulders of yours—and *we* need you to get it together!"

They stood looking at each other, silent. Finally, Brock broke the silence and the tension. "Some sky, huh?"

Thirteen

Lawrence Newman had an idea. He had caught on to something that had escaped him until now—and he couldn't believe he'd missed it. Though it had been many years, Michael Auzman had fought too hard for the whole project to have argued and then simply let it go. That meant, quite probably, that Brock Auzman was no ordinary kid. And he had an idea on how to find out if his theory was right. But he would need some help, and he thought he knew the one he could use.

First, he would need Stoker's help—something that would be easy to obtain. All it would take would be a bit more of his empty flattery and veiled promises.

"William, I have to say I'm very impressed by your leadership, and the changes you've made over at Batterson. Quite impressed. And so are many of my friends—friends that I'm sure could help you make even more improvements."

"Why, thank you, Dr. Newman. I take that as a high compliment coming from you."

Stoker was actually blushing under his beard as much from the wine, which he was highly unaccustomed to drinking, as from the compliment being given him, and the hope of some donations from Newman's high-level friends. Sitting in Lawrence Newman's plush office was another thing Stoker was unaccustomed to. In the ten years they had served in their respective positions, Stoker had only been in a handful of social settings with Newman, and never in his office. He stole a few glances to notice the rich collection of Armani figurines and the original Monet. Little did he know that every time he was looking, Newman was smiling inside, knowing that Stoker was drooling. He'd seen Stoker's office. Quaint, but nothing he'd ever want to spend any time in, and certainly not to entertain supporters in. He could tell

Stoker was quite uncomfortable—but not just because of the setting, or even because of the wine. He had invited Stoker on the premise of discussing the Batterson Discipline Council decision about that kid Turner, and knew that Stoker was still smarting from the dressing down he had taken.

"Please, it's Lawrence. And, William, relax. I'm not upset with you about this Turner thing. It certainly wasn't you that let that kid get off with his insolence. I know your hands were tied, but not your tongue, from what I hear. Thank you for trying to stand up for me. I know you're as upset about someone like Turner getting off with what he did as I am. Especially after the changes you're working on—changes you've made."

"Thank you again, Lawrence. Yes, I've made some changes, and I'm pleased with the way things are going. And, yes, I'm quite upset that The Council felt the need of giving Mr. Turner such leeway on his behavior, especially concerning his rudeness to you. In fact, I'm appalled, and am willing to do whatever I can to rectify this situation. You mentioned you had something you wished to say. I'd like to hear it."

Newman smiled, savoring the moment. He loved these times when he knew his scheming was working. He felt like those old cartoons where the cat had the mouse cornered, knowing the end result.

"William, let me be frank. It's not John Turner that most concerns me. It's that friend of his that defended him. What was his name?" Newman, of course, knew the name, but he also knew how to play the coy game.

"You must mean Brock Auzman. He's a fine young man, though I, too, must question his choice in friends."

"Auzman, that's it. Yes, I'm sure he's a fine young man—one that Batterson prides itself in training. I'm sure *he* could do you proud. Unless, of course, people were to find out a bit more about his past...who he really is. No—who *they* really are."

Stoker was clearly surprised. "I'm not sure I know what you mean. We do a thorough check on each of our students, and Auzman came through our screening with flying colors. Strong family. Strong supporters of our school, even though neither Mr. nor Mrs. Auzman are alumni."

"You know that Brock is not Michael Auzman's son. But did you ever wonder why he would send their son to Batterson? Ever wonder why they would do that—*and support the school*—when they had no history there? As you state, not alumni?"

"Why? Why not? Batterson is a good school; we give a quality education. We have one of the highest Ivy—"

"Oh get off it, William! I don't want to hear about your percentage of graduates in Ivy League schools. We both know those numbers don't really mean as much as you would like them to. Do you honestly believe *that* is the reason a family like the Auzmans would send their son to a private academy hours away from their home? A place where they know they will not see him for months on end? A place where they can turn all disciplinary responsibilities over to teachers, deans, and you yourself, with just a simple signature? Especially the ones on the tuition checks?"

Stoker was taken aback once again by Newman's words, as well as his tone. "What are you getting at, Dr. Newman? Do you know something about this family; this young man? Something I should know?"

Newman let out a long sigh. "Oh, William, I probably should not be the one to tell you these things. In fact, some would say I only do so because of sour grapes, or some such thing. Perhaps they're right. Maybe I do carry some bitterness over what Michael Auzman did; what Michael Auzman *was*, in a 'past life.' But this is today, William. I'm not going to let something that happened nearly twenty years ago cloud my judgment today. Nor should it cloud yours. I'm sure Brock Auzman is a fine young man. But I'm not so sure that he comes from such a 'good' family. Certainly not the family you must think they are. You see, I knew Michael Auzman years ago. And I know for a fact that, though he sends you checks, he doesn't send much of anything to young Brock— especially not in the form of love. He doesn't care about him, William. They don't care."

"I think you're wrong, Dr. Newman. I think you are very wrong. They are here, like other parents, as much as they possibly can be. And I see nothing but the most profound respect for their son."

"Respect? That's what you see? Come now, William. You have

sons, don't you? Do you think they would be happy with respect? No, that just does not do, and you know it. He doesn't love him, sir. He doesn't want him. He doesn't care about him. I'm telling you, I know Michael Auzman. He has sent him here to be rid of him."

Newman could tell Stoker was shaken. He knew that the headmaster prided himself on his knowledge of each student, each family. And that he liked to think of himself as some sort of surrogate father for 'his boys'—though probably very few of them looked at him with any kind of respect, let alone real relationship. It was time to bring up his main reason for this little meeting.

"His roommate. The Turner kid. They're very close, aren't they?"

Stoker was nodding yes as he looked up.

"I'm sure they've had some very close talks, and I'm sure young Mr. Auzman has shared some of his frustrations, his emptiness, with Turner. Why don't you call him up? Ask him. Tell him what I said. See if I'm not right." He handed Stoker his phone.

"Now? You want me to call him right now?"

"William, I'm concerned about that boy. I think he might be heading for some sort of trouble if you—if we—don't take some action right away. I don't want to see your school tarnished by some sort of incident that could have been prevented. After all, we really are in this together—whatever happens to Batterson certainly affects Newman. So let's stop whatever might be happening before it happens."

Stoker took the phone. He was visibly shaking as he dialed his office and, speaking to his secretary, told her to locate John Turner. Knowing that it would only take a few minutes, he told her he would wait, so she placed him on hold. "I'm not sure I should be doing this, Lawrence. Though his parents would be impossible to reach—they're missionaries far off in some god-awful place—I'm not sure I should allow you to talk to him without some sort of permission."

"Of course you're concerned. But I think you'd feel far worse if you found out that Brock Auzman was close to some sort of breaking point, and you hadn't done all you could have when you had the chance. Relax, William. I just want to ask Turner a few questions. Find out if he's noticed any strange behavior in his friend. I think he owes me that much."

Stoker heard his secretary come back on the line. "Dr. Stoker, I have John Turner here in my office. Would you like me to put him on?"

"Thank you, Maggie. Yes." He heard her hand the phone to Turner. "John, I'm sorry to pull you out of class, but I have something that I need to speak with you about."

"No, Dr. Stoker. Please let me speak with him." As Newman took the phone he could hear Turner, apparently confused by the few moments of silence as Newman gloated inwardly.

"Dr. Stoker? Dr. Stoker?"

"No, John, this is Dr. Lawrence Newman. We need to talk."

Fourteen

John figured this meeting—arranged just a few hours after that strange phone call—was Stoker's way to get what he had wanted: an apology to Newman. He knew Stoker wanted to stay on Newman's good side, so he had probably arranged this meeting to force John to apologize in spite of the Discipline Council's stand. But it wasn't going to work. He walked into Dr. Stoker's office ready for battle, which meant he wasn't ready for what happened, as Newman got up from his chair, walked over to him, and hugged him.

"John, I want you to know I have no hard feelings about your outburst at the game. I was an athlete once upon a time, and I fully understand game-heightened adrenaline. Not to mention the rivalry factor. I expect no apology, and that is not why I've asked to meet with you."

"Then why did you want to meet with me? I'm confused." In fact, he was also angry and quite suspicious. What was Newman up to?

"John, I wanted to talk to you about your roommate, your friend Brock Auzman. Dr. Stoker and I were talking about our shared concerns for him and hoped you might be able to give us some insight into what you might know about those concerns. You probably know him better than anyone, and I'm sure you only want what's best for him, as do we."

John simmered. How dare this pompous windbag act like some sort of savior! But he was torn, for he truly did have concerns as well. He had watched over these last few months as Brock had become more and more withdrawn, even from him. They talked—or rather, Brock talked—but it was almost always after lights out, when John couldn't see Brock; couldn't see the pain that he knew was on his face as he shared, again, his emptiness, loneliness, pain. Brock rarely laughed any more and only looked at John with dark, almost hollow eyes. His brilliant smile was almost nonexistent these days, and his wardrobe, usually crisp to the point of obsessive, was a bit slovenly. Yes, John was concerned, but did he want to share that concern with these two? He figured it would do no harm to at least hear them out.

"Exactly what are your 'shared concerns'? And why should *you* care?" he spat out.

"Good question, young man. I'll tell you why I care. I've seen too many young men who seem lost, with no purpose, no drive. Wasted potential, and all too often, wasted lives. Young men who don't feel loved, don't feel valued, and often, don't feel like living any more. And, frankly, I'm afraid your friend might be headed there. Honestly, John, he reminds me of myself at his age—of where I was, and where I was headed, until someone took me under their wing and gave me purpose."

John had a hard time not laughing at how overly serious the whole tone was, while at the same time he had a hard time not yelling. How could this guy bring out so many different emotional reactions just by sitting there with some sort of pained expression, like he truly cared? To John, however, he was far less empathetic than plain pathetic, acting like he was going to be John's *and* Brock's best friend all of a sudden.

"So you think Brock is wasting his life, but you're going to save him. Sorry, sir, but in spite of your inflated view of yourself, I don't see you as being the one who's going to swoop in and 'rescue' Brock from himself. Nor do I think he would be all that enamored with hearing that he's just like you were—'cause I don't think he wants to end up where you are now. I know you think you're something special, and obviously you've been able to fool a lot of people—or at least enough to have made it where you are. But you don't fool me. I don't know what other people see in you, but I see someone who makes me sick."

Dr. Stoker was having a hard time believing what was happening in front of him. He knew he should stop Turner from being so disrespectful to an elder, but he couldn't help but enjoy watching Newman being taken down a few notches. Turner had nailed it on the head. The man was so full of himself. Nevertheless, he knew he'd better intervene if he hoped to be invited to anything by Newman.

"Mr. Turner. That is quite enough. You will not be disrespectful, no matter what your feelings might be. Now I want you to answer Dr. Newman's questions regarding Brock, and I expect you to do so with proper respect. Am I understood?"

John took a long, hard look at Dr. Stoker, then turned the same hard look to Dr. Newman. He may not like either of these men, but he understood the need of respecting authority. "What do you want to know, *sir?*"

Newman looked the young man over before responding. He *was* a big kid, but he was just a kid. He had almost laughed out loud as he saw firsthand what he'd been told—that the kid always wore those gray sweatpants. Since it was after school hours he didn't have a tie on, but still wore his uniform white shirt under a very tight Batterson blazer. He sat rigid on the overstuffed chair he had taken upon invitation, and he shot daggers with those strange golden brown eyes of his—eyes like a wolf that Newman clearly remembered seeing through the facemask of the young man's football helmet when he had climbed that fence and verbally accosted him. He knew he must tread lightly at this point if he hoped to get any useful information, or he could lose the kid. Realizing his body language was probably offsetting—Newman had been sitting back in his chair with his leg crossed—he uncrossed his legs and leaned forward with his elbows on his knees. Placing his hands together in an almost prayerful manner, he touched the tips of his forefingers to his lips, imploring.

"Young man, you've made what you think of me and about me quite clear. I understand you have your opinion, and you obviously have every right to your feelings. But I hope you'll set those feelings aside for a few moments and work with me...with us—" he glanced Stoker's way—"to help your friend Brock. Here's what I'd like to know, John. Have you noticed any strange behavior? Drinking? Drugs? Have you seen any problems with Brock, or talked with him about problems, or his feelings about himself? I know you've seen Brock as a leader, but have you seen him do so with, perhaps, a bit too much of himself, like he feels he *has* to do something, rather than really caring about the cause? In other words, have you seen Brock just not being himself lately?"

John had seen all of this and more. Brock himself had discussed many times with John how he hated what he was seeing in himself—and hated what he was feeling almost all the time. He continually talked about feeling empty, lost, and drifting. John was always trying to talk him out of these feelings, telling him what a great guy he really was. Then he would watch Brock be a completely different kid when he was with people. It was like Jekyll and Hyde—one person when they were on their bunks talking into the late night, another completely different person when he stood before a class, or convo, or even in the Commons, challenging the other guys on whatever was the subject of the day.

Brock could make the world follow him on his charm alone, but he also seemed to say the right thing, at the right time. And it came so naturally—that big old crooked grin, perfect white teeth, the "aw shucks" demeanor. Like the old saying, he could sell ice cubes to Eskimos. Then the lights would go out, and the charm—as well as the confidence—was gone. The empty, questioning, almost frightened kid came out, and John would go through what had become the nightly ritual of repeating Brock's own words of the day to him—the ones that had caused many just a few hours prior to look at him with awe and wonder. And now he was supposed to "share" these oddities with a man he couldn't stand?

"Dr. Newman. Dr. Stoker. You have just described Brock to a T. How can I help him?"

Newman smiled inside. He didn't dare let this kid—this opinionated but all-too-insightful kid—see that smile. He'd lose him, right when he could sense that he now had him on his side, at least where Auzman came into play. If he could get to John Turner, he could get to Brock Auzman, and from there? After all these years, he might be able to get even with the contemptible, conniving Michael Auzman, and—who knew? Maybe even higher up the chain than that....

Fifteen

Graduation was only a couple of weeks away, and again, John was worried. At times Brock seemed worse than ever, but then there would be the switch. That switch was often more worrisome than the status quo, as John watched each "mood" become more pronounced each time. Newman had given him the assignment of keeping a journal, writing down all the conversations he'd had with Brock, recording each time he observed him go from Jekyll to Hyde, as well as the severity of the swing. Maybe Brock's attitude had been this bad before John had started keeping close tabs; perhaps he had simply overlooked it. But there was no doubt in his mind, now that he was being more observant, and the more he saw, the more it weighed on him.

So again he was worried as he watched a moody, sullen Brock reluctantly prepare for the Senior Reception—a formal event put on by alumni and supporters. Brock would have normally been pumped about going; these were the events where he could really shine. These were people who usually mattered to Brock—the "movers and shakers," as he like to call them. People who could help you get places. Brock was going to be given a special award and had been asked to give a brief speech after the presentation so John, who ordinarily would have skipped the event all together, wanted to make sure he was able to go. He had even worked at losing some weight—nothing but salads the last few days—so he could fit in a borrowed tuxedo loaned to him by one of the larger professors. Now, as they were getting ready to leave their dorm and walk over to the dining hall, which had been transformed into a fairly impressive banquet hall, Brock nearly backed out.

"You know it's just a bunch of—what do you like to call them? *Windbags?* Most of these guys are people who simply like the sound of their own voice, and apparently like to hear it a lot. Let's just skip it—

go shoot some pool or something. Anything."

"What's your problem, man? You know you can't skip out on this thing even if you want to. Stoker will track you down. He's so hot to give you that award—to show you off to the alumni and supporters. You, my friend, are his goose of the golden egg variety, and he's looking for a lot of gold tonight. So come on, let's get going. I'm actually hungry enough to eat that infamous rubber chicken, and, quite honestly, I can't wait to hear your speech."

"Speech? I'm supposed to give a speech? No way! Now I *know* I'm not going. I didn't prepare any *speech!*"

John had turned toward the door but stopped cold in his tracks. "Are you *kidding* me? Are you telling me you didn't know you were going to be giving the acceptance speech for the Prestige Award? There's *always* a speech. Dude, you *know* that! You go to these things. You *had to know that.* Someone had to have told you that!"

"Clops, settle down. I was yankin' your chain. I know there's a speech. What do you think I've been working on the past few weeks? I know I gotta give it, but that doesn't mean I *want* to give it. I know Stoker's expecting me to wow his cronies, and I know they're all sitting there expecting me to be the next great Batterson biggie, whatever that means. And *that* is why I don't want to go. I'm sick and tired of being used by other people for *their* purposes. I'm sick of being someone's big answer to whatever big question they think is out there. Dude, these people are talking 'the future president.' The *president!* And I'm eighteen years old. I haven't even lived yet, and I'm sure not thinking about being the stinking president!"

John, still reeling from his friend's idea of a joke, was nowhere near ready for the outburst. But he was especially caught off guard—no, *shocked*—to hear that the people he'd be with in just a few minutes were actually talking about Brock Auzman someday being the president! *Whoa!* He didn't *dare* say out loud what he was thinking: that he, himself, had thought on many, many occasions that Brock would make an excellent president. He'd thought that so many times lately that he wondered now if Brock hadn't actually read his mind, or that, perhaps, he'd talked in his sleep.

Had Brock actually been told the same thing by others? Were

others thinking his same thoughts? And what if they were doing more than thinking? What if they were people who could *do* something about it? What if, indeed? He stood there with his mouth gaping wide open, staring at Brock Auzman, "the wizard." Could he potentially be a future candidate for the President of the United States? *Could he be the future President?*

"Hey, earth to Clops. Why the crazy look? I *told you* I was kidding. I know I'm giving the speech! It's okay, man—you can breathe!"

John did. He took a couple of deep breaths as he looked at his friend in a new light, then spoke: "I think I'd better ask you something, my friend. What exactly are you planning on saying? Wiz, tell me you really did prepare for this speech!"

The Chancellor of Batterson Academy was Duncan Collier. As such he was expected to attend—and almost always did—the Senior Reception, missing only rarely due to other higher engagements. But he wouldn't have missed this one for the world. He knew all of the students: the slackers, the hard-workers, the brown-nosers (perhaps especially the brown-nosers and their parents!) and, of course, those who truly were the future leaders. Beyond that, however, he knew all about Brock Auzman, this year's Prestige Award winner. He should, of course. As chancellor of Batterson, as well as head of the denomination to which it was affiliated (though some radical antagonists referred to it as more of a cult than a denomination), he was the one who chose the award winner each year, and he had chosen Brock.

In reality, however, Brock had been chosen for far more than this simple award long before this. Duncan was anxious to hear young Auzman's speech tonight—his "coming of age" speech—as he had not seen any tangible signs of the promised *wunderkind*. Certainly not what he had been promised, and certainly not anything worth the huge investment he had poured in so far. That investment went far beyond the financial capital. In reality, Collier's very legacy was at stake, and if he didn't start seeing some sort of return soon—as in *tonight*—he was going to be very tempted to pull the plug on the entire project.

Collier had been head of The Haimaelien Brothers for the past forty years. Back then he had been driven by many of the same dreams and ideals that he would, no doubt, hear from the various award winners tonight. He, too, believed that this was a place where anyone could accomplish anything if they simply tried hard enough. And he had tried. It hadn't taken as much in his younger years. Blessed with a certain charisma, fairly good looks, and a commanding voice, he had risen to the top leadership positions of The Brothers in short time. His quick mind had also helped, but he knew that you only got what you worked for, even if you did have certain ancestral advantages such as being the son of the former leader. His good looks, his booming speaking voice, and even his family name alone would not have gotten him to the place he was today. But where he was still was nowhere near where he wanted to be—where The Brothers needed him to be.

Collier no longer had the good looks or the youthful enthusiasm to depend on to get him into the places he needed to go. He was sick, and there was no hiding it. He had lost too much weight, lost too much hair, and his face was sunken and sallow save for the ever-present bags under his sunken eyes, making his eyes look too big for their sockets. Nothing about him was anywhere close to the former handsome face. The weight he could live with—he still looked pretty good in the hand-tailored suits given to him earlier in the year by a faithful follower in Atlanta. He knew he needed to put on some pounds in spite of his health, but he had no appetite. The sickness had also taken its toll on his bones, especially on his knees, leading to a bothersome limp. But he could live with that, too. He didn't like the puffiness around his eyes, nor the sagging jowls where his once strong chin had been. Even that, however, didn't bother him as much as it should have. Not that there was much of anything he could do about any of it.

The one thing that *did* bother him was the loss of his once glorious full head of hair. It had turned white at a relatively young age, which had accented his steely blue eyes and even his strong, cleft chin. He had often been compared to Burt Lancaster—to which Collier had ambivalent feelings. On the one hand he was considered a handsome actor, but on the other hand, he had played the role of a crooked and dishonest preacher in one of his most well-known parts, Elmer Gantry, the very persona that Collier had fought years to dispel. Well, he certainly didn't have to worry about that comparison any more. Not as bald as he was. He could wear a rug, but he knew it would look strange on his shrunken head. The once striking feature was now completely gone, and the man who used to enjoy practicing his speeches and sermons in front of a mirror now avoided them as much as possible.

Fortunately, in spite of all the surgeries, the medicine, the radiation, and even the fatigue, Duncan Collier still had his strong voice. It was amazing. People would see this feeble, bent shell of a man struggle to get out of his chair, limp to the podium, and grip the sides for support, then sit back in wonder as the still powerful voice belted out the familiar message. Collier took pride in the fact that people still came out to hear him, came to the meetings to support him—and that he could still deliver.

He also took pride in the fact that he had built The Brothers into the force that it was today. Once an unknown, misunderstood, and maligned "cult"—oh, how he hated that accusation, that name!—he had brought The Brothers into the new century with a new vision. Then he'd been presented with an unheard-of opportunity to go way beyond that vision. And now they just might be on the verge of being a world religion that would have to be recognized as far more than *a* religion, and certainly far more than some cult that could be ignored and relegated to nothingness. And he would be recognized as the leader he felt he truly was. No more critics! If his advisors were right in their prognosis, and he felt that they must be, the time was very, very soon.

Collier also knew that his doctors were right in their prognosis: he was getting better. His liver was still diseased, and he had no business being alive with the onset of lung cancer. Between the surgeries and the radiation he *had* nearly died. He had almost given up the fight after the third round of chemotherapy, but he could look back now and see it had been the correct call. He was feeling stronger, and knew that he would not only get his appetite and strength back, albeit slowly; his hair would also re-grow.

Most importantly, he had never lost control of his position—his power. Several efforts had been made during his most difficult bouts by men trying to gather a following and take control. And he had been approached by representatives from The Council on two different occasions out of their "concern" that the progress he'd made for The Brothers would all be lost, should they have to go through another messy battle for his position; a battle that could be avoided if he would simply name his successor now. But he wasn't ready to do that, even though he very much wanted to. Actually, it wasn't that he wasn't ready, for he wanted to name his own son, Jason. He knew he could not take that step yet, for Jason, his own son, the "rightful" heir, was nowhere near being ready—being the leader he had hoped for. And the other plan—The Council's plan—was even further behind than that, at least so far. But perhaps tonight would give him hope. Yes, he would get better—this time. But he knew he would not be around forever, and he knew there certainly wasn't time to start over…not in his lifetime anyway. This one had to be *the* One.

As he continued to get dressed for the reception, he let his mind drift back, like it so often did, to those days so many years ago. He had been chosen for the role as head of The Brothers—a role that should have been his naturally as there was a history of "original succession." He was the son of James Collier and the grandson of Jeremiah Collier. In fact, a Collier had sat at the head of The Brothers for over two hundred years. Yet for several years he had continued to fight for his position with everything he had in him. He had sat on The Council for only eight years before his father's sudden death and would be one of the youngest heads of the denomination ever chosen.

Largely because of his inexperience, but also because of his natural assumption that he would automatically inherit the position, there had been an ugly fight. But he truly had a vision for The Brothers and, quite frankly, none of the others fighting for the position did. Most of them felt that their role was to stay the course. Keep the ship afloat. But Collier wanted to get The Brothers out of their tiny clapboard meeting houses and, especially, out of the books on cults, and into public acceptance. Granted, most of the other candidates held much stronger convictions on the faith issues. But he saw the importance of making their message, as well as their image, more mainstream. In the end, he had been chosen as the candidate to take them there.

The fight hadn't ended with his appointment, however, for he had no son. He had fought hard for his role under the name of "original succession"—the belief that the head of The Haimaelian Brothers was a direct descendant of the man who first brought forth the blood—so there was a constant battle for his position from various ones who would argue the well-known reality that *he himself* had no son. His wife had been unable to carry a baby to full term, having had several miscarriages. He couldn't put her through that again. They had talked about adoption, but Collier just didn't feel right about that—he didn't feel that he could bring an adopted son forth in original succession. Then came his plan...though it really hadn't started out as a plan...more of an itch.

Marie Foster was only twenty-four, but her excitement made her seem even younger. Yet she was so committed to the faith! She had been brought to Collier's office to meet him when she had visited Chicago. A cousin worked in the office and asked on her behalf, telling Collier that she was a devoted disciple whose one wish to complete her trip was to meet Duncan Collier himself. Collier had a few spare minutes so agreed.

He was struck by her exotic beauty the instant she walked in. Actually, in her anticipation and enthusiasm, it was more like she bounced in, with a beautiful, worshipful smile. Her long, black, curly hair was pulled away from her face, making her round, deep brown eyes seem even bigger, if that was possible. Her eyebrows were arched with awe. It was clear she was enamored. In the course of their conversation he realized he could have anything—*anything*—he wanted from her.

And there was something he wanted. Needed. He needed a son. Though it didn't happen immediately—of course! She was an innocent *child,* for heaven's sake! But she readily jumped at the job he offered her that day, moving within days from her home in Kansas to Chicago to room with her cousin. It was only a matter of time before she started working in the executive suite, usually directly with him. He began pointedly giving her projects that required staying late, and he himself started staying later as well. It wasn't long before they began sharing meals and, not long after that—due to their deepening mealtime conversations—he was able to talk to her about his need.

In only a matter of weeks he was able to convince her that she could be the one to help him. She could give him a son. His wife had started the adoption talk again, and he felt he needed to do something soon or she would start some proceedings on her own. If Marie would carry his baby, then give him up for adoption to him and his wife, he promised her she would be rewarded handsomely now, and in the afterlife.

It had taken a bit of convincing, but that was what Duncan Collier was best at. She moved back to Kansas during the pregnancy, keeping their knowledge of who the father was a total secret from anyone in The Brother's leadership. Duncan and his wife were, of course, thrilled to help a young woman from their denomination who was "in trouble." They would be more than pleased to adopt her baby. Only Collier would know that he was doing far more than a charitable act—he was continuing the original succession. What his wife didn't know—must never know—wouldn't hurt her. This was for the greater good.

When they arrived at the hospital in Kansas to pick up their new son, whom they'd already named Jason, Duncan met with the weeping young mother privately. "I promise—I'll make it up to you."

Little did he know at that point how soon he would have the opportunity to do so. It seemed The Council had a plan of their own. Since he and Marie had kept their plan a secret, he was able to recommend her for theirs.

And tonight, that plan just might come to fruition.

Sixteen

Brock and John sat together, of course, but they were quite surprised to find themselves at the same table as *the* Duncan Collier! Why wasn't he at the head table? It was a bit disconcerting to be with the man who had built Batterson into the school it was today. Obviously, John would not be pulling any pranks tonight.

"Dr. Collier, it is a pleasure to meet you, sir. I wasn't expecting to have you at our table, but I'm glad I get the opportunity to thank you personally and privately for the Prestige Award. I expected to only be able to do this on the platform. I truly am grateful for the award, but I'm especially thankful for your trust in me. I'm truly honored, and I only hope that I can live up to all that the award implies."

"That sounds an awful lot like a speech, son. Shall I head on home and make it an early night? Or will I hear something new when you receive the award?"

"I'm sorry, sir. That did sound a bit canned. I'm just a bit surprised to have you sitting here. Might I ask, sir, why *are* you sitting here? Shouldn't you be up there—at the head table?"

"With the *windbags?* Isn't that what you called the president and the dean, Mr. Turner? That letter to the editor was from you, wasn't it?"

Duncan Collier took delight in watching people squirm. Problem was, John wasn't squirming. He was staring straight into Duncan Collier's eyes with a hard, angry look.

"Yes sir, that letter was from me. I'm glad you read it. I presume you also saw what I called you, and my only apology is that I could not say it directly to your face. I believe something like that should be said in person, but I was not allowed into your office. So, sir, I, too, am glad you are sitting here."

"I have to say I wasn't as surprised that you would call me a *charlatan* as much as that you knew how to spell it," Collier said coolly. "Perhaps your time at Batterson has done some good. I'm sure your parents are proud of your graduation. They've served our mission long and hard to get you to this point. I hope you're thankful for at least that. And now, if you'll allow me to continue my talk with Mr. Auzman."

"I'm sorry, Dr. Collier. John gets very passionate about anything he considers out of whack. But his bark—loud as it might be, and usually is—well, I don't think he's bitten anyone lately. I apologize for him, sir. You certainly did not sit here to be insulted."

"Don't mention it, Brock. John, again, you are entitled to your opinion. And I am entitled to mine, which is this: Brock, if you intend to become what many people have worked hard to make you, you had better choose your friends very wisely. You are known by the company you keep, and I did want to sit with you—not fully aware of who else might be sitting here—to warn you, to encourage you, that as you move on from here, you must be careful. People will look for any possible opening to drag you down. You don't want to give them that opening. And choosing the wrong friends...let me put it this way. Presidents Carter and Clinton had no choice regarding their brothers, but you *do* have the choice regarding who might bring you down. Choose wisely, young man. You have a great future—greater than you could possibly imagine. I'd hate to see it lost because of someone else."

Both Brock and John appeared stunned, but that didn't mean John was speechless.

"So, Dr. Collier, I'm wondering who the heck you hung out with that made you the *charlatan* you became."

In spite of himself, Collier had to laugh. "Turner, you may have one of the sharpest tongues I've heard—besides my own! There might be hope for you after all. So, instead of warning Brock, I'm going to warn you. You need this friend of yours, but he does not need you. You are nothing without him, and..."

At that very moment Dr. Stoker stood to the podium and announced the presentation of the Prestige Award and called Brock up to the dais. He wasn't sure it was the best time for him to leave John at the mercy of Duncan Collier, but he had no choice. People were applauding, and it would only look like he was purposefully extending it if he didn't get up from his seat right now.

"Go ahead, Brock. You need to get up there. Dr. Collier and I will be just fine. Let's hear your speech."

Brock, head down partly because of his concern for his friend and partly because he didn't like being applauded, headed up to the platform. After the perfunctory thanks to the faculty, staff, Dr. Stoker, and Dr. Collier, he began his speech. For the most part it was a fairly simple challenge to listen to the next generation—his generation: a challenge that they weren't just kids but leaders in the making. But then, in his usual style, he hit a home run.

As I was handed the envelope stating that I had won this award, I was asked to answer the question, "What is your place in history?"

Thinking about the words to share with this class, about what's next, about what's possible, and what opportunities lay ahead, I think it's not a bad question to ask ourselves: "What will be our place in history?"

In other times, other places, this question could be answered with relative ease and certainty. As a slave in Rome, you knew you'd spend your life forced to build somebody else's Empire. As a peasant in eleventh-century China, you knew that no matter how hard you worked, the local warlord might come and take everything you had—and you also knew that famine might come knocking at the door. As a subject of King George, you knew that your freedom of worship and your freedom to speak and to build your own life would be ultimately limited by the throne.

But we now live in a different time, and a different place. A place where destiny is not a destination, but a journey to be shared and shaped and remade by those who have the drive, the tenacity to believe that, against all odds, they can form a better place at this time.

Have we failed at times? Absolutely. Will we occasionally fail when we embark on our own dream? We surely will. But the test is not perfection.

The true test of the dream is whether we're able to realize and learn from our failings and then rise together to meet the challenges of our time. Whether we allow ourselves to be shaped by events and history, or whether we act to shape them. Whether chance of birth or circumstance decides life's big winners and losers, or whether we build a community where, at the very least, everyone has a chance to work hard, get ahead, and reach their dreams. People like us have faced this choice before.

Today we have to decide. This time, it is our turn to choose.

So much is possible, but none of it will come easy. Every one of us is going to have to work more, read more, train more, think more. We will have to slough off some bad habits. We'll have to reform institutions—even private schools like Batterson—that were designed for a different time. It won't be easy, but it can be done. It can be our future. We have the talent and the resources and brainpower.

But we need each of you. Students, faculty of Batterson Academy, honorable alumni.

Now, no one can force you to meet these challenges. If you want, it will be pretty easy for you to leave here today and not give another thought to places like Batterson and the challenges they face. There is no community service requirement in the real world; no one is forcing you to care. You can take your diploma next week, walk off that stage, and go chasing after the fanciest education, the best job, the biggest house, and the nicest suits, and all the other things that our money culture says that you should want, that you should aspire to, that you can buy.

But I hope you don't walk away from the challenge. Focusing your life solely on making a buck shows a certain poverty of ambition. It asks too little of yourself. You need to take up the challenges that we face and make them your own. Not because you have a debt to those who helped you get here, although we all have that debt. Not because you have an obligation to those who are less fortunate than you, although I do think we all have that obligation. It's primarily because you have an obligation to yourself. Because it's only when you hitch your wagon to something larger than yourself that you realize your true potential.

And I know that all of you are wondering how you'll do this, since the challenges seem so big. They seem so difficult for one person to make a difference.

But we know it can be done. It's been done before.

Today, on this day of possibility, we have in our presence a raw-boned man with little formal education who once took this very stage and told the graduates and school leaders of his day that if they did not rise up to the challenge facing them at that point, there would be no school, no alumni, no leaders of this faith and its principles that are timeless and all-inclusive. Dr. Collier, on behalf of all Batterson graduates and alumni, thank you.

My hope for all of you is that as you leave here today, you decide to keep these principles alive in your own life. We will be tested. We won't always succeed. But know that we have it within our power to try. That generations who have come before us faced these same fears and uncertainties in their own time. And that through our collective labor, and through God's providence, and our willingness to shoulder each other's burdens, we will continue on this precious journey towards that distant horizon, and a better day.

To thunderous applause, Brock Auzman—a brand new Brock Auzman in nearly everyone's eyes, sat down. Even John sat in stunned admiration of his best friend.

And Duncan Collier knew his advisors had been absolutely correct. It was time.

Seventeen

Brock was going to spend the summer working for Duncan Collier. He had accepted the invitation—offered immediately after the Senior Reception—to be Collier's intern, working at the international headquarters in Chicago. It was an easy choice, not only because it was better than spending the summer home with Michael's attitude, but because it seemed to be the first thing he had done in as long as he could remember that actually made Michael and his mother happy. In fact, when he called to let his parents know about the invitation, Michael had offered to drive him to Chicago himself.

"I haven't seen Dr. Collier in several years, and I'd like to thank him for taking you under his wing for the summer. Son, this is a fantastic opportunity!"

"How do *you* know Dr. Collier? I've never known about that."

"Brock, there's quite a bit you don't know about me—or your mother. We've both worked very closely with Dr. Collier. Very closely. I can tell you that you will learn much from him, as well as from The Council. You should come out of this summer with some tremendous debate skills, if nothing else, but I know you'll come out with a lot more than that. Much more. Brock, you possess something that only a few men in all of history have had. Something that can't be explained. Even should I try, you would call me crazy. Maybe I am crazy for believing it—and for trying to tell you."

"Okay. You've got my curiosity piqued. What are you talking about?"

"Tell you what, Brock. Your mother and I will be there for graduation. Then we'll put her on a plane home, and you and I will drive to Chicago together. And we'll talk then. It will be good for us to spend some time on the road."

Brock wasn't quite as sure it was going to be fun, but in retelling the conversation to John, his best friend thought it would be a very great thing indeed.

"Wiz, are you kiddin' me? What an opportunity! You yourself say you never get to spend time with him. No wonder you don't know anything about him or your mother. I know you've been ticked off about them sending you away to school, but you gotta admit, it's been a great thing for you. Look at where you're going this summer. And who knows where *that's* going to lead? Man, you are going places!"

"Hey, you, too! In fact, I really wish I was going with you. The sun, the beach, the native women."

Laughing, John replied, "Yeah, right. The sun beats down on you worse than you can begin to imagine, cooking you like a lobster; the beach, what little there is of it, is usually covered by dead fish stinking to high heaven. And I'm not sure if you've seen where my parents work in any of your geography studies, but I don't think I'll be seeking out time with any of the native women. But you, my friend, are quite welcome to come down and give it a shot yourself."

They both got a good laugh at that one.

"In all reality, it would be great to have you there," John said. "But oh, you're going to be hangin' out with *the* Dr. Duncan Collier; way too good for us lowly commoners. But if you'll still have me—*if* I can still approach the stratosphere called you—I guess we'll have to settle for plan B: I'll come see you in August. And you'd better have Cubs tickets, or I'll tell Collier a thing or two that just might knock you off that pedestal he's got you on."

"Cubs? Lookin' at you, I'd take you more for a Giants fan. Or maybe, considering that mouth of yours, the Blue Jays—they never shut up either, right?"

"Alright, alright—cut the sarcasm and just get the tickets, okay?"

John realized they were joking around to keep from doing anything crazy like crying. They both knew this was the last night that they would be together as roommates; probably the last time they would have this kind of innocent banter. Brock was heading for Harvard after his summer internship in Chicago. And John, miraculously, had gotten a football scholarship to Dartmouth of all places. He had no idea what New Hampshire was like, and playing for The Big Green wasn't exactly at the top of his list. But in all reality, the more he heard about the school and its history, the more reasons he had for saying yes when the recruiter came knocking. And, of course, it wasn't that far to Cambridge to see Brock as often as possible. It would be much easier than if he was at State.

"Clops, I think I know what you're thinking. You know I'm coming up to see you every game I can make—not just when you play Harvard. We'll still talk. No way can I make it without your ranting and raving about everything under the sun."

"Rantings? Ravings! Oh, my friend, you know you're gonna miss a lot more than that. Who's gonna keep you in line? Who, besides yours truly, can ever put up with your smug, condescending, pretentious personality? As bad as you are now, I can hardly imagine how you're gonna be after spending a summer being trained by the king of pompous!"

"Hey, Clops, hold on. All joking aside for a second. You know, you give that guy a lot of grief, but I think you're wrong about him. Do you think I'd be spending this summer there if I thought he was as bad as you make him out to be? He might not be the warm cuddly person that you are, but he has done an awful lot of good, ya know? Lots of people are living a better life because of him, his teaching, and his church. He's one of the good guys. You call him money hungry—but that money is used for good."

"Oh come on, Brock. You call all that he's doing good? Flying in his own private jet? Being driven around in chauffeured limousines? Wearing those fancy suits? Hey, I know the guy's sick and all, but I don't think that qualifies him to take people's money and use it for his exorbitant lifestyle. I was joking about him being the king of pompous—but not really. He's sick all right. And he makes me sick. I'm sorry, Brock. I know you like him, but I just don't. I don't trust him either. So, to be honest, I *am* a bit worried about you. And I'm glad we're going to be somewhat close next fall. Maybe I'll have some opportunity to de-program you."

So many times they had been here before: John standing firm and on the edge of angry over his strong, unbending principles, not afraid to say what he felt; Brock trying to hit some sort of middle ground, always trying to say just the right thing in just the right way, compromising to the point of appeasing. It was truly amazing that they had remained such close friends for so long. Standing toe to toe and nearly nose to nose, finally, like always, Brock broke out in that big smile of his, punched his big friend on the shoulder, then laughed out loud.

"You jerk. Yeah, you need to go off to the jungle, smoke some banana leaves or something, calm down. Then you can come de-program me—and maybe even Collier himself, huh? After all, you really won him over last week at the reception. I'm sure he'll welcome you with open arms. Get out of here, man. I'll see you in August—with Cubs tickets in hand."

"Smoke some banana leaves? You are really too much."

And just like that, they were friends again.

Eighteen

"He told you to smoke banana leaves? Why? What's that supposed to do? I don't understand why he would want you to do that."

John's mother didn't have much of a sense of humor, and certainly not a sense of youth culture. They were sitting in the kitchen—such as it was—in their mission home. The house itself was very small and plain, though it had high ceilings to help with the oppressive heat. Ceiling fans circled slowly in each room and helped stir the air some, but they were always suspect due to the constant government ordained power brown-outs. Sometimes the mission compound's generator kicked in, most times it didn't. Fortunately this was one of those times when it was on. The small, whitewashed kitchen seemed even smaller with John's massive frame filling most of one side of the room. John had been gone for over two years, but nothing had changed, including, thankfully, his mother's cooking.

"Mom, it's a joke. He just wanted me to calm down. I get a bit heated, and Brock knows what to say to cool me off. He's like that. He's a good guy—one of those guys who always knows what to say. He can talk to Duncan Collier as easily as he can talk to me, you, or some little kid. He's just smooth."

"Is he too smooth, John?" Before John could interrupt, his mother held up her hand and continued on. "Let me explain. You said he hit it off with Duncan Collier—and you didn't. You said he always says 'just the right thing.' But is it always the *right* thing? You know—is what he says right? Or is he just saying what people want to hear? And you also said he has a charisma that makes people follow him even though they have no idea what he actually stands for. Did his speech really say anything, or did it just make people feel good? I don't know, John. Something doesn't sound right. I'm glad you want to help him make something of himself, and that you're so concerned that he's—what did you call him? lost?—and needs someone like you. But Son, I don't want to see him pull you away from who you are. And believe me, someone who's going to spend a summer—and mark my word, it will end up being a lot more than just a summer—with Duncan Collier? To put it bluntly, I don't trust him. I'm not sure why. I only know what I feel."

"Whoa, Mom. In all reality I couldn't agree with you more about Collier..."

"Doctor Collier, John. No matter what you might think of him as a person, I still want you to be respectful of him as an authority figure. I may not agree with a lot about him, but he is still the head of this church, and as such we must respect his position. Now, you were saying, regarding *Doctor* Collier?"

"Okay. Fair enough. I couldn't agree with you more about Dr. Collier. I don't trust him either. I really wish Brock would have said no to the internship, but he was so excited. And even more, his dad was so excited. They were going to be able to spend a lot of time driving to Chicago together, and I sure didn't want to say anything that would stop that. Brock can't stand his dad, but I think they just need to spend some time and get to know each other better. So it was like I couldn't say anything about Col—uh, Dr. Collier. But Mom, you don't know Brock. He's a *leader.* Yeah, he says the right thing. I can't tell you if it's always right—who knows? Sure, sometimes he seems to say things that just make people feel good, but is that all wrong? Again, I don't know. I only know it makes people like the guy, and follow him. I've told people before, I think they'd follow him to *hell* if he told them..."

"Jonathon James Turner! I will *not* have you saying such things! I don't know what that school has done to your good values, but you know very well that neither your mother nor I will stand for such talk; talk of sending someone to hell! Apologize to your mother, and to your Lord." John's father had walked in to the kitchen after waking from a short nap. The drive from the airport was long, and their old Land Rover had never been comfortable. The years hadn't helped the comfort level any, and Mr. Turner was not a young man. And right now he wasn't a very happy man either.

"I'm sorry, Pop. I really wasn't saying someone should go to hell. I was saying that Brock—you know Brock Auzman, my roommate? That he's such a leader that people would *follow* him to hell. Pop, you know I wouldn't ever wish someone there. I'm sorry, but you missed a big part of the conversation."

"Well, if we're talking about someone leading others to hell, this conversation is over. That's not a conversation topic that should ever, ever be taken so lightly, and I'm afraid that way too many of this generation do take it lightly. Do you not realize that you are talking *eternity?* If your 'friend' (his dad actually made air quotation marks as he said the word) can lead people there, exactly what do you think that makes him?"

"Pop, Mom, it was a figure of speech. Obviously a very poor one. My *point,* sir, was that Brock is a leader. He's just a kid, but it's like he's some great person walking around in this kid's body. He walks in a room, and people not only look at him, notice him, but they stop talking. Kids, yeah, but adults too. You should have heard the speech he gave at the Senior Reception, Pop. Yeah, Mom, it made people feel good, but it did say something. It made you want to be a better person. To change things. To be changed. I gotta tell you—it's a great privilege to be his friend. He's going somewhere, and I'm ready to go with him."

John's dad took a seat across the table from his big son. He was noticing, once again, how much he had changed. He still had that wild shock of black hair that they'd never been able to control, no matter what they tried. And now he was growing a beard; he had told his dad it just didn't do any good to shave anymore, as he always looked like he needed a shave even if it had only been a couple of hours. His hands had grown strong, and the weightlifting he had been doing for football showed in his massive arms and shoulders, not to mention his neck. But most impressive were his eyes. *Piercing.* That was the only way to describe them. Though they would probably be described as caramel brown, they seemed to have a smoldering fire behind them. John's dad looked into those eyes and saw the passion of conviction.

"I believe you are, son. Your mother and I just want to make sure you know exactly where that is."

Mrs. Turner spoke up again, directing her concern-laced words to her husband. "Brock is spending the summer as an intern for Duncan

70

Collier."

John's dad was physically shaken. He looked like he'd seen a ghost.

"Pop, what is it? What's wrong with him working for Dr. Collier? I know I don't think too highly of him, and I heard from Mom that she feels some of those same things. But he is the head of the church, right? Is this just because he's your boss? Is he the one who sent you guys here? To this jungle?"

"John, we came here because we truly felt this was where we should be. Yes, Duncan Collier assigned us to this place, and though we might have seen it at first as punishment, we have come to see it as providence. We have had a good ministry here. And we've made an actual difference. But John, there are things about Dr. Collier that you need to know. And things about us as well—your mother and I. Think you're ready?"

Wide-eyed, leaning forward with his elbows on the table, John shook his head.

"Yeah, you're ready. John, the biggest change we've made here has much more to do with us than with these dear people we work with. We came here—rather, were sent here, as know-it-alls, not that much different than Dr. Collier himself. Though he had been in his position as head of the church for quite some time, it was obvious to many of us that he had no leadership abilities. He looked at his position as a birthright—which, in a sense, it was—but he did nothing to keep it. He simply took all the perks of the position and gave very little back, feeling like he was invincible."

"I called him a charlatan in a letter to the school paper."

"John, you didn't!" His mother appeared ready to begin another lecture, before her husband interrupted her.

"Mother! He is one, and you know it. And you also know that this son of ours has never been afraid to tell it like it is. And, beyond that, he's always had a great sense of discernment. And this time, son, I'd have to say you were right on. Charlatan. I'll bet he liked that! Do you know if he read it?"

"Oh yeah, he read it. He sat at our table at the reception and called me on it. You'd have been proud. I pretty much told him what you just said: that I call 'em like I see 'em. I think he actually liked that. He started to threaten me, I think, just before Brock got up to speak. Something about me needing Brock more than Brock needing me."

Both his parents were taken aback this time.

"That's exactly what he said to us just before sending us here. Though I hadn't called him a charlatan—but only because I don't think I knew that word—I did call him a few other choice things. And, similar to what he said to you, he let us know that we needed him a lot more than he needed us. I was challenging his leadership before The Council and hadn't realized just how much support he had from them. I honestly thought they were seeing, realizing, the same things your mother and I, and many, many others, were. This guy couldn't have led a snowflake to the ground, but here he was trying to lead The Brothers. We thought, then, that he would destroy all that we and so many others believed in. And, in all reality, he did. But I have to tell you, Son, that was the best thing in the world—not to mention the world beyond—that he could have done for us. Yes, he's a charlatan, a fraud. But the fraud goes way, way beyond him."

John, usually never at a loss for words, knew he needed to sit back and let his father continue. But he was struck with something that just came to mind. "I hate to interrupt, Pop, but I have to ask something. Was Lawrence Newman any part of this?"

"How do you know Lawrence Newman?" His mother was, again, shocked.

Using his hands to demonstrate a widening gulf, he answered "Looonnnng story, Mom. I'll save it for later. Much later. But my question is, do you guys know him?"

"Obviously we do, or did. Yes, he was part of our challenge to Dr. Collier's leadership. A big part. He was our voice, the one who stood in front of The Council to present our argument. And he was the natural choice to do so. The man could talk! But usually that was all he did do; talk, that is. He wasn't exactly a guy who took any real action on things, or acted like he had any real belief in what he argued for. Usually. But he did have passion on this one—he *really* wanted to see Collier gone."

"Dr. Collier, Pop. Let's respect the position even if we can't respect the man." He stole a sideways glance at his mom, who just rolled her eyes.

His dad was a bit perplexed, but plowed on in spite of the interruption."O-kay, Dr. Collier. At any rate, Newman stood up to *Dr. Collier* and his spokesman, and lost. He left The Brothers at that point and pretty much started his own branch or sect—or whatever you want to call it—of the church. Though we disagreed with his methods then, and still do, we certainly understood his motives. He, too, would most likely have been banished like we were, but there's no way a man like him who demands the public eye could have ever survived out here. Not that we deserve some gold medal for having done so…. We took our punishment as an opportunity to get out of what we saw as a sickening situation. My only regret is having lost any voice with The Council, thus letting Dr. Collier have his way these past couple of decades. We stay out of it all;we obviously have little choice. But I can't help but feel we've done very wrong by doing so. Our silence has probably allowed The Council's project to run unhindered and who knows what's going to happen because of that. There's a time, John, when you must speak out against something you know is wrong, no matter what it costs you."

"Okay, Pop, you've hinted around the edges long enough. What the heck are you talking about? You've told me a lot of stuff, but that's only left me with more questions. Exactly who is Dr. Collier? Who is Lawrence Newman? What is The Council? And who are you guys—and what have you done with my parents?"

"Tell you what, John. Let's get out of these uncomfortable kitchen chairs and take a walk. Your mother hates this kind of talk, and I need your help on a few things out in the compound. If we're going to talk about dirt, let's go out and get dirty."

Nineteen

Brock kissed his mother good-bye as she stood up to board her flight back home. Final boarding call had just been announced, and they could wait no longer. It had been great to spend the last few days with her, and they both teared up a little as she gave him another hug. She reached out and touched his cheek, looking up into his teary eyes.

"You be patient with your father, Brock. He's doing his best, and he's as nervous about taking this road trip with you as you are. Don't sit in silence. Talk to him. I think you'll be surprised at what you might learn from him."

"Mom, enough. I'll talk. I'll listen. Do I have any choice? You and I both know that Michael will talk whether I pay attention or not. I don't know why he wants to take this trip with me, and I don't know why you're not coming with us. But I have to admit that I'm anxious to hear more about Dr. Collier from him."

At that his mother's face clouded over. Brock interpreted the look as sadness over their separation.

Marie Auzman was troubled at the mere mention of Collier's name. Though she had known the time must come for her son to hear the truth, and from what Michael had hinted, this trip might lead to at least some of that truth, she was not ready for it. Certainly not for all of it, or for what might become of it. She didn't know if Brock was ready for it or not, but she didn't think that she, the one who had been so willing so many years before, would ever be ready for it. She looked at his strong, handsome face, into those dark, usually brooding eyes, softened this time by tears and his deep smile as he gazed down at her.

Like so many times before she looked and longed for some sign of similarity; something that showed herself in him. And, like always, she was disappointed. There was the obvious skin color difference—she was so white she was pale—but so much more. His angular face, his lanky frame, his tight, curly hair, currently cropped close according to Batterson Academy standards, and, of course, those eyes—all so different. He was growing into such a handsome young man, and she could already tell that his smile, his charm, his natural charisma, would get him into places that most young men his age would never go. Like so many times before, she wondered about where those places might be, and, like so many times before, she worried.

"Mom, there you go again. You haven't even boarded the plane, but I can see you've already taken off into that distant place you always visit. Earth to Mom!"

"Oh Brock, I'm sorry. I'm just thinking what a handsome young man you are. And, honestly, thinking about what great things lay ahead for you. I can't say I'm as excited as your father about this summer internship. I'd so much rather have you home before you head off for—well, for whatever. But I do know, and do agree, that you *need* this. It will be one more step toward the greatness you are destined for. But I had hoped we could spend so much more time together first. I'm going to miss you so much!"

Holding her hands, Brock looked down at his mother. She still looked like he'd always remembered her. She still wore her curly, black hair long, just past the shoulders, parted off to one side, clipped in the back with a tortoise-shell barrette to keep it out of her eyes. Not too much makeup—just a bit of mascara to highlight the green of her eyes. Always in a dress even when most women her age were always in pants or jeans. She had been called Mrs. Cleaver by more than one of his friends as he grew up. Though he *had* grown up, and now towered over her, she hadn't changed at all. Standing in the middle of the busy concourse, they might as well have been having this conversation at home in the kitchen, two years prior.

"And I'm going to miss you too, Mom. Now go, before you miss your flight, and before Michael has a stroke waiting for me." Grabbing her for one last hug, he told her, "Mom, I am well aware that anything I might become will not be because of Duncan Collier. I am what I am, and will become whatever, only because of what you've made me—what you've taught me. So...thank you."

Marie joined the crowd headed to the jetway to board her flight with tears in her eyes, partly because of their parting, but more because she knew the truth: that it was *precisely* because of Duncan Collier that her son even existed, and it would probably be because of him that Brock would be the leader he was destined to become. But she felt something else: that truth, once he knew it, would more than likely cause her to lose the young man she knew as her son.

Brock turned to head for the exit and find Michael, who had chosen to drive around the airport while mother and son said their good-byes. Never one for sentiment, not knowing the true source of his mother's tears, he knew it would be better this way; better than letting her make one last wave before she headed down the jetway. Better than standing at the huge window hoping she was able to spot him through the porthole, knowing that was the main reason she had chosen a window seat. Exiting the terminal, he spotted Michael and flagged him down. As Michael slid the Buick toward the curb, into the line of cars picking up and dropping off passengers, Brock jumped in, barely waiting for the big car to come to a complete stop.

"That was good timing" was all he said, and they were off.

Michael knew the young man was far more emotional than he liked to let on, so he stayed quiet, allowing Brock to get his emotions in check. He knew better than to try and say anything that would only lead to the all-too-sudden switch from sadness to anger. He had watched this young man go from happy to sad to angry to near violent all too many times.

They drove for several minutes in silence as Michael maneuvered through the traffic, exited the airport, and headed to the interstate. There would be plenty of time to talk. Michael had planned a three-day trip, which could easily be cut down to two should Brock remain his usual sullen, moody, and angry self. Michael was surprised, therefore, when it was Brock who broke the silence.

"Mom was concerned that we wouldn't talk. I guess that's our usual M.O. But honestly, Michael, I'm anxious to hear what you have to say. Since I'm going to be spending the summer with Dr. Collier, I need to know exactly who he is. I'd also like for you to tell me exactly who *you* are, Michael Auzman. And, as long as we're at it, I'd like for you to tell me exactly who I am."

Twenty

Half a world away, two men were in a very similar conversation. They had been clearing brush for over three hours in the hot sun and needed the break. John was helping his dad prepare a site for yet another building on the mission compound—a hoped-for medical clinic. They might never get the funds for the medical supplies and would most likely never see a doctor or nurse make the sacrifice to serve in such a remote place for no money, no fame, and very few successes as far as helping the sick. Yet a clinic would provide a place for those who suffered from so many illnesses to find a place of compassion, at the very least. Jake Turner still believed in that, and, in reality, much of what The Brothers had taught so many years ago. It was only a few things that he could no longer accept. But they were big.

As they sat in the limited shade of a ramshackle shed that would soon be torn down to make room for the clinic, they drank water from a jug that had been brought out to them by one of the young boys living on the compound. His eyes had been as huge as saucers as he looked up at John and whispered "Goliath?"

John must have looked every bit as much a giant as Goliath, a story the boy had certainly heard taught by Mrs. Turner time and time again. She loved telling the old Bible stories and was a master at making practical applications from each one. As John took a long drink of the now lukewarm water, he thought about how David had brought provisions out to his brothers on the battlefield, then took on the giant that dared to mock his God. Often John himself, in spite of his size, felt like a little boy taking on God-mocking giants. He could not sit silently and allow someone to run roughshod over his principles—truths that had been taught to him on this very compound so many years before. Yet now, here was his own father, one who had taught him so much, telling him that they had been wrong.

"I know this is all a bit hard to take, John, so let me back up a bit more. Long before Duncan Collier, or even his father and his grandfather, messed things up, The Brothers had it wrong. John, they started out wrong! They were so close to the truth, but they missed it. I know you've heard the story many, many times, but I want you to hear it again—only listen this time with new ears. Listen to what *isn't* said as much as you hear what *is* being said. Use that discerning mind of yours, and hear truth."

"Pop, I get it! I understand that you and Mom have been out here, away from the teachings of anyone else, only yourselves to discuss these things with. And I'm sure you've had a lot of opportunity in this blasted heat to think about all Collier has done to you, and I'm sure it's caused an awful lot of anger at him and The Council. I don't blame you for wanting to walk away from what they teach."

"No, John. That's not it. I told you, this might have started as punishment, but we look at it now as the hand of providence. The hand of God himself! Yes, it is true, we are away from the teachings of others. False teachings. And because we have been away from what basically amounted to brainwashing, we have had the opportunity to think, to study, and to learn truth for ourselves, rather than what was crammed down our throats. We have not been in a vacuum, John. We have had plenty of opportunity to not only search the Scriptures to see if these things are true or not, but to see that truth in action. John, please, do the same. Listen, then test it for yourself."

"Okay, Pop. I know you, and I know Mom. So I know you haven't lost your minds. So, tell me. What's the story?"

"You know that we worship the blood. But do you know why? I know you understand that there is a difference between right and wrong, and that 'wrong' must be punished. But all too often the standard for right and wrong, or who sets that standard, is all too subjective. It can, and has, become 'majority rules,' both in selecting the standard, and in selecting the ones who set the standard. Much of western society, of democracy, is based on such a fluctuating standard. What was wrong last decade can be completely accepted as right today if enough people decide it is so. Or if the influential leaders of the society—whoever they might be or whatever they might do, just as long as they are popular, beautiful, rich, or charismatic—say something is right or wrong, people will follow them. There are people who will set the standard for western society just because they starred in some movie! Their whole life may be an act, but they become the mouthpiece for the majority simply because they *can* act—or at least sell a few tickets. We're not so isolated out here that we don't already see and hear such things. It's appalling to us, John, that so many people base their beliefs and their actions off of what is told them—without thinking."

"You mean like being against a war, not because the war is wrong—since the cause itself may be much worth fighting for—but because *somebody* is against it...even if they don't understand its reason, its cause, but happen to be popular?"

"Exactly. That's it. Right and wrong are all too often way too subjective, and all too often based more on the majority or, even, the loudest minority, rather than the truth. That's why it has been good for us to be away from that kind of influence, John. You see, we had fallen into that same trap. We believed simply because others did. We followed simply because others did. We were young, idealistic, and passionate. But we were stupid.

Jake Turner sighed. "Oh we *thought* we were the smartest people to come along since Einstein...or at least Sartre, or any number of philosophers. We had the answers—we thought—because our leaders had them. As long as those 'leaders' were handsome, or charming, or rich. And Duncan Collier was all of those, but he was no leader. He talked a good talk, but he was as blind as we were, and like you were saying when I walked in on your conversation a few hours ago? We would have followed him into hell, 'cause that's exactly where he was leading us, John, until we discovered—way out here, in what many of the 'beautiful people' would consider hell—the truth."

John was in awe. He had never heard his father speak this way. Normally soft spoken and a man of very, very few words, he couldn't think of a time that he'd heard his dad say this much in one setting, unless he was teaching a class. And never had he heard such conviction, such passion. He realized he was no longer leaning casually against the rough wood of the old shed. He had changed his posture to that of a student sitting at the feet of a master teacher, sitting on his knees, hands folded in his lap, and leaning forward as if he could gain more knowledge by bending toward the teacher. He was afraid to break the rhythm of his father's lecture, but he felt as if he were expected to ask the next question—the question that would lead to more than just words, but to answers.

"So what is the difference? Why do you feel that you have discovered what really is right and what is wrong?"

"No, John. That is the wrong question. You see, that's what we thought we were looking for. Right truth, wrong 'truth.' Right people, wrong people." He was using his hands like a scale, held by Lady Justice, measuring what was right and wrong. "In reality, John—in *truth*—it is not always whether something is right or wrong; rather, does it bring honor or shame? You see, that is more the mindset of the Middle East—the mindset of the writers of Scripture. To be sure, we have had other books added to our 'faith' and claimed as Holy Scripture, but by whom, John? I'll tell you: by the very ones who would gain from those writings. Again, by those who were trying to tell us right from wrong, but what usually only came out as their version, their interpretation of right—what benefits *me*—and wrong—what harms *me*.

"Yet when you read the Bible, written by God, it is what brings shame upon his name, his character, or what brings honor. And what brings shame must be atoned for. Do you know what the word *atoned* means? 'Covered.' The shame of Noah was covered by his sons in the story of how he got drunk and naked after leaving the Ark. And the one thing, the only thing, that can cover our shame—and here's where I want you to truly listen, John—the only thing that covers our shame is blood. Innocent blood. God instituted the sacrificial system to cover our shame...shame caused by, yes, wrong actions. But wrong that was established by His word, His commandments, His law—not by what the popular or the majority determined.

"You see, he didn't leave us in our shame, unable to stand in His presence. He gave us a way—no, *the* way, to be covered. That, John, is why Jesus, the very Son of God, came to this world. And what was it that your namesake, John the Baptizer, said when he saw Jesus? 'Behold, *the lamb of God*, who comes to take away the sins of the world.' He didn't do that with his teaching, nor his good life. He couldn't do it with those things, for the Bible also makes it clear: 'without the shedding of blood there can be no remission—no covering—of sin.' No, Son, he did it with his shed blood."

"Right. I know all that. You've always taught me that, I've heard all that. Okay, I admit, I've never heard this right, wrong, shame, honor stuff, and that is good. I've learned a lot of *why* there had to be the covering, but I've always heard about the shed blood. Pop, remember? That is why you told me that we are Haimaelians—followers of the blood. So what's so different about what you're telling me now?"

"That's just it, John. We—rather, they, The Brothers—are 'followers of the blood.' They started when Jesus shed his blood—blood from his wounded side that poured on to the cloak of the very Roman centurion who had led his crucifixion detail. And that is where they went wrong. Don't you see, it wasn't that literal blood—that very human blood of the very human Jesus—that saves. It was the *shedding* of his blood—the sacrifice, and the obedience. And it is our faith in his obedience, his act of obedience—dying on that cross—that saves us. Not our faith in just the blood. Yet, for all these years, *that* is what we have falsely followed. That is what we have put our faith in. An artifact, covered in blood. Did you know that, John? And did you know that I have held it?"

"The cloak? *You* have held it? Pop, I thought only a handful of people in all of history have actually seen the cloak up close, let alone *held* it! How? When? What was it like? How did it make you feel? *Pop! The* cloak!?"

Jake Turner looked again at his son. The pride he had felt a few hours before was now mixed with so much sadness. He should have expected no less of a reaction, for he knew that he, himself, had taught the young man when he was just a boy the legend of the cloak. And it had been he who had shared that very fact that only a few in all of history had seen "it." But to hear his son now—to watch him literally change into a different person at the very mention of *an artifact*—

saddened and worried him.

"John, it's a cloak. I know you've been taught that it is something far more. I know *I* taught you. But it is only a piece of cloth, with blood on it. True, it is the blood of Jesus, the Son of God. But John, I'm sorry to break this to you. It's just blood. Not something to be worshiped. Not something to be bowed down to. And certainly not something to build an entire denomination, an entire people of faith, on.

"Son, we worship God. The one true God who sent his one and only Son, Jesus—God incarnate. Remember what that means? God *in the flesh.* And we worship that God in the flesh, Jesus, who came to this earth for one reason: to shed his blood to atone—to cover—our sin. But we don't worship that blood, and we certainly are not to worship a piece of cloth that has that blood on it. His blood was precious. I know that. I know it was his blood that saved my sin.

"But John, that cloak did not save, cannot save, and never will save anyone. Yes, I saw it. I held it. I was part of a team that was making a very important decision concerning it. And, sad to say, I worshiped it. I thought I was entering into the very Holy of Holies when I was allowed into the room where it is protected and preserved. I shook with anticipation.

"But it was only a cloak. Oh, I tried to make it more. I tried with all my heart to believe that it was more. But when I actually saw it, held it, examined it—it was just a cloak. Then and there I realized what I've been telling you, yet I made a conscious decision to work at forgetting what I'd felt—or rather, did not feel. I continued to work for The Brothers. I continued to minister and came here as a missionary under that umbrella. But I finally came to the realization that I simply could not live this lie any longer. I have submitted my resignation to The Council. I will no longer accept funds from any supporter who does not know about my resignation. And I will do everything in my power—no, John—in the power of my Lord and Savior Jesus Christ, to tell everyone I can the *truth.* That *Jesus* saves us from our sin—not that cloak."

"So you just walk away from years of what you've taught. Including what you've taught me. And now I guess I'm supposed to walk away from it all too. Well, I'm sorry, Pop. That may all be fine for you. But honestly, I don't care."

John stood, fists clenched, and walked away angrily. There was no way he was going to spend the rest of the day in this heat with a crazy Bible banger.

Twenty-one

The subject was not brought up again. John got up the next morning and went back to work with his dad, clearing brush, and did so for the next several days as well. They were attempting to clear over two acres, and though there were several other people from the compound who came out at various times to help, most of them had other tasks to attend to; thus, the majority of the job was left to John and his dad. Even though it was a large lot and the work was tough and slow, John knew that he was being a big help. There was simply no way his father could have done this project without him. He also knew it would be extremely rude to work completely on the other side of the lot, so he worked alongside his dad. Often his dad would use the shovel and dig around an especially tough bush while John, with a rope tied around the base root ball, would pull with all of his strength.

They worked in silence for the most part, broken only by an occasional discussion about how much hotter this day or that day had been compared to any other day, though they were *all* hotter than blazes as far as John was concerned. He simply wanted to avoid any conversation that went deep. Every once in a while he saw his dad watching him, observing him, and several times John could tell his dad wanted to say something, but thought better about it each time.

After they had worked the morning, they would head to the house for lunch, followed by a nap while it was the hottest part of the day. There, too, the conversations were strained. His mother kept the conversation going by asking John to tell various stories about the school year. She was mortified at the things John had eaten for money and teared up to think he had done that because they had been unable to send him any spending money. They laughed at most of his stories, but nearly rebuked him for others, especially his verbal attack on Dr. Newman of Newman College.

"Oh, John. Haven't we taught you better than that? Did we not teach you to respect your elders? To respect authority? You may not like Lawrence Newman, which isn't too surprising given your discernment. But that doesn't give you the right to verbally accost him. I hope that you apologized."

"Actually, Mom, he told me he didn't expect one. I met with him a few weeks after the game in Dr. Stoker's office."

John's dad hadn't been too involved in their conversation until now. He had been clearing the table but sat back down at the table. "Why did you meet with those two? I don't know Dr. Stoker all that well, but I can't imagine why Lawrence Newman would want to be in his office unless he had some sort of ulterior motive."

"Oh, yeah, I forgot. You guys *know* Dr. Newman. I forgot he was once a part of The Brothers." Sarcastically, he added, "But then, I guess you're not anymore either."

"John! You will not talk to your father that way. We've talked about your discussion the other day, and I don't blame you for being upset. But you will not be rude. He may not be your friend right now, and certainly not your hero at this point, but he is your father."

There was a tense moment as John, sitting across the table again from his parents, looked at both of them. They were older—he had been a late-in-life child. They had tried so many times to have children, and John had heard the stories of how sorrowful and disappointing each effort had been. John knew they had been very active in The Brothers before their mission assignment and knew now that his father had been much higher up in the leadership than he had ever imagined. *He had seen and held the cloak!* He still couldn't believe that—and that news had been followed immediately by the revelation they no longer had that faith. All he'd believed had been pulled out from under him. Admittedly his faith hadn't been all that strong—it was more hereditary than owned. But it had been a stable point in his life. His parents had been so giving, so trusting, so trustworthy. How could he doubt them now?

"I'm sorry. You're right, Mom. And Pop, I've done a lot of thinking about what you said. It all just hit me wrong. It's hard for me to think I've been wrong—*you've* been wrong—all these years, especially to realize that the whole reason you're out here in this God-forsaken place is because of those wrong beliefs. I feel like you've thrown away your life for nothing!"

"John, there is so much for us to talk about; first, that we most certainly have not thrown our lives away. Anything but! We've been spending a lot of time out in that hot field of rocks, but we'll take a break this afternoon, and I'll show you some of the things that have been happening here. I think you'll be impressed. Also, I don't want to push you, and we should have plenty of time to talk much more about it, but I want to discuss so much more with you about what genuine faith is—or, rather, faith *in* the genuine. I'm so glad you're willing to at least give it a fair examination with an open mind and, hopefully, an open heart.

His father paused. "But before we get sidetracked and forget your original point: yes, we know, or knew, Lawrence Newman. He was my best friend, and he almost married your mother before I wooed her away from him with my charm. See, John, he *was* a member—a very influential member—of the same group that I was in The Brothers. He was rather impulsive and, honestly, way too brash…always just saying the first thing that came to his tongue without making a stop at his brain. It was my job to mentor him in some of the finer points of debate and tact, but it didn't take long for him to take over my position as the main presenter. He was good, but not always good enough. We were part of the group that studied the cloak, and made a very important, very persuasive, but, unfortunately, very unsuccessful presentation to The Council regarding that cloak."

"Was it the same stuff you talked to me about out in the field? That whole 'shame versus honor' thing?"

"No, no. Remember, John, I said *we*, your mother and I, had only come to *that* realization recently—or, at least, only recently came to the commitment involving that realization. And I honestly don't think Lawrence would have been arguing that point—certainly not before The Council. No 'content points' with that argument, right, Mother?"

John's mother smiled. Then, as though she'd pictured such an event in her mind, she laughed out loud. "No, Jake. And Lawrence truly would have lacked passion on that presentation. He would have melted on the spot when steam started coming out of those men's ears! And believe me, John, there would have been steam! Oh, and before I forget *your* little comment, Mr. Turner, I did *not* almost marry Lawrence Newman. I saw from the beginning that he was nothing but an empty shell. A handsome shell, but a shell nonetheless. I never could have fallen for him. But I did fall for your plain old dad. He was simply the better choice."

"Well thank you, *Mrs. Turner*, for that ringing vote of confidence. But the point I was making—before that outpouring of love—was that Lawrence Newman would *not* have been arguing for any change in doctrine. In fact, what we were arguing for at that point, so many years ago, was to keep the doctrine and practice the same, as opposed to what was being argued from the other side: a proposal that was going to be the most unbelievable change that The Brothers could have ever imagined in its two-thousand year history. I say 'we,' but it was actually Newman who did the majority of the arguing. I had simply been the one who had done the research. Newman was always the better presenter, but he was lousy in the research library. He always felt that he could win more on presentation than on content, but he rarely did. And, sure enough, just like always, he got beat that day. The only problem was, this time it really mattered."

"What was that issue, Pop? Why did it matter so much more?"

"We were arguing over the continued preservation of the cloak, John—the cloak that had been so very carefully preserved for the past two thousand years. But also something so much greater. There was an effort afoot to do some very unique scientific experiments on it…experiments that would damage the integrity of the cloak. This was the very foundation of our faith. Comparatively, it would be like blasting a hole through the Gordon site in Jerusalem—the supposed tomb of Joseph where Jesus laid for three days after his crucifixion."

"Something that serious sounds like it would have been listened to. Why on earth didn't you win?"

"The other side, the side Collier was pushing for, had a presenter who was something else, John. He wasn't nearly the orator that Lawrence was—nothing like him at all. But on this occasion he had passion, eloquence, and, perhaps most importantly, vested interest. And he was backed by the research and knowledge of a group of scientists—men who were part of The Brothers and had been funded for these experiments for quite some time by The Council at Collier's request. We all had the chance to examine the cloak to determine whether the integrity of the cloak would be compromised, and Lawrence and I felt there was no way that their experiment could be done without considerable damage. Further, we argued that it *shouldn't* be done. Their experiment was too risky, too damaging to the cloak, and it didn't seem ethical, no matter what the outcome. In fact, my argument was it should not be done quite specifically *because of the outcome.*"

John's curiosity was overwhelming, but so was his awe. As close as he was to his parents, or thought he was, he had never known this part of their life. He had only known them as the quiet, secluded missionary couple in this backward place—a place that seemed to fit them and their lifestyle perfectly. Now, to hear that they had been active and even in leadership in the denomination? He couldn't even fathom it!

His dad had stood before The Council! That was hard to picture—his dad hardly talked in front of John and his mother. His teaching at the mission was usually limited to a handful of people, and John had seem him actually shake in fear when the crowd was any bigger than twenty. The Council wasn't all that big, but they were some of the most influential people in the country, let alone the denomination. His mind was whirling to think of this quiet man arguing with any one individual, let alone that collective group of leaders.

"Pop, I gotta say I've got a ton of questions, but obviously the main question: what was the experiment? What outcome were you afraid would happen?"

"How much do you know about Duncan Collier, Son?"

John put his forefinger to his thumb to represent a big zero: nothing.

"Are you aware that he is quite ill, and has been for quite some time?"

John shook his head no, indicating with a roll of his hand that his dad should simply continue the story.

"Okay, okay, I'm getting there. All right. Duncan Collier had the money—rather, his supporters have given to the point that he has built up quite a kitty—to utilize quite a bit of experimental medicine. But medicine wasn't helping. Not regular medicine. He has a very bad liver. I don't want to pass any judgment on why, 'cause I don't know for sure. Could be hereditary, or could be because of any number of reasons. All I know is he's been sick for a long time and hasn't gotten any better over the years. Because he is rich, he has always been the favorite patient and target of shysters and quacks—but also of legitimate doctors. It was the latter kind, John, a very legitimate doctor, who approached him when liver transplants were on the cutting edge. He offered to put Collier on the national transplant list, but he warned him about all the known risks, especially the overwhelming chance of rejection. In fact, the doctor only gave Collier a 40 percent chance at best of surviving more than five years. Collier asked if there was any way those chances could be improved, and the doctor told him there truly was only one way, and it was barely off the drawing boards, let alone fully developed enough to guarantee any success.

His father drew a deep breath. "It was cloning, John. Doctors felt that if an organ could be cloned from the person in need of the transplant, there would be far less risk of rejection, thus greatly enhancing the chance of survival. Collier had enough medical researchers on his payroll in various areas of the world that he was able to put them on this unbelievable project."

"Okay, hold on a second, Pop. You're losing me. Dr. Collier needed a liver, so he put his research scientists and doctors to work at growing him a new one? From himself? And people didn't think he was crazy?"

"Actually, John, he's been heralded as a groundbreaking genius for doing so. He's given more private money to independent bio-genetic research than the government would probably ever give. Yes, it's for his own selfish gain and it wasn't really his own to give, but that's never stopped him. Through his own giving and through his speeches to many organizations and politicians, though they probably hate to admit relationship with him, he had raised so much money and awareness. Hundreds of thousands of other people have been, or will be, helped by such research."

"So what's the problem? I mean, if it was truly going to help so many people, why not do it? That seems like the right thing to do."

"Ah, so we're back to our discussion of a few days ago: the difference between what's right or wrong, and who, or what, decides the difference? So something might be right for someone...but what if it hurts someone else? Is it still right? What if it helps a thousand, but hurts one...literally takes that someone's life? Is it right *then*? Or is it still wrong? What if it helps only one, but that one is, say, the President of the United States, but it's going to cost the life of that someone else? Is it right then? Or is it still wrong? See, John, that's why it's called *situational ethics.*"

"Got it, Pop. I understand where you're coming from on this, and you're right. I see how easy it is to fall into that trap. Whoa, and I thought I had strong principles."

"You do have strong principles, John. But it's very easy to be swallowed up in a worldview that's so prevalent that says, basically, majority rules, not principles. What happens is much like an old story I read a long time ago, where some men broke into a store to steal things—only they didn't walk out with them. So they slipped into hiding places until the store closed, then spent the night changing price tags. When the doors opened the next morning, they simply went to the checkout stand with their newly priced—very low priced—goods, leaving behind things of no real value that now had huge price tags on them. John, the world has changed the price tags on values today. What should be very valuable—life, marriage relationships, parenting—has largely been devalued. And things that really have lesser value, especially self-appeasement, have been given tremendous value. How wrong! Yet how popular to the majority."

"Okay, so did these doctors clone Dr. Collier and give him a new liver?"

"Actually, they tried the cloning but couldn't make it work. Then something happened that no one could have ever in a million years—or at least, two thousand—thought of. And that's where the real argument came into play. After many, many failed attempts, one researcher came forward with an idea that was so bizarre, so unbelievable, so out of this world, that it should never have been given audience. But it was. And it was given audience all the way to The Council. To make it even more unbelievable, they approved the idea, and the entire plan, which was where Lawrence Newman and I came in. Their plan involved taking blood from the cloak—the blood of Jesus—and cloning *him*. Then, well, I'm not sure exactly what was to happen then. Give Collier a blood transfusion? Give him part of this cloned Jesus' liver? All I know is that their plan involved taking a four-inch square out of the very center of the cloak, which, obviously, ruined its integrity, which was our argument. Besides that, Son, it was so wrong. All those previous efforts were playing 'god' with life. But now they were playing god with God Himself!"

"I can't believe it. How could anyone have felt like this was the right thing to do? How could they have thought such a crazy thing would work? It *didn't work*, did it?"

"Did it work? I don't know, John. Due to our fight, our presentation that was rejected, Newman left The Brothers, and we were banished here. Collier didn't take too kindly to my outspokenness about how nothing, not even his life, made this thing right. We were gone fairly shortly after the vote. Quite honestly, I've never heard if it worked or not. I know it was a far-fetched dream, but there's no way they could actually do this—everything before this had failed. But whether it worked or not wasn't what mattered. We simply didn't think it was right, or ethical to even try, let alone the damage it would do to the integrity of the cloak. Again, remember, at that time the cloak was the foundation of all I believed in. It was my holy grail, my crucifix, my Shroud of Turin."

"Pop, why doesn't anyone know about this? How could they have kept an experiment to clone Jesus Christ a secret?"

"It must *not* have worked, John, or they couldn't have kept it a secret. And there's no way The Council was going to let the word out that they had allowed such an experiment—a *failed* experiment, let alone a damaging experiment—to be done on the cloak. It wasn't just the foundation of my faith; it *is* the foundation of an entire movement of faith. They would have had a revolution on their hands if word ever got out to the faithful followers that the blood from that cloak had been cut out and placed in some scientist's beaker. Collier himself would have been crucified!"

Twenty-two

Chicago was hot. It had been over 100 degrees for ten days. And humid. So humid Brock was thinking he might as well have gone to the jungle with John; it couldn't be much worse than this. Though he was absolutely correct in assuming that John was experiencing the same discomfort, there was no way he could know that John was also going through much of the same emotions he was feeling right now...his continued shocked reaction to the news he'd heard from his stepfather on their drive. He had always known Michael was not his father, but to find out he had *no* father? At least not one that anyone would have ever known about. And that his mother was actually a surrogate mother—she had only carried him to birth? He was a *test-tube* baby! Whatever that was. He'd never heard of such a thing until Michael patiently explained it to him.

At least it helped him understand why he'd felt so empty, so lost! His life was a joke. He was a freak. The void he'd felt so often—a feeling of being completely disconnected from anyone and everyone—was true. As a result, he had very mixed feelings about the upcoming visit from John: on the one hand he couldn't bear to see his friend, feeling that John, with that uncanny discernment of his, would see right through his very empty shell and call him out for being the fraud he'd actually been all this time. Yet on the other hand, he realized he desperately needed his friend right now. John always had that way of making Brock believe in himself, find the best of his self, and be what he should be. John had, on more than one occasion, been his north star, and if Brock ever needed guidance to find himself, it was now!

First, however, he had something else he had to take care of—the end of his internship. He had been busy all summer following Duncan Collier. The older man was slow, due largely to his illness, but he still met with a lot of people every day. Brock was responsible for knowing the purpose of the visit, briefing Collier and providing him with a set of crib notes, plus whatever it was that was being asked for, then greeting the visitors and ushering them into the plush office. He would brief the visitor on exactly how they were to greet Dr. Collier, what they were allowed to say—and not to say. And he would make sure that they knew how sick Dr. Collier was, so they were not to get too close to him.

On more than one occasion over the several weeks so far he had been the one who kept someone from entering the office over such a simple thing as a cough, or runny nose, or, heaven forbid, a sneeze. He also had stopped the ongoing parade of people on several days when he could sense that Collier had simply had enough. He was just too weak to continue. But the visitors never stopped coming. There would be more tomorrow, and the next day, and the day after that. People came to bring gifts, but those gifts usually came with strings. Something was wanted in exchange: a blessing, a benevolent need met, a baby blessed, or simply advice given for a new business venture. Brock would meet with them, give them the ground rules for their brief meeting, then, after briefing Dr. Collier, usher them in, while he went out to repeat the process with the next visitor.

The good thing was he was busy—too busy to do much thinking about all that he'd learned, at least during the day. But he hated the nights. He hated any time he was alone. He also hated that this summer had been nothing like he'd anticipated. He had hoped to spend a lot of time with Collier himself—not spend all his time introducing everyone else to him. He hadn't spent more than fifteen minutes all summer alone with the man. That wasn't to say he hadn't learned anything; he had sat in on many of those meetings and watched the man speak words of comfort, of hope, of blessing, of wisdom to visitor after visitor. He had stood in awe as this man, so sick himself, had reached out to someone and touched them, prayed over them, blessed them—unless they had something that was contagious, of course.

There were times, though, he had to admit, that he had heard Collier speak of those very people with disdain after they had left his office. He had also watched the old man be far more perfunctory in his prayers and blessings than "real"—almost as though he were simply going through some empty motion rather than a heartfelt ministry. The people he touched didn't seem to care, as they were usually overwhelmed to simply be there. But over the weeks it had come to truly bother Brock. He knew that many of the people waiting to meet Collier had not only traveled from a great distance at great expense, they were so hungry for what they were seeking that they were willing to come back day after day if their appointment was broken due to Collier's erratic schedule. Appointments meant nothing to him, as he would decide in the middle of the day that he'd had enough, or that he needed to watch something on television, or that he needed to make some phone calls. It would be left to Brock to break the hearts of all those waiting in the large foyer for their time with their leader.

Brock found himself intermittently loving the man and longing to be near him, then hating him for his rude and seemingly selfish behavior. It was during one of the better times that Collier called the young man into his office "for a little chat." Brock was not sure what that meant, but he dutifully followed the halting, faltering old man into his office.

"Brock, I know your time here is almost done. I hope you've enjoyed the summer, and I want you to know you have done an outstanding job. It isn't easy trying to meet the needs of so many people, but you were extremely patient, humble, helpful, and—perhaps most importantly—compassionate."

Seeing the surprised look on Brock's face, he continued. "Oh yes, I've noticed. I know we haven't had much time to talk, but don't think I haven't been watching. I see how you look at the families that come in, and you always take time even for the youngest of children, or the oldest of men. The many needs that come in these doors—blind, deaf, or lame—you have empathized and sympathized with them all. I can tell that you have experienced pain of your own, for you treat those who are in pain so kindly, so patiently. In addition, Brock, I have observed, and have greatly appreciated, how patient and kind you have been with me. I'm not always the easiest to work for—or so I've been told. People grow impatient with me, and perhaps you have as well. But you've never shown it. Nor have you shown impatience with our constituents. You know I'm not well, but I feel I must continue to minister to these faithful pilgrims, and you obviously feel the same way. You have a unique way about you, young man. You are truly a very special person."

Brock had been standing in deference to the elderly leader, but the compliment took all the strength from his legs. He nearly fell into the chair facing Collier's desk. Realizing Collier was waiting for him to respond, he swallowed hard and tried to find his voice. "I have wanted so badly to talk to you all summer, sir. I greatly appreciate all the kind words you've said, and I also greatly appreciate the chance to talk with you now, though I'm not quite sure what to say. I came here this summer as a confused kid, and I can't say that I'm ending the summer any better. I was hoping to find something that would give me purpose, direction. I was hoping you could help me find that. But I know you are so busy, not to mention sick. I'm not sure anything would have been any different even if you weren't sick, or busy. The problem hasn't been yours—but mine. I honestly don't think there is anyone or anything that can help me. I think I am the very definition of helpless."

"No, young man—you are anything but. You are not helpless, for I've seen you take many matters into your own hands and help so many, without waiting to be told what to do or how to do it. But you must learn that others cannot do for you what you are not willing to do for yourself. You are waiting for someone else to give you hope and purpose? Well, young man, I can tell you from experience that you must stand up for yourself, and make your own purpose, find it for yourself. You do have one. I would certainly not have brought you here this summer if I did not believe that, but that does you no good. *You* must believe it, and must believe in yourself. You must know it. Here's what I do know, Brock. You are special. I've said that already, but let me explain. You have something within you, within that heart of yours. You have blood coursing through your veins that contains something you'll never understand."

No longer overwhelmed, Brock leaned forward in the chair, eager to hear more—to learn more about his origin. "That's part of what's bothering me, sir. My stepfather only recently—on my way to Chicago earlier this summer—told me about my birth, and it's all just too weird for me."

96

"Weird? In what way?" Collier was afraid of what Auzman might have said.

"I'm a 'test-tube' baby. My mom isn't really my mother, she's my surrogate mother—she only carried me. I don't even know who my real dad is, and my stepdad obviously married my mom and got stuck with me—the freak. I don't understand why they had me that way...why they even had me at all!"

Relieved that Brock still didn't know everything, Collier contemplated exactly what he should tell him. Obviously he needed to know enough to not give up on himself, but he couldn't be told the truth. Not all of it. Not yet.

"I know about you, Brock. I know your mother, and your stepfather. You say he married your mother for her? Not true, young man. I know that he fought to have you, to raise you, as his very own son. And I know he did so because he was convinced, even back then, that you would be a great leader, and he wanted to be part of your development. He literally sacrificed his own career—a very promising career—to be able to raise you."

Brock took a long look at his mentor. Collier's little speech only led to more confusion, for several reasons. He wasn't sure, again, what Collier's real relationship with his stepfather entailed. Michael had attempted to explain to Brock that he, too, had worked at the international office under the tutelage of Duncan Collier, and that he owed him much, but wouldn't elaborate. In addition, he was confused by all this talk of his greatness and the knowledge of it from the beginning of his life.

But he was mostly confused by Collier's talk because he had such a hard time believing him. All too many times over the past couple of months he had seen this man say just what people wanted—needed—to hear. Like a benevolent grandfather patting a child on the head before handing over some candy, Collier took little thought to what harm his advice or false encouragement might do. Seemingly he simply wanted to meet with as many people as possible, as though it made him feel better to make people feel good. He certainly didn't see what he was doing as lying or deceiving—only as encouraging.

Brock, however, had come to realize that you could hardly ever tell when he was actually telling someone the truth as opposed to what he thought they might want to hear. So, was what Collier was saying truth now? How could it be? If his stepfather had fought to raise him, why did he then pass him off to Stoker and Batterson Academy? And why would he want to raise him in the first place? He was a kid who apparently came from nowhere.

"I'm not exactly sure why he would do that. Why would anyone give their life up for someone else unless they were going to get something out of it?"

"Actually, Brock, there are people who do such things because they see the good that they can do—that the sacrifice of one can help many, many others. Your mother understood that. And someday you will too. But, yes, your stepfather did gain. He gained a purpose for himself by helping to shape your purpose. He gained a new understanding of himself. And he gained a son—you. Michael Auzman might never have had a child on his own, Brock. But by taking your mother as his wife, he gained a family, a purpose, a cause. He knew what he was getting into. And he fought for it."

"How do you know all of this? Up until a couple of months ago I didn't even know my parents knew you—or even knew of you. Now I hear that you know the intimate details of their life. Why? How?"

"I've known your parents for quite some time, young man. Your mother worked for me right here in these very offices as one of my most loyal followers and dedicated servants. And your stepfather argued for many more things than the right to raise you. He was one of the best, the brightest, of our young student leaders. I have heard him present facts on subjects that would—how do you young people say it?—'blow your mind'? He was able to see things in the present and project the future outcome like no one I've ever known. He wasn't the most charismatic speaker. I imagine you can tell that from how he probably still is today. But I'll tell you what set him apart, Brock. It was one simple, yet profound, thing: conviction. What he presented, he believed. And he had a way of making you believe it, too, because he presented with such conviction. Few people possess that ability, but I'm convinced that you might have it, too."

Leaning back in the chair, Brock realized his posture, with arms crossed, was communicating defiance. Uncrossing them, he continued. "Okay, so he believed in what he was saying. But is that all it takes? Is that enough? I've seen some people pretty convinced that what they believed or believed in was right—totally and completely. They had conviction, but they didn't have facts to back up their belief. It was, pure and simple, blind faith. Yeah, I've seen my stepfather absolutely convinced of what he was saying, and pretty convincing, too. But how he said what he said doesn't matter if what he's saying is just plain wrong, does it? And he's been wrong on some of those things. Lots of things! Does a person's passion or, as you put it, conviction, truly matter if there's not something substantive behind it?"

"Well put, Brock. Yes, I do believe you have some of that persuasive ability. Your speech at the Senior Reception convinced me of that, but you have shown further proof several times over the summer, and that was just one more proof. You know how to see beyond the norm and ask the tough question. You'll go far."

Now Brock was defiant. He realized Collier was blowing smoke, and he had had enough. "Okay, there's my point. I asked you a question, and you gave me an answer that is not an answer, at least not to my question. You avoided the question by giving an answer that redirects toward another topic or thought. And as much as you say you've seen me give proof of your belief in me, I've seen the same thing with you, sir. Only I don't believe positive things about you, Dr. Collier, or this empty religion you lead. It's no wonder people call this thing a cult. It feels like there's this unknown code that is spoken, things said that never directly answer a person's deepest need, or quest. But because a symptom or a separate need *is* answered, most people leave here with some sort of satisfaction, yet never what they sought in the first place. It's like watching someone at a carnival play the shell game, hoping for the giant stuffed teddy bear but leaving, and somehow satisfied with, the kewpie doll. I don't know how you do it, but I do know I want no more of it. I need real answers, not empty accolades that mean nothing in the long run."

Collier was more than a little hot under the collar over the brashness of this young man and nearly lashed out in that anger. But he knew this type and, more importantly, he knew Brock. He knew Brock could go far—would go far—if he was pointed in the right direction, and mentored along the way. Michael Auzman had argued that very point nearly twenty years ago, and he had been right. Collier couldn't afford to get in an argument with Brock and risk losing him. He needed to stay on course with Michael Auzman's argument from back then: Create, develop, train, and send.

And above all, keep the truth from this kid and the world for as long as possible. If he found out too soon, he would not be ready. And if the world found out before he was ready, there was no telling what would happen. Brock was not ready to be sent, but Collier was finding the development and the training far more complicated than he, Auzman, or the rest of those who developed this plan could have ever anticipated. Michael had obviously already opened the proverbial bag of beans during their drive to Chicago. Collier wanted to make sure he didn't tip it over and start the spilling. Not yet.

"Brock, you are absolutely right. I did not answer your question, and you deserve an answer, not a diversion. You are correct. Eloquence, conviction, and argument mean nothing without substance. We pride ourselves on presenting our argument of faith, but that argument—and more importantly that faith—means nothing if there is not something of substance to back it up. Faith must have its object. For us, The Brothers, we know that we have such an object of faith. Brock, we have the very blood of Jesus. Believers have made pilgrimages for centuries to bow down before the cloak. People have been healed in its presence, changed, transformed. This is no cult, son. This is no empty promise. The object is real, people's faith in what it does is real, and the results are neither a kewpie doll nor a cheap carnival trick. They, too, are real."

"Are they? What proof do you have of these real results? What is the measurement of real? And how do you know that whatever happened to people who made that pilgrimage happened because of the cloak? How do you *know* it's real? I mean, I'm here, right? And the cloak is here, right? I came here with a need, I've made my 'pilgrimage.' And I've done my best to believe. But I've had no change. So is the problem with me? Or with the cloak. Who knows, maybe all the magic has been used up. What I *do* know is it hasn't done anything for me. I'm still empty, and so are your answers."

"Stop right there. I don't like your tone, Brock, or your challenges. Maybe the problem is you. Maybe you don't have the faith necessary. Or, maybe you're looking for the wrong thing, so you haven't found it. But I will not let you blame the cloak. And your insolence borders on blasphemy, young man."

Collier held his breath. Had his anger gone too far? Had he pushed Brock out the door—out of the project—before it had even had a chance to really start? Would the plan, set in motion two decades earlier, be stopped, just because Brock Auzman had pushed his buttons? Would he now die without leaving a legacy—or at least without leaving the legacy that he had longed for: that The Brothers would be recognized not as a cult, but as *the* one true faith? He had to do whatever he could to keep the dream alive.

"Brock, we need to take a walk. Perhaps you should actually see the cloak."

Twenty-three

"**D**ude, these seats are awesome! How did you swing this? You must have done some serious schmoozin' with one of Collier's supporters to get seats like this!"

Brock and John were sitting four rows up from the field, first base side, just a few sections over from the visitor's dugout. It hadn't been Brock that had done the schmoozing; their old rival Jason Collier, whom Brock now worked with at the international office, had gotten them. Jason had simply mentioned the request to his father, and the next day Brock had been handed an envelope with the "Club Box Seat IF" tickets inside. It was only after they had entered "the friendly confines" that they both realized IF meant infield—and just how great the seats were. They each got a couple of Chicago-style hot dogs and a soda apiece, then sat back to enjoy the game. John had been looking forward to this day all summer and couldn't wait to catch up on all the happenings with his best friend.

Brock, however, was not so anxious to talk. Nothing that had happened this summer had been as he'd hoped. No answers had been given—only more questions raised. And he was afraid that John would be asking questions of him; questions that he could not possibly answer. Brock just missed catching a foul ball—it ended up in the hands of a middle-aged man two seats over—then they, along with the rest of the crowd, sat back down. The sun was warm, the ivy was beautiful, the scene was surreal. They were tired and the game was a bit boring, but they wanted to enjoy the whole game, especially the traditional seventh-inning stretch singing by the famous announcer up in the press box.

"Okay, Wiz. You've been quiet this whole game, and if you'd had any life in you at all you could've caught that ball. Heck, a little old lady could've beat you out of it. I don't know what's eating you, but you're making me feel like you'd rather be just about anywhere but here."

Brock knew he should have known better than try to act happy with his friend. John had always been able to see right through him—and even though it had been a few months since they'd been together, he should have known that John hadn't lost any of that sensitivity.

"Sorry, dude. Trust me, it's not you; it's me. Lots has happened since graduation, and I'm still trying to figure it all out. But this isn't the time or the place, so I'll..."

He didn't finish. John grabbed his knee and squeezed hard, and got right in his face. "No, this *is* the time, so I guess that means this has to be the place. I came here to watch baseball, relax with my best friend, catch up on our summer, take in some of this famous ballpark, and wrap up the end of my so called 'carefree' preadult years by not dealing with any adult things whatsoever. But, like always, you and your constant internal turmoil won't let any of that happen. I hoped—I *prayed*—that you'd get over it this summer, but I guess I knew all along that wasn't going to happen. So here you sit, still feeling like everyone's against you, everything's destined to ruin your life, and you've got it worse than anyone else in the whole wide world. Well, get over yourself, man. Life—*your life*—ain't that bad, but you'll never know it if you keep looking at that half-empty glass. Look around you, Brock. Look at this place. I know it's not reality. I know we can't sit here for the rest of our lives and do nothing with our lives. But we *can* enjoy this—here and now. I *want to*. And you should want to also. But you can't. Or won't. You'll sit here feeling sorry for yourself and miss out on what could have been one of the best memories of this summer, just like you missed that foul ball."

Brock flared. "Back off, Clops! Don't play psychologist on me. You have no idea what my life is like—what *is* eating me. My life may not be bad in your eyes, but you don't see it through mine. Okay, you wanna know what's eating me? I'll tell you. On that 'glorious' drive that you so highly recommended I take with my stepfather—remember that advice?—I was informed that not only am I not *his* son (probably the only good news that I got all summer), I'm also not my *mother's* real son. She was, as my stepfather so eloquently put it, my 'surrogate' mother. She carried me, apparently, but I'm not really her son. But wait, before you interrupt on that one, let me tell you more, Mr. Know-It-All. In reality I'm *no one's son*, unless you want to count some test tube in Dr. Frankenstein's lab as being my parent."

Brock glowered. "That's right, your best friend, the one who's supposed to get over himself, is a test-tube baby—created, not born! I'm a freak, John, and you wonder why I'm feeling sorry for myself? At least it helps me understand why my parents sent me away and obviously didn't care to have me home for the summer. I guess you're right: I *should* be happy. I finally know why they don't want me around. So *that* question is answered! *Woo-hoo!* Let's celebrate, Clops! Let's throw a party right here over the fact that the freak of nature now knows why his parents don't want him!"

"Wait a minute. Do you hear yourself? This is *exactly* what I mean about getting over yourself. You get this news, and you automatically jump on the negative side of it. Can you not see that maybe, just maybe, your mom was willing to do whatever—even unbelievable things—to have a baby precisely because she did want one so badly? Hey, anyone can have a baby the regular way. She went to great lengths to have you. She did all she could to bring you into this world, sparing no expense, no effort. So before you get all stupid and complain again about how that makes you a freak, think. Maybe, just maybe, it makes you the special person that they believe you are, and that I believe you are too. In fact, Wiz, it makes you exactly that: a very special person."

Brock threw his hands up in the air. "Special person! Do you know how sick and tired I am of being called a special person? Like some trained monkey? I'd love nothing more than to sit and enjoy a game; lots of games in fact. I'd like to go to school this fall and simply study, learn, go on some dates, watch you play football—live! But I can't just do those things, 'cause I'm *special!* And what's so special about me? Certainly not my past—there isn't one!"

"But maybe that is what *makes* you special. Remember when I went to your parent's house last spring and your dad and I talked? He told me some interesting things, but they didn't mean a whole lot to me at the time. I guess he was telling me what you're telling me now: that your birth was no ordinary birth. He tried to tell me that you had some special background, but he didn't tell me—I don't think he knew—who your father was. But obviously, Wiz, it's someone pretty special. Okay, okay, I know, you're sick of hearing that. But I don't think being special means you can't live life. You've got a life, and you need to live it to the full. Let's get another hot dog, and get ready for that guy who sings during the seventh-inning stretch. And other than that? Unless you're willing to start talking some sense, and believing you are what you are, who you are? Shut up, man! Just shut up!"

Brock looked at his very best friend, the kid who always had a way of making sense of the senseless, and shook his head in wonder. So his stepfather had talked to John about the same thing he had hinted at with him? And how did this all tie in with what Collier was telling him a few days ago? And what he had felt when he held the cloak? Maybe he was special. What if John was right that all these things didn't make him a freak? What if all these things were actually working together to make him—well, special? One thing he knew, regardless of how "special" he might be: he still needed his best friend, who was now intently, but angrily, watching the ball game.

"One last question, genius. Just why do they call it the seventh-inning stretch?"

John just smiled. It was his friend's way of saying they were back. All was forgiven. Once again, their friendship would survive and probably even be strengthened by their honest challenge to each other. Never taking his eye off the game, he answered.

"You're pronouncing it wrong, but most people do. It's not seventh inning—it's 'Sventé Ning"—named after the only Swedish-Japanese baseball player to ever make it in the majors. He was pitching in the 1908 World Series and, tragically, was killed by a line-drive right to the middle of his forehead. People stood right on the sidelines during those days so they all stretched to see what had happened to him, and if he would get back up. He didn't. It was tragic. It happened to be the middle of the seventh inning, and baseball fans everywhere have stood at that time in his honor ever since then. They call it 'the Sventé Ning stretch'. I'm surprised a smart kid like you didn't know that."

Brock bust out laughing. "And I thought Collier was full of it."

Twenty-four

Jason Collier had been angry when Brock had been brought on as an intern, but he was livid when he found out that John Turner was coming for a visit. He was working at the International Headquarters as well, but certainly not in the executive office suite. His dad had told him that he couldn't afford accusations of nepotism so he would have to work his way up to any higher position, especially since he only worked during his summers home from college.

Now in his third summer in the mail room, khe couldn't believe Auzman had been given the prestigious internship right out of high school. What a jerk! He watched Brock get all the attention from the various guests coming through the headquarters, most of them on pilgrimage. He knew from his dad that Brock spent time with some of the biggest supporters of The Brothers, and was often handed huge checks to deliver to Collier himself—while about all Jason got to do was open envelopes sent in by the faithful, usually with no more than a few dollars of support.

He was sick and tired of hearing his dad talk about how great a job Brock was doing, especially when he would add the usual assessment that Brock was truly headed for leadership. He had seen Brock a few times over the summer when he had headed up to the suite for various errands, or simply when they had arrived or left the building at the same time and happened to run into each other. But they had rarely spoken more than a casual greeting or remarks about the hot, humid weather. One of their longest times together had happened just a few days ago when they both arrived at the perpetually slow elevator and had waited for what seemed an eternity. Brock was heading up to the executive office suite, of course, while Jason was on his way to the basement mail room. Jason, figuring they would only have the same inane small talk, was about to give up and simply head for the stairs when Brock dropped a couple of bombshells on him.

"Hey, I was thinking about what happened just before the Discipline Council last fall. When I punched you?"

"Yeah? What got you thinking about that? Guilt?"

Brock laughed. "Yeah, sure, that was it—guilt. Sorry, Jason, but it most definitely was not guilt. Though I guess I probably should apologize. I was pretty frustrated with the whole thing, and you didn't help with your attitude. A bit too smug as I recall, and that's why I punched you. But that was wrong, and I'm sorry."

Jason couldn't believe "the mighty Oz" was talking to him, let alone apologizing. Maybe there was a chance for working with Auzman after all, now that he was away from John Turner.

"Apology accepted. I couldn't believe you hit me, but, yeah, I probably was a bit cocky. I really thought Turner was going to get it, and I couldn't believe he didn't. He's such a jerk, and had no business being at a place like Batterson, let alone graduating and becoming an alumnus. We all know he was only there because of his parents and the charity shown by The Council. I just didn't think that charity would go as far as it did, allowing him to stay in school after what he did to Dr. Newman. That whole thing was a farce as far as I'm concerned."

"Actually, that whole thing is what got me thinking about you. I was thinking about why I hit you—how you put John down and wanted him to stay there. I was thinking about all that because John is coming here later this week. I'll be sure to let him know how excited you are to have him as a fellow alumni."

And with that Jason Collier had succeeded in doing what he could not afford to do—pushing Brock Auzman even further away. He could have cared less about Turner, but he knew he needed Auzman, even though the thought of being chummy with him made Jason nearly throw up. He couldn't stand him. As hot and humid as it was, even in the air-conditioned offices, Brock always wore his suit, though he wore no tie. Yet he always looked cool as a cucumber. Nothing seemed to bother him, which really bothered Jason. But he knew that if he was ever going to win points with his dad, points he desperately needed, it was going to be through the golden boy. He might not like him, but he needed him.

"Turner's coming here, to the International Headquarters? What on earth for—pilgrimage? He doesn't seem the type."

Then Brock had told him about John's upcoming visit and their "pilgrimage" to Wrigley Field, along with the rest of the things they had planned. Perhaps there was still a chance to gain some favor with Auzman by using what limited influence he did have. He'd volunteered to get field level box seats from a supporter he knew of, and Brock had jumped at it, claiming Turner would go nuts over it. Apparently he had, for when Jason heard them coming into the interns' dorm later that night, they were telling anyone who would listen what great seats they had, and what a great game it had been. Jason wasn't purposefully hiding from them, even though they would have probably questioned why he was hanging out in the dorm instead of heading home after work. So he was glad they hadn't seen him behind the dividing screen when they sat down in the student lounge. He was able to hear every word they were saying as they drank their coffee, and he couldn't believe their conversation.

"The problem is," Turner said, "whether they know it or not, they're asking me to make a choice between them, or this. I've known nothing else but this faith, faith in the cloak, and in the words of our prophets—not to mention *their* words! They taught me this faith. I know I haven't been the most faithful, but this feels like being very, very *unfaithful*. And I know they also said that it's my choice, but this feels an awful lot like heavy handed persuasion, even if it's being done from thousands of miles away."

"So how are they going to get support if they leave The Brothers?" Auzman questioned. "What are they going to do about money? How will they get back home?"

"That's just it. They don't intend to ever come back here. They said they can make it on their own there, and the people who have left The Brothers with them are helping them with whatever needs they have. They're old, Brock. They don't want to pick up after twenty years there and try to restart here. They say they will live—and die—there."

"Clops, I'm sorry. I don't know what to say. All I can think about is all you've said about them and their strong faith, and their faithfulness in serving Collier."

"Yeah, then to find out they weren't there because they were serving him or the faith. I can't believe he banished them to that place. They have never said a word about that until now. I admire them for that. But why now, after all these years? Don't you think you would have rebelled and left the guy way back then? Yeah, I admire them, but I also think that's crazy!"

"So what are you going to do? Are you going to go back there? Are you going to stay in the faith?"

"I'm afraid of how they're going to take it if I don't follow them in this newfound faith, you know? Wiz, dude, you should have heard how they prayed for me the night before I flew out! I gotta say, I've never heard them pray like that before. Maybe this thing they've found *is* real. It got to me. I can't go back there. I'm going to Dartmouth, I'm going to play football, and I'm going to live my life. I'm going to do all that, my friend, because quite honestly, I don't know what else to do."

Jason Collier wasn't sure what he was going to do either. Not right now. But he knew he was going to do something, and before he had discreetly left the lounge just a few minutes after Auzman and Turner finished their coffee and headed up to Brock's room, the plan was taking shape. This was the gold mine he needed to make his dad turn some attention on to him, instead of his precious project, Brock Auzman.

Twenty-five

Brock's first day at the John F. Kennedy School of Government was unbelievable. He couldn't believe he was finally at Harvard; even more, he couldn't believe how much he hated it already. The place had so much history and so much anticipation that he knew there was no way he could ever live up to the expectations of his parents, Dr. Collier, or even himself. But worse, he didn't want to. He didn't want to be president of the freshman class, like that would ever happen, let alone of the United States. He just wanted to be normal—whatever that was.

He had always thought John was normal—in his own weird way, that is. Sure he was huge, and ate far more than anyone could have ever imagined. And, of course, he had absolutely no boundaries when it came to speaking his mind whenever, wherever, and towards whomever. But he'd always seen John as normal when it came to his life: parents who loved him, fairly healthy emotions, and a constant drive to be the very best at what he did. Even though he now realized that not all those things might apply to John as much as he once thought, he still saw them as being signs of normalcy; signs that he most certainly did not have.

What, after all, was normal about being at Harvard? Thousands tried to get in but failed; thousands more made it and went on to careers that were unbelievable. And then there were the rest. Students who were in this amazing place, standing at the threshold of the greatest opportunity imaginable, who would just get by—not only in regards to their education, but in life. They would use their Harvard education like a thief uses the tools of his trade, gaining access into places they didn't belong, flaunting a piece of paper that had a name that represented truth and honor, but their reality was full of shame. At the very least, the shame of wasted potential.

Everyone else's opinion to the contrary, Brock felt that he was destined to be part of that last group. So he wanted out now, before he blew this chance and disappointed everyone. They might be disappointed that he had walked away from such an opportunity, but that would be better than failing. In just a few hours he had seen an amazing array of people whom he was sure were already on their way to greatness, and he figured there were probably many just like them who had not been admitted to Harvard. Why should he fill space that could be made available for someone who could be so much more than he would ever be?

And then, everything changed. He was standing in line, just like he'd been doing nearly all day, when he saw the most beautiful girl he had ever seen. She was coming out of the very building he was waiting in line to go in to, alone. Everything about her was unbelievable! And what he did next was too. He got out of the line that he'd been in for nearly forty-five minutes—the line that he *had* to be in to get in the class that he *had* to take—and walked right up to her. Brock Auzman, the kid who went to an all-boys school and hadn't talked to a girl his age in six months—and that was just a couple of other interns—walked right up to this goddess and said the first thing that came to his mind: something he'd heard John say a couple of times.

"Is your name Mona Lisa? 'Cause you are a work of art!"

Only then did he remember that it had *never* worked when John said it. Never.

Twenty-six

The hallway of the executive office suite was exactly sixty steps long, from the window behind Duncan Collier's desk to the window at the far end of the hallway. And it took Collier exactly five minutes to go from end to end. A younger, healthier man would obviously make it in much less than that, but Collier was neither young nor healthy. His window overlooked the staff parking lot and the path that wandered through the Japanese gardens beyond. It was a nice view during the day, but it was now close to two in the morning.

The view from the window at the other end of the hall wasn't much better at this time of the morning, yet Collier continued his pacing from one end of the hall to the other with lengthy stops at both ends. The main reason for the stops was, of course, his health. He was feeling somewhat better most days, but he still couldn't walk those sixty steps without stopping at each end to sit and catch his breath. Though the view at the far end was only of more buildings of the upscale business park and the Oakbrook Terrace water tower in the distance, it was enough to take his mind off of his thoughts for at least a few moments. Then he would start the slow walk to the other end of the hall, and the thoughts, concerns, frustrations and worries all came back.

This certainly wasn't the first time someone had left The Brothers, even from the mission field. In all reality, he was amazed that the Turners had stayed "faithful" for so long. After all, he had sought advice from the Committee on Expansion before sending the couple to their current field; specific advice as to which field the Committee was having the most difficulty breaking through. That's where they had been for nearly two decades, and from all reports they hadn't made much progress. That had to be frustrating and even a bit demoralizing—which had been Collier's hope when he'd banished them to that place.

But that was only part of what was keeping him up right now. Jason had told him about the conversation he had overheard, and his plan. It was that plan that was keeping him awake and pacing now, specifically the part of Jason's plan that involved him. He didn't think he could face Jake Turner again, let alone bring him up for public rebuke. Losing his breath as he neared the end of the hall, he remembered how hardened Turner's face had turned when he told him of the banishment. Thinking such action would crush and humble the man, he was shocked when he had responded with quiet resolve, telling Collier that he would welcome any place that took him far from here. That had been all right with Collier as well. But now Turner might be coming back—back to face the very Council that had banished him twenty-some years ago.

Jason's plan had merit. Perhaps the public rebuke and expulsion that went with it was what Collier should have done back then. Of course, he didn't have any valid reasons for doing so, but, then, he didn't really have a valid reason for the banishment, other than the fact that Turner had stood up to him, battling against him over the Messiah Project. Turner, and even more so, Newman, had argued effectively and passionately, but Collier's argument—and presenter, Michael Auzman—had won out in the end, even though the victory had cost him dearly. He had lost Newman, Turner, and even Auzman—three of his best students ever. It had actually decimated the debate cadre, resulting in an unplanned hiatus, if not outright death, of the long-standing form of counsel. Most decisions since that time had been unilaterally made by Collier himself, with the rubber stamp approval of The Council. In all reality most decisions had been made that way even under the old system, but at least more people were involved in the process, if not the outcome.

Collier mused on that process now. He had to admit that he was quite impressed that Jason had spent time in the library at headquarters, researching the debate process, even if his motivation was one of pure hatred. Jason had presented his plan to his father to use the debate process once again. And he knew exactly whom to use as presenters, pitting himself against the Turner's own son, John. He had one unique twist to the old process, however, obviously based on his confidence that he would easily defeat the big kid: the loser of the presentation would also be publicly rebuked and excommunicated.

Having caught his breath, Collier began his long walk to the other end of the hall as he continued thinking about Jason's plan. John should be easy to convince. The two young men had been at odds ever since the big kid had been allowed to attend Batterson on a mission scholarship. Even though Jason certainly didn't pay his own way, he didn't feel that John should be getting that same free ride. The kid hadn't worked a day in his life, but he hated when anyone else got any perceived privilege—even if the other kid might be extremely deserving. Duncan didn't think he'd have any problem getting the Turner kid to agree to any presentation that would involve the potential of affecting Jason negatively, not to mention the possibility of casting his parents in a much more positive light

A coughing fit caused Collier to stop midway to the office end of the hallway. He held onto the doorknob of some subordinate's office while the cough racked through his frail body. Finally gaining control, he continued to stand for a few minutes to regain his strength before attempting to get to his office. As he stood there, he noticed the nameplate on the door he'd been resting his forehead against. It was the office of the interns, and it still had Brock Auzman's name on it. A new idea gave him renewed strength to walk the rest of the hallway to his office. He would ask Brock what his opinion was regarding the plan.

Brock, however, would probably be difficult to persuade. Not only was he the best friend of John Turner, which would obviously cause him to be completely non-objective, but he was already away at school. Would he leave Harvard just to come back for a presentation? And would he even be in support of his friend's parents? He was, however, in the Kennedy School of Government's Institute of Politics; perhaps the opportunity for debate experience would intrigue him?

Collier finally made it back to the end of the hallway and entered his spacious office, where he nearly fell into his desk chair. It was way too late to even think of going home and getting any sleep, but it was way too early for him to try to contact Brock and give him the challenge. Though exhausted, he wasn't at all sleepy, but he knew he had a very full day ahead of him so needed to get some rest.

As he lay down on the plush couch in his office, he couldn't help but think of all that had transpired in such a short time, and how everything was coming together. Marie, sweet Marie. So willing to do anything to help the cause, even sacrificing her own body, her womb—twice! His thoughts clouded as he thought of her being with Michael Auzman now—especially now that his own wife was gone. Marie could have been with him, and with their son, Jason. Oh, but that would complicate things. Jason, or anyone else, could never know that truth! He thought, too, of how *that* decision had turned out so wrong, so disappointing. How could he have known that Jason would not turn out to be anyone that he could turn the reins of The Brothers over to? And how could he have known that Auzman and the others would come to him with their plan, the Messiah Project? So now he had Brock; he, The Brothers, and ultimately the world.

Twenty-seven

er name wasn't Mona Lisa, of course. Fortunately for Brock, Mary Roller had laughed at what she considered a great sense of humor, and it was only later—after they had shared a cup of coffee that led to the beginning of their relationship—that she found out he was actually thinking the line was meant to impress her!

She *was* beautiful, and Brock really did think of her as a work of art: short, petite, almost fragile looking, yet she carried herself with a certain air that shouted confidence. Her hair, black as coal, was cut in a manner that outlined her square face, nearly coming to a point under her short chin. Her full lips were usually slightly parted in a perpetual smile that revealed brilliantly white, perfect teeth, and her blue, "sleepy" eyes sparkled. In addition, she laughed the most beautiful laugh he'd ever heard, even though she was usually laughing at something stupid he said or did. Probably because of the combination of all of this, he seemed to do and say a lot of stupid things around her.

But their conversation at this moment was anything but stupid. Brock had received the phone call from Duncan Collier nearly a week earlier and had been thinking of what he should do nearly every waking moment since then—alternating between anger that Jason Collier had eavesdropped and outrage that he had called for the public rebuke and excommunication. He hadn't seen much of Mary since that call, but they had set a time to meet for coffee. Thankful for the opportunity to get her opinion over what he should do, he told her about John, his parents, and the efforts by Jason to have them brought before The Council, as well as Collier's request that he come to Chicago to give counsel, since he knew both young men so well.

"Brock, you have no choice. You have to go back. You can't let them have that council. From everything you've told me, it will kill John to see his parents treated like that, even if he doesn't completely agree with their change of heart."

"I know. You're right. I've got to go back. Only I'm not going back to advise Dr. Collier against having the council. I think there needs to be a time that the Turners are brought before those who banished them. They need to face their accusers."

"But Brock, they'll be crucified!" Her blue eyes weren't sparkling or sleepy now. They were on fire, as though imploring Brock to share her passion—which, of course, he already did.

Though they had known each other only a few days, he was falling for her. What had started as attraction was moving very quickly into a desire to know more of this girl, what made her tick, and why he already had such strong feelings for her. He saw something in her, in those fiery eyes, which he felt he lacked: an inner drive. It seemed that he could say the right things to people and could make them like him through his natural charm and charisma, but he didn't think he could ever have what she had—that fire in her bones. She didn't even know John or his parents, but she was passionate about her feelings for Brock's best friend, and those feelings came through loud and clear. In that regards he realized she was a lot like John—that same deep conviction that led to action and challenge.

"Interesting choice of words, Mary. Isn't it something that whenever we think of someone being persecuted—even if only emotionally—we bring up crucifixion? Look at what Jesus went through! I'm sure he would have much rather just faced the men who taunted him and mocked him rather than being nailed to a cross!"

Mary started to protest again, but Brock held up his hand to stop her. "I'm not going to let them do that, Mary. I'm not going to let Jason Collier have his field day 'crucifying' my best friend or his parents. I'm not going to even let them make a mockery of John by having him defend his parents. I will accept the invitation by Dr. Collier to give him some advice on how to handle this, but I'm not sure he'll like or take my advice. He's wondering if he should follow his son's plan and allow The Council to either publicly rebuke the Turners and John or not even have the presentation at all. I'm going to give a third option that will blow *his* mind."

"Brock, what are you planning? What options do you have?"

Twenty-eight

The only option Brock thought feasible was finalized, along with his presentation, on the flight to Chicago. He was scheduled to meet with Collier later that evening…and with Jason as well. The Council had been forewarned that they might be called for argument, so should be ready to meet within the next few months. Most were quite surprised that Collier was using the old form of counsel, and nearly all were very pleased that he was doing so. When they heard who would be presenting, however, there had been quite a stir. The majority did not like the change in rules—that the losing presenter would receive public rebuke—but they were moved that the participants would be the "sons" of the principal characters from the last argument ever to have taken place before The Council. There was quite a bit of discussion over the phone lines regarding the subject matter—the public rebuke of Jake and Elizabeth Turner. Hadn't they served long enough in banishment to be left alone? All Collier would tell them was that he was seeking counsel himself to determine the best course of action, and he would be back in touch with each member by the next evening on when, or whether, they were to head in. He would let them know as soon as he had met with his "advisor."

Collier was amazed as he listened to Brock's plan. It was perfect—giving The Council the opportunity to weigh in on what to do with the Turners, but also the chance to meet and see this outstanding young man. Brock's recommendation was to bring the Turners before The Council and present their rejection of the standard of faith but to allow him to be the presenter, not John. The plan pleased Collier.

Jason, on the other hand, was anything but pleased. It was obvious that he still wanted a chance to humiliate John Turner, but it was equally obvious that he was aware that he would have a very difficult chance, if any, of beating Auzman. He had set the stakes—

excommunication for the loser—based on opposing Turner, whom he clearly figured he could defeat. His first argument was to change that condition, which Brock had no problem with. Neither did the elder Collier, for he had no intention of losing either of these two young men to the cause. He had no desire to excommunicate his own son. He couldn't afford to do so to Brock.

It was the second part of Brock's plan that was pure genius, but he didn't reveal it until he was actually arguing before The Council, several weeks later. Time had been given for the Turners to arrange their trip, as well as to make sure their mission was covered. It also took some time for council members to arrange for the unscheduled meeting, but there was not one absentee.

Allowing Jason to go first, they listened as the smug, condescending young man brought out every detail of the Turners' "apostasy": how wrong they were to deny the faith, how wrong they were to have served even one day, let alone what he presented as years, under false pretense. He stood up for the cause and the need of defending the cause, closing, as was customary, with his final appeal.

"Gentlemen, I am a young man, but I know right from wrong, good from bad. I have no doubt but that these were good people who attempted, over the years, to do many good things. They have no doubt sacrificed, served faithfully, and surrendered many of the creature comforts we are all accustomed to. I'm sure they have helped many people in their years of service. I'm sure they think that such service, such sacrifice, entitles them to a few liberties; after all, they have so few."

He paused, heightening the drama. "However, while all of you surely remember that they were sent to their field of service because of impertinence, it appears that they have forgotten, or at least have chosen to not remember, or repent. Though they have been on the field of service, they have apparently served their self-interests. Though they have sacrificed, they have also stolen. Yes, gentlemen, they have stolen the principles and ideals, the very foundations of our faith, from the heathen to whom they were sent. They have abandoned the blood, the cause, and the faith itself. They must be held accountable, and you, gentlemen, must be the ones who will hold them accountable. I plead for public rebuke, to take place at the next General Session of The Brothers, complete with excommunication."

The Council heard his impassioned, surprisingly eloquent, plea, and it was obvious from the numerous nods and veiled smiles that most of them were in full agreement with all that Jason said. Many of them looked over at the Turners throughout Jason's argument and couldn't help but notice the contrast in appearances. They were obvious in their discomfort with not only the proceedings taking place over them, but their wardrobe as well. It was clear that they had not worn such formal clothing in quite some time. Holding each other for comfort—though, strangely, not crying at all—it was like the Turners were already being punished, just by being forced to be here. Tired, old, and a bit unkempt, they were clearly thankful that they, themselves, did not have to speak. Jason had been correct about them, though. They weren't sitting with a posture of humility or repentance. Jake Turner held his head high in confidence, as did his wife, in spite of her rather humble dress.

Jason, on the other hand, was handsome in appearance. Though adopted, of course, many of the older Council members saw an uncanny resemblance to what his father had been in earlier years. He had the same dazzling blue eyes, same cleft chin, and the same strong forehead that his dad once had. One very noticeable difference, should anyone bother to compare a picture of the two men when the older Collier was young, was the hair. The father had once had a shocking head of blond, then prematurely gray, then white, straight hair; the son had very dark, curly hair, which accentuated his pale complexion. He also lacked the strong voice of his adopted father. His argument, though most agreeable, had been weak.

The next presenter stood and introduced himself, causing no small stir among the men sitting before him. Most had guessed that the presenter would be the only son of the Turners, John. He was known only in name to most of The Council, so they had assumed the young man sitting next to the Turners was he—especially since Collier had told them the son of a presenter from the last argument would be presenting today. Now, as soon as they heard the name Auzman, they understood. A few had heard Brock speak at the Senior Reception but until now had not paid enough attention to recognize him. Those few leaned forward in anticipation, remembering how dynamic that speech had been. The others, even though they did not know him, likewise sat up in anticipation. It was obvious now why Collier had chosen to renew debate. And it was especially obvious why *now*, and why this young man. They had not been told his name until he introduced himself, but now that they all knew who he was, they all knew this was going to be something very, very special.

And they were not disappointed. His argument was anything but special. He merely agreed with everything Jason had presented, stating that his counterpart's argument had been flawless in content as much as in presentation. But then he made his final appeal: to not rebuke the Turners, but to thank them for their years of faithful service. Show mercy. Take the higher road. Be the bigger man.

The Turners sat in stunned silence, as did most of The Council, along with Duncan Collier, who had not expected this at all. But not Jason. He was on his feet instantly, charging forward to the presentation podium.

"This is an outrage! *Thanked?* You want these *apostates* to be thanked? They deserve to be...must be...rebuked and excommunicated!"

The Council disagreed, voting unanimously in favor of Brock's appeal.

Jason was beat. He stormed out of the room and out of the building. He would never set foot in that place again, not even if his father begged him. Let them have their precious Brock. He didn't need The Brothers, The Council, or his hypocrite of a father—the man who had never appreciated who he was, or what he could do. At least not since Brock Auzman had shown up.

But he knew someone who would appreciate him, as well as all that he knew about The Brothers and Auzman. Oh yeah, he had learned quite a bit in his research in the library—more than just how presentations were brought before The Council. He had learned exactly what that last presentation had been about, who had been the presenters, and exactly who might be very interested in some new information. Jumping in his car, he peeled out of the parking lot and headed for Newman College.

Meanwhile, Collier and The Council recognized that their project was ready: Christ-like. The plan to take Brock Auzman into the role he was made for could now move forward.

Twenty-nine

Ten years later

"If the tickets came from Collier, my friend, I'm not going."

"I had hoped, John, that we'd be able to have just one conversation without you getting huffy about Collier. Did it occur to you that perhaps I am now able to afford pretty good tickets on my own? No, the tickets did not come from Dr. Collier."

They hadn't seen each other in three months, so Brock had made the first move, buying tickets to a hockey game. Neither of them were the greatest fans of hockey, but the game was only an excuse. Brock had hoped he and John could spend some time together and thought that a game that meant nothing to them might be the best place to talk. He knew John would find a way to get out of just about anything else, but the man did like sports. Even hockey. So Brock had taken the chance.

"So—nosebleed seats, huh? Yeah, it had occurred to me that you might be able to afford tickets on your own, but knowing your salary, perhaps you should let *me* buy the tickets. I'd like to see the game, not just ants on ice."

"Does that mean you'll go? I don't give a rip where the seats are as long as we can talk, man. It's been too long!"

"Ahh, Wiz! You care! Wow, I'm touched. I didn't think you missed me. Yeah, yeah, I'll be there. Don't get all sappy on me. And it hasn't been that long. We were just with you and Mary at that thing, remember? That speech thing you invited us to downstate. It sure was memorable to me—but I guess not to you, huh?"

"That speech thing was the Governor's State of the State. I'm glad it was so memorable that you can't even remember what it was! Besides, that was over three months ago. I'm not trying to be sappy. I just need to talk to you about something, and I figured a hockey game would be the right place to do so, where we won't be disturbed by anyone."

"Sorry, man. I was just playing around. This sounds serious, and you know I'm there for you—or want to be. So, my ride or yours?"

After the second period, they finally had the opportunity to get serious. Watching the zamboni clean the ice, Brock took a deep breath and plunged in. He told John he was tired of waiting. He was ready to announce that he was going to run for Congress, as the next step of his political career.

"I've been working at the state legislature in that run-down office for five years, and I'm not making a bit of difference in anything there—especially in my own life! I feel like I do nothing but mop up—never doing anything that really matters."

"Brock, you know they want to bring you along slowly. You're not ready to run yet, especially not against Newman. He'll cook you, and you'll be remembered for losing. Not that that's always bad. It seemed to work for Lincoln. You might learn something from it, but so will voters. And you don't want them learning too much yet. Win some local battles, man, even if they're mop-ups. Serve on some committees that help the down and outers. Do the charity work thing, like they've been telling you. Run for a state office, like State Senate…but not even that yet; not this election. Wait for it."

Brock watched as the action on the ice had started up again. Two players were going at it in a slug fest, and the other players, as well as the refs, were letting it happen. Why did they do that? Neither team would benefit, both guys would be sent to the penalty box, and the game would continue on without them, at least for a few minutes. Did they need the rest, so chose this method to get it? Or did they actually hope that they would hurt their opponent? It made no sense, and that's exactly how Brock felt about his life. He didn't think he could stand any more time in what he considered his own penalty box of a life. He needed action, something to give him purpose, and he felt that the only action that mattered for him was in the national political field. Enough people had talked to him over the years about it, and had been supposedly grooming him for it, that he couldn't understand why he had to keep waiting.

"I don't think I can take one more inane committee meeting, one more late night listening to people talk, talk, talk about absolutely nothing, or worse, things that could have been and should have been done by the people who elected us in the first place. Why do we spend so much time and money electing people we consider to be the best possible, then tie their hands by over analyzing decisions that they should be making? I'm sick of it, John, and I don't think I can take it anymore. If that is truly what it's going to take to get into office someday, then maybe I'm not cut out for it. I just want to get there and start doing something, making a difference *now*."

John looked at his friend. Their relationship was not as close as he'd like, and he knew it was mostly his fault. Brock had tried. He called on a regular basis and even came by John's work whenever he was in town. They would talk, but it wasn't the same. How could it be? Though it had been seven years, John was still convinced that the death of his parents had been no accident, and he still felt very, very strongly that Collier was behind it. He didn't know how, at least not yet, but he would not rest until he found out. In the meantime, he had a difficult time being close to Brock as long as he kept working for, or at least in the same office as that man.

But now he was having very mixed feelings. He knew Brock needed him, for many reasons. And he knew he owed Brock his help. He had never forgotten Brock's help, even though it had been ten years. It was Brock who had gotten him off when the board would have kicked him out of Batterson—and he would never have gotten to Dartmouth if that had happened. Then it was Brock who kept him, and, more importantly, his parents, from being publicly humiliated at the hands of The Brothers. Though it might not have affected him too much, it sure would have affected them, and he knew it was only because of Brock they were spared that pain. But then, just three years after their return to their mission field, he got word that they had been in a terrible accident. Again, it was Brock who came through with the money to fly him, and fly with him, for the funeral. Yet as much as he tried, not only knowing how much he should but also wanting to have their old friendship back, he still held back. All because of Duncan Collier. Well, it was time for him to get past that. Brock might not like all he had to say, but at least he deserved having a friend who would tell him what he needed to hear.

"I want you to listen to me, old friend. I know you want to get moving, but you gotta ask yourself why. Okay? You gotta ask what is your motivation. Is it because you have a vision? A purpose? Or is it because you just want what you want? Seriously."

"Are you kidding me? Man, you are one of the ones who have been on my case for ten years to lead, to 'be what you're meant to be.' What was that all about? Now you're gonna tell me I'm doing this for *me?*"

"No, Brock. That's not what I'm saying. I'm saying you've got to do it for the right reason. And I'm not so sure, friend, that you *own* that right reason."

"You're wrong. John, you're wrong. I know I'm ready. I do own the right reason, and I am a leader—a 'natural born' leader I think you've said. Besides, I'm a quick learner. What I don't know, or feel, I'll learn. I—"

"Hold it, Brock. Several things you've just said. First of all, I, I, I, I. 'I'm a leader,' 'I own the reason.' That's typical of most of your statements—pretty 'I' centered. Second, yes, you *are* a natural-born leader. But Brock, that's not going to be enough. You depend too much on what *you* are, or what you can do, and—on your own—that's just not much. So third, you need to be at those committee meetings, and taking on those causes you don't want to, because a huge part of being a leader is learning to be a servant. You seem to have a lot of compassion. I know you feel for the people who have less than you, people who have needs. I'm one of them. But you lack this: though you have compassion, you don't *do* enough with it. You care, but you don't serve, unless it benefits you. You're great with the photo ops, but what do you do, really, when the cameras aren't there? Do you even show up?"

"Twice now you've said 'friend.' Wow—makes you realize where the saying 'with friends like that who needs enemies' comes from.

You've got some nerve saying I don't *do* anything with my compassion. Do I need to remind you of the things I've *done* for you, John?"

"Of course not. I'm well aware of the many things you've done for me, as well as my family. In fact, those exact thoughts were just going through my mind. I was thinking how much I owe you, which is exactly why I was willing to say some very difficult things to you. I know they are hard to hear, but they are equally as hard to say. But if I really do care—and I do—I have to say, and do, the hard things. You're right. You've done a *lot* for me, and I can never, ever repay you."

"I don't expect you to…"

"Let me finish. I happen to know I'm not the only one you've helped. You actually do a lot, considering your limited personal funds. But you do them for people you known. For people who do stuff for you—or people you know might be able to someday. Again, like me. I may not be able to give back to you what you give me, but you know that I'm going to be here for you no matter what. Now, I don't do what I do because I feel like I owe you or something; I do what I do because you are my best friend—my brother. But believe it or not, you do a lot of what you do for those you do it for because somewhere, in that constantly working mind of yours, you know that they—people like me whom you help, will feel obligated to you."

"Exactly whom *should* I be helping then, John, if not the people who matter to me? I don't expect anything back. I help because I care. I don't want people to feel obligated to me!"

"Maybe. Maybe not. I don't suppose you do it on purpose, but you do it. And you just showed me your true feelings when you said you're tired of sitting on committees that only talk. Yet, what are *you* doing? Just listening? Joining in the talk? Or *doing* something—even if it is merely showing support for the causes being presented? Volunteering? Standing up to the other members of the legislature and challenging them? Or just complaining about the way things are done. See, Brock, you don't *do* anything. You say you care, but there isn't much action to back up those words."

John could see the muscles working in Brock's jaws as he processed, and his eyes had become slivers as he continued silently watching the game. He wasn't sure if Brock was contemplating punching his lights out, or arguing, or agreeing. He doubted it was the latter, so he was surprised when Brock finally turned to him and spoke.

"How do you do that? How do you say *the* thing that most gets my goat? I could have sat here all night and just watched hockey, stated my rather ambitious announcement about feeling ready to do something, and left tonight with your utter and complete support. Instead? I'm challenged that my announcement is not ambitious; it's arrogant. My feelings are not altruistic; they're self-serving. And your support is anything but utter and complete. Yet, instead of anger, which I must admit I have at least a little bit of, I'm challenged. I will prove you wrong, John Turner. So let's get out of here. I've got some causes I need to get started on, and the committee meeting discussing homeless shelters is tomorrow night. I need to prepare a speech, then roll up my sleeves."

Thirty

Brock was as good as his word—for two weeks. He had heard a plea from the board of the Inner City Mission and was ready to help them find a new director by making some strategic phone calls. He dialed one of the key supporters of The Brothers, knowing the man had supported many such causes, even if they were not directly related to the work of The Brothers. The man happened also to be Senator Ross Russell. Brock had first met him during his internship at International Headquarters and had kept an informal relationship with him over the past ten years, mainly by Senator Russell's initiative. Brock had been his guest at several political events and the senator had always encouraged him to stay active in the public eye. He had also helped Brock with several fundraising efforts in the past, so there was nothing unusual about the call.

"Brock! It is so good to hear from you. I have you at the top of my to-do list to give you a call today. Did you have some sort of premonition or something?"

"Sir? I'm not sure what you're talking about. I'm calling you regarding the Inner City Mission and our search for a new director, and thought you might know of someone to recommend."

That got a laugh from Senator Russell. "That's a good one, Brock. What really happened? Did one of my loose-lipped staffers have a little too much to drink and let my announcement slip?"

"Again, sir, I have no idea what you're talking about. What announcement?"

"Wait a minute. You truly do not know? Brock, I'm announcing my retirement from the senate, effective the end of this term. That gives you time to run for Congress against old man Newman next November, serve your term, get your feet wet here in D.C., then announce that you'll be running for this office. And I'm recommending to my supporters that they elect you to take my place. I think it's about time you got started in the big leagues. You've got a lot to give, and our state needs you here. This *country* needs you, young man. And though I haven't passed this by Dr. Collier just yet, I think he'll agree that you need to be on your way. Whaddya think? Ready to toss your hat into this proverbial ring?"

Senator Ross Russell had been a mainstay in the Senate for four decades and had talked retirement just prior to each of the last two elections. He had waited both times until it was, in reality, too late for anyone to mount any kind of campaign, thus assuring that the party leaders would beg him to stay. For him to make an announcement this far in advance could only mean he intended to follow through this time.

"Senator Russell, you have no idea how ready I am. But are you sure—is Dr. Collier sure—that I'm ready? I thought everyone thought I needed more time, more experience in the state legislature. Especially in the area of charity work."

"Son, you can get your experience here, and get a whole lot more done from this hill I'm sitting on right now than anything you'll do there. And for you, Brock, this is just the beginning—the first step of many. Let's meet for supper this weekend and discuss what you need to get started. Hang on while I send you back to Jenny. She'll make the arrangements with you."

"I don't know what to say, Senator. I'm stunned!"

"You don't have to say anything to me, Brock. All I want to hear from you is the 'so help me, God' that comes at the end of the oath of office when you're sworn in."

"Thank you, sir. And believe me, if you're going to hear that—if I'm going to have the opportunity to say that—I'll need your help."

Brock's next call was to John. There was no way he was going to believe this, or like it—or so he thought. To Brock's surprise, John was as happy as he was.

"Brock, that's awesome! See, this is just what I was saying. You didn't have to push that door open. I knew that when the timing was right, it would open for you. I just can't believe it opened that quickly! So, what's the next step?"

"I'm having dinner with Senator Russell this weekend to discuss that very thing. And I want you to be there. I've already cleared it with him and his secretary made the reservations for all three of us. You and I will meet him there, and we'll start planning when to officially announce, what to say, and how to start raising some money for the campaign...starting with your check, big boy!"

John was quiet for a moment, thinking if he should say what instantly came to his mind, knowing that it would probably upset Brock. As usual, he decided it was better to say it than to think it and watch the train wreck happen.

"Uh, buddy? I think you left out someone pretty important. Shouldn't you include Mary in this meeting?"

"Mary? I don't think so. I don't think we want to bring her into this right now. I mean, I know she's eventually got to get on board, but if you think you were negative about me running when we spoke a couple of weeks ago, how do you think she's going to be? I don't think we want her to burst the balloon before it gets off the ground, do we?"

"Better now than later, Brock, and you know it. I think you owe her that much, since she'll be carrying a huge load of responsibility once you guys get married, especially since we all know this isn't the final step of your political career."

"Political career. How does that sound to your ears? Are you ready?"

"Brock, seriously. Talk to her. You've got to know what's more important to you—your relationship with her, or your ambitions. It's gonna come up and bite you later if you don't take care of it now. Remember that story my dad told me about the thieves and the changed price tags? You've got to know right now what your untouchable values are, because your chosen 'career' path is going to constantly challenge those values. Get it right right now—or kiss them all good-bye."

"John, do you *always* have to preach? Do you ever lighten up?"

"Thankfully for you, my friend, that's a big negatory. Especially when it comes to you, project numero uno, I will not lighten up. 'Cause you and I both know that you don't want me to. And one reason you don't want me to is because you don't want to be just like so many other politicians, acting like a street magician who will do anything for a buck. You have to be different, man. So start now, or you won't be. Hang up, buddy—then make that call."

"Ease up, Clops. I'm already dialing."

Thirty-one

Convincing Mary was going to be no ordinary feat. Not only did she have a huge problem with all politics and pretty much all politicians, even on the state level, she had made it abundantly clear that she didn't want Brock running for national office, at least not until they were married. She had never given him her reasoning, but she certainly had her reasons.

She knew what the press would do to both of them and was afraid that Brock would back out of marrying her when they found out about and publicly revealed her past, causing him to see it—to see her!—as too much of a liability to his future. Being married wouldn't change her past, but it might assure her future.

Brock didn't know all of that—not yet—but what he did know was that she would be very upset to think that he was contemplating a run; she would be especially upset to find out he was meeting with Russell to discuss actually being his replacement someday, and what getting there meant.

"It's exploratory, Mary. I'm simply finding out if there's any chance at all for me to win—and what winning might mean down the road."

"I already know what it means, Brock. It means our life is no longer ours. It means that everything about you *and* about me is no longer private. It's fair game for every tabloid out there. It means my mom can never go out in public again without wondering if someone's going to stop her, look at her funny, or whisper behind her back. That's what it means, Brock, and you know that. And you know what it means to us. This is different than being a state representative, Brock. This puts you on the national stage—and me right there beside you."

He had been holding her close as she said most of those words into his chest, more sobbing than saying. He now held her away so that she

133

could look right into his eyes. Wiping tears away from her eyes, he almost changed his mind about considering the run. But only almost, for he realized at this moment that he was truly willing to give up anything and anyone—even her—to have this chance.

"Mary, sometimes to get what you know is important, what is best, you have to give up other things, even good things. Yes, we'll lose some of our privacy. Yes, we'll be fair game. But that doesn't mean we run and hide. It doesn't mean we don't do the right thing, the important thing—the thing that I feel I've been shaped for all of my life. I'm in this thing, Mary, and I want you in with me. But I have to do this, even if you don't want it. You are important to me; you know that. You also know *this* is important to me. Don't make me choose."

Mary Roller was going to be sick. For nearly all of their past two years together she had done everything she could to try to talk Brock out of this move but had known all along that she would not change his mind. He could say it all he wanted, but she knew which was actually more important to him. If she did make him choose, which she would not do, he would choose politics. The choice was actually hers: join him, no matter the cost, or lose him.

Taking a deep breath to keep from getting physically sick, she looked up at Brock's handsome face. Mary had fallen in love with Brock the first time she had seen him and he had used the corniest pick-up line she'd ever heard. They became fast friends instantly, but the relationship stalled after that, becoming the typical "'on-again-off-again" type, until just two years ago. She had found herself at the absolute end of her rope, ready to give in to the most unbelievable thoughts anyone could have imagined. She had always been fairly self-confident and driven but had entered into a number of relationships that had brought most of those feelings to a rapid end.

At the very worst of those times, seemingly out of nowhere, Brock had come back into her life. Standing in line at a coffee shop, she felt, more than saw, his presence. Surprisingly the feeling she had was not a warm one, but she knew it was him. He had listened to her sad story, then reached across the booth and touched her cheek, telling her he understood, and she didn't need to be alone ever again.

She loved this man, but she wasn't so sure he loved her, at least not more than he loved himself. She loved how he gave himself to charity work, doing so much pro bono legal work that she was amazed he still had time to do everything else that being a state representative entailed. He especially loved to work for organizations that she believed in, so maybe he was doing that as a gift of love to her? If so, he never told her. She didn't even know if being with her was simply another act of charity. Yet, what would the press do with those acts of charity? And worse, at least as far as she could think or feel right now, what would they do with her acts—her choice of going to one of those places to make a decision, and take action, that she swore she could even now still feel in the depths of her womb.

Neither of them had any idea that it would not be Mary's past that would become the issue—a relationship that had ended badly, made worse by choosing to have an abortion. At that point in her life she had felt she had no choice—how ironic that it was called the right to choose. She made the only choice presented to her in the women's clinic and ended the life growing inside her. She had never gotten over it. And now what had been a personal choice would more than likely become anything but personal. She knew that no amount of "right to privacy" laws would matter when the press hounds were released, and Brock's decision would release them. Perhaps she should just make her own press announcement before they forced it, handling it her way rather than theirs. The shame would still be there, but she could at least control how it came about.

She allowed Brock to hold her a few moments longer, then pulled herself away. She couldn't believe how much her life had changed in the past ten years. But she knew it was about to change a whole lot more.

"All right, *Senator* Auzman. Let's do it. But if you're going to get us in this thing, you better win."

Dinner was at Wildfire, and, quite surprisingly, Senator Russell was already in the dining room when the three of them arrived. He was roving from table to table, shaking hands, squeezing shoulders—doing what had come so naturally to him for so many years that he continued even now, though he was not going to run again. Seeing Brock and the rest enter behind the *maitre d'*, he called out in a voice far too loud for the intimate setting, announcing what Brock himself was not completely sure of just yet.

"I'd like everyone to meet Brock Auzman, candidate to become your next United States Congressman!"

Polite applause, whispered buzz, and more than a few handshakes followed Brock to their table. Senator Russell was still making his way across the room to them, still singing the praises of his "hand-picked candidate," but Brock was liking the prospects of this kind of life less and less.

It had been one thing to run as a state representative. He had basically been appointed rather than elected, as his opponent had dropped out of the race just a few weeks before the election due to family problems, and no one else had chosen to run. Life had not changed much in this position, but from what he already felt, it would never be the same once he made this choice. Perhaps Mary was right in her reluctance.

Clapping him on the back, Russell nearly shouted, "Brock, it's good to see you. And who is this lovely young lady, and this giant next to her?"

Russell was no small man himself but didn't have the height to carry the bulk like John did. Balding, ruddy faced, bulbous nose, and puffy eyes, he looked every bit the part of a man who had spent too much time being wined and dined by his constituents. But he had been able to get things done, and those constituents loved him for it. They would expect no less from whomever took his place, and if it was to be Brock, he would have to start learning some of the tricks of the trade. That was one purpose for this meeting tonight, but there were other things that needed attending to as well, or Brock would never have the chance to start that learning process.

"Senator Russell, I'd like to introduce you to my fiancé, Mary Roller."

"Fiancé, huh? You didn't tell me you were engaged. That makes this even better! Oh, you might lose a few votes from those single gals out there and even a few of the moms who like to think you might've married their daughter, but most people like a good love story. It ought to play well in all the papers, especially if you plan on getting married sometime during the campaign."

The fact that John hadn't even been introduced yet didn't stop him from speaking out over what he saw as rudeness. He didn't care if this was a United States Senator or the President of the United States, it was none of his business when, or even if, Brock and Mary got married.

"Excuse me, sir. With all due respect..."

"Horsefeathers. I know better than to think you've got *any* respect for me, son. Oh, don't look so surprised, like I don't already know who you are. I'm not sure why you are here, though I can take a pretty good guess that, as Brock's best friend, he's asked you to serve on his campaign staff in some capacity. But I, for one, think that would be a mistake, for precisely the reason I just stated: you have no respect for this office, let alone for me in it. You've got quite a reputation as an outspoken critic of any and all organized rule, and that reputation will do nothing but harm Brock, should you be attached in any way to him. You don't know how to play the game, kid. It's way over your head. But go ahead. You were saying something about 'all due respect.'"

John wasn't about to back down. "Senator, *with all due respect*, I don't think Brock and Mary's marriage is any of your concern. Nor is his choice of campaign staffers, though I would advise him to listen to you in that regards—if he truly wants to win, that is. You may not be much of a leader, in my eyes, but you do know how to play the game, and to run a campaign. But before you think I'm telling him to emulate you, you should know that I *do* think he should listen to you as to how you campaigned, then *do the exact opposite.* He may not win, but at least he would lose without surrendering his integrity."

It was hard to tell who was more surprised by John's statements: Russell, who was beet-red and apoplectic; Brock, nearly as red-faced as the Senator but for a completely different reason, who had simply kept his head down during John's tirade; or Mary, who was equally red-faced from stifling laughter. John gave her a wink, then, with a look of bemusement—lips pursed, eyebrows raised—stared hard at his friend, challenging him to say something. Clearing his throat out of nervousness, Brock looked Senator Russell in the eye.

"Sir, I want you to know that I am grateful for the opportunity that you are giving me, but I will not compromise who I am simply to become what you or anyone else may want me to be. Honestly, I'm not even sure who I am all the time, but I do know who these guys are. They are my friends and have helped me through some very difficult times. I will not use my marriage as a political tool. And I will not turn my back on friends. If that means waiting to run for Congress, or running now but without your backing, then so be it. I'm pretty sure I would rather run, and win, on my own anyway."

"Who said anything about running without my backing? People love backbone, son, and you've got it." Turning his attention to John, Russell continued. "And so does your *campaign director*. Turner, that little lecture of yours shows you might be a bit naïve, but you are spot on. This business will suck the moral character right out of you, and if you start out that way, there's simply nothing there to give from the get-go. You stay with this friend of yours, and never let anyone draw *you* away from who you are. He's going to need you as his moral compass, bringing him back to center every-so-often when some contributor, colleague, or even opponent tries to pull him away. If you drift, he has no hope. It will be tough enough as it is, but your role is vital. Never forget that."

Now it was John's turn to be stunned. He certainly hadn't expected *that* from the man sitting across the table from him. He was actually speechless, so was thankful when it was Mary who spoke up.

"Which still leaves the matter of our marriage, sir. I too, intend to be by this guy's side throughout. As much as I might want to get married now—right now—I, too, will not allow our marriage to be a political fiasco, so I'm stating here and now that we will not set a date until *after* the election. But *you*, Brock Auzman, had better still be there when the dust settles, or you'll only think you've already faced your toughest opponent during the campaign."

Though she was smiling, it was through clenched teeth. Brock got the message.

"Well, this has been a great start to our first campaign planning session," laughed the Senator. "Let's order our food and get down to some serious business. We've got a lot of work to do, and a lot of money to raise. I'll help you get started by paying for dinner. Except for yours, Turner. I don't think that even I can afford that."

Thirty-two

Marie Auzman was as proud as she could possibly be. She knew that Brock was not really hers, but she *had* given him life, she had raised him, and she had taught him so much of what he was now living and proclaiming. It was one thing to hear him when the news carried a sound bite, but to be sitting in the very same room, hearing him answer questions and state his positions? She had goosebumps. She had tried to get him to wear a tie, but, as usual, his casual ways won out. It was clear; he would be his own man, and no one—not even his mother—was going to change him. For that she was extremely grateful, and proud.

But Marie Auzman was also sad. Brock still did not know the full truth, and each day that he lived in that forced ignorance was another day of reckoning; or a day that made the day of reckoning even worse. When he finally found out the truth—and he would—his anger over having been lied to and lied about would explode.

And Marie knew that she would be part of the fallout. This young man she loved with all her heart, and had given so much of herself to, would hate her. He already hated her husband, knowing Michael was not his father. What would happen when he found out that she had been more than just the carrier of the experiment, but had been a very willing participant? What would happen when he found out there was none of her in him—that there was nothing of anyone that he knew?

He was constantly searching for and asking about his roots, struggling with his feelings of having no connection to his past...looking for what parts of it had made him who he was now. His emptiness had led him down some wrong paths already—paths of self-abuse that, had they continued, could have ruined everything. What would happen if—when—he found out the truth?

Marie looked around the large auditorium where Brock was

140

holding his press conference. They had chosen such a large room, in spite of the sparse crowd, to show the press an object lesson. They would fill that auditorium, Brock had told them, with people who believed in a new direction, new leadership, and a new leader. He had invited all of the press to be back in this very room in just a few months when they would be reporting on his victory, and celebration party would be held here. He told them to look at all those empty seats now, because they would be filled then. The prototypical red, white, and blue bunting was everywhere, as were similar colored helium-filled balloons. She smiled as she recalled John, in the ready room just moments before they walked out onto the platform, sucking the helium out of one so he could loosen things up with his rendition of "we represent the lollipop guild." Watching the giant kid attempt to imitate a munchkin had accomplished the intended purpose of making Brock laugh, but it hadn't helped her relax.

She honestly didn't think anything would, ever, until the inevitable happened—until Brock knew the truth. It would be painful, but she didn't think she could take living this lie much longer. Had it been up to her, Brock would have been told long before now. But it was not her call, nor had it ever been, and she knew it. The time was near, so she knew she had better enjoy what time was left—time for this man, this unbelievable leader of men, to know her as mom, and time to know him, for at least a little while longer, as her son.

She was enjoying him now, watching him answer some fairly tough questions, nodding in that humorous way he did just before he answered—like he had heard some answer from within or even from above and was now going to give it to the masses. He was in his element, in control. Once again, she realized the dichotomy. Alone, or in the company of those closest to him, he always seemed so insecure, unsure, questioning, even moody.

But in this setting, or any setting where he felt he could lead, he was a changed person: calm, assured, confident. He would give what appeared to be absolute and full attention to whomever he was in front of, whether a supporter, a potential constituent with a need or simply asking a question, or, like now, a member of the press. He gave them the feeling that, though surrounded by a crowd, *they* were the most important thing in the world to him at that point, and they loved him for it. Though he had never held office or done very little of anything that merited such praise, he was already way ahead in every poll and showed no signs of letting up, and the press was making sure it stayed that way. She was very proud, but she also couldn't completely explain it, and wondered just how long it could all last before someone started asking why this young man was special—why he was being given so much so early.

Her thoughts must have somehow drifted down to him on the platform. In the middle of answering a question he looked up at her and broke into that wide, engaging smile of his. His long arm stretched upwards toward her and, with sudden horror, she realized he was about to introduce her. Why had she sat there? Why not stay back in the ready room? Why had she, or Duncan Collier himself for that matter, not thought what the consequences of his actions—his running for a national office—would be up until now?

With that introduction would come the inevitable flash of cameras, along with the whir of the various mini-cams of the news crews. They would play those tapes, print those pictures, and give their caption proclaiming her as the mother of the candidate, but she knew there would most certainly be someone who would see that news report or see that picture and know who she *really* was—or had been!

These weren't reporters from the *Quincy Herald Whig* or the *Wauconda News*; these were from the national news outlets. Even though they were two states away, someone, somewhere, would see her, and know her, and would remember her as that poor single young mother who had been forced to give up her baby for adoption. *Why* hadn't anyone, including herself, thought of this before *now*? There would be no more secret, no more hiding the truth from Brock, or Jason, or anyone else, after this!

Covering her face like some sort of accused criminal leaving a courthouse arraignment, Marie fled from her seat and ran up the stairs to the nearest exit. She was fairly confident that the only picture any of them had gotten was of her backside. Let them all—the photographers, the news crews, the audience, even Brock—think she was just camera shy. Let them laugh; even let Brock shake his head in wonderment. He might ask questions later, but she could handle them then. She knew she had to take some drastic measures immediately or all of their hard work up until now would be for naught, and she could not let that happen. It simply wasn't time.

Thirty-three

Sitting in his office in Washington D.C., Lawrence Newman was also watching the press conference. He was fascinated that, through satellite TV, he could keep up with the local news as it happened, and had been keeping a close eye on the announcement. He knew there were others who would also attempt to run against him who would be opposing Brock in the primary race. Not that there was much of a race to it, as it was clear that Brock Auzman was going to win in a landslide. What of it? What could that kid do to him? He hadn't done anything of much importance as a state representative. The mayor of Chicago and the county supervisor had more impact on what truly happened than that kid would ever have. He might be hot stuff right now, but he'd be yesterday's news as soon as the election was over. Newman was sure of it, and continued to work hard at convincing himself of it.

He watched as Auzman pointed up to the rising seats of the large auditorium and the cameras followed. Who was that woman, and why was she running out? He turned up the volume and heard Brock, in that grating, laughing voice of his, announce that his mother obviously had a previously unknown shy streak to her. His mother! That was Marie Auzman he had just seen flying out of the press conference. He hadn't seen her in over ten years, but he would have recognized her even if they hadn't identified her.

But why was she running out of there? This was her moment to shine, and for Michael to gloat. From what he'd learned, Brock being elected to Congress was the first step toward fulfillment of the goal laid out many years before. A lot of time had passed, and Newman had been stonewalled from any real information, but he had his strong opinions—opinions that had been somewhat supported by information brought to him a decade ago by Jason Collier. He had attempted to dig deeper and get real facts, but even Jason, son and presumed successor to his father's role, though not a natural heir, was no longer welcome on the campus of The Brothers' International Headquarters. When he'd stormed out of that council meeting so many years earlier, he had sealed for himself the same fate that Newman now lived.

They made a good pair, though the younger Collier was driven more by hatred than cause. Sometimes that worked for Newman; most often it was a liability. It had nearly cost Newman his election to Congress for his first term, as Jason had blown up in a press conference very much like the one on TV right now, when Newman himself was announcing his candidacy for Congress. Jason had attempted to control the line of questioning regarding his relationship with Newman, and the press read into it exactly what they were looking for—that he was protesting too much. Newman had been able to keep Jason pretty much under wraps since then, which was one reason he had been able to secure his fourth term at the last election. His long-term plan was working perfectly. After he won this term, he would seek what would surely be the open Senate seat, vacated by the hopeful retiring of Senator Ross Russell after his current term.

But why was Marie running from her son's moment of glory? What had made her so afraid? Newman hadn't really been paying attention to the drivel that was Brock Auzman's announcement, but he'd have to get the tape to hear what was said. Or, better yet, put Jason on it. That's what the boy did best, after all, because that was when his hatred could be utilized. Give him the opportunity to drag someone down and he was like a rabid dog, relentless in his pursuit.

He had proven that when he was given permission to go after the Turners. It had taken some doing, but Newman was convinced he had been successful in covering up that whole sordid event. Beyond their son, John, and a few of the people they worked with on their mission compound, hardly anyone even knew them or took notice of their death, which had been ruled accidental. There was no investigation; no reason for one was given. No one would have suspected that they were forced off the road. Every indication was that either Jake Turner had fallen asleep at the wheel, or had lost control. Their Land Rover was quite ancient, so the local police attributed their accident to exactly that—a loss of control. No one was the wiser, and Jason had his revenge, at least on them. But Newman couldn't afford to let him go after John. He was simply too high profiled, and this wasn't the jungle of southern India. He would let him go after Marie Auzman, however. He wanted to find out why she was so afraid of the public eye.

Michael Auzman, having chosen to stay home and watch the press conference on TV so he could hear what the talking heads would say in summation, was wondering the same thing as he watched his wife run out of the auditorium. He had never seen her act so strangely, and knew for a fact that this was one of her proudest moments ever. Why was she so afraid of being recognized publicly as the mother of the hottest thing to hit politics since Kennedy? The news camera had caught one small fleeting glimpse of her before she turned and ran, and she looked like she'd seen a ghost, leading to Michael's confusion. What was she afraid of? No one, outside of him, her, and Duncan Collier, knew that she was merely the surrogate mother of Brock.

The only other person who could have known, the doctor who had performed the procedure, was long dead. True names had not been used, so no official record could reveal anything. They had taken great pains to make sure that the truth would not be known until it was the proper time. Thus, for all practical purposes, every person now watching knew her only as Brock Auzman's birth mother.

If anyone had reason to stay away from the carnival that was campaigning, it was Michael. He was the one who would be pestered with questions about not being the "real" father of "the great and mighty wizard of Auz." He was the one who would be the nothing, the nobody, the stepdad who had nothing to do with the already assumed greatness of this young man. They would laud praises on his mother, relegating him to a role comparable to the rabbit in a greyhound race— necessary, perhaps, but not the main show.

Michael had known that such would be the case all along, from the very introduction of the project and his involvement in it. For the most part that had always been okay with him; he wasn't a man who needed to be in the spotlight, and never had been. From his first presentation until now, he truly had no desire to do anything but his job. Yet, he found himself—quite often, in fact—a bit jealous of Brock, while at the same time admiring the young man tremendously. As he watched him now, he was simply thankful that it was not he who had to answer the questions and put on false appearances. No, if anyone should be running away from this, it should be Michael, not her.

In his heart, however, he still knew what the truth was, and just how important of a role he did play in all that was happening right now. And someday, perhaps sooner than later, that truth would be known to everyone and then he would be recognized, even honored. He might not be the charismatic leader that his stepson was, but he knew there would be no Brock Auzman if it had not been for him. Marie might have been the surrogate, but he had been the one who had convinced Collier and the others that this could be, and should be, done. Though no one else would ever say it, and there was obviously no scientific or any other physical reality of it, he knew in his heart that he was the true father of Brock Auzman, the man who, if everything continued to work according to the plan he laid out thirty years ago, would someday be president. Then, and only then, would Michael be recognized for the great man he felt he was.

There was one other person who watched in amazement as Marie Auzman fled the press conference. Only he understood her reasoning. Duncan Collier was amazed that neither of them had thought of the ramifications of her face being spread across the evening news, and he was equally amazed that she had realized it in the nick of time. What if she hadn't? What if someone had recognized her, recognized her still, and told the press that they knew her—not as Marie Auzman, but as Marie Foster, an unwed pregnant girl from Kansas? People would dig, and they would learn too much—far too much!

Collier inhaled. The Council might find out the truth of his relationship to Marie. His followers would question everything he had ever done. Jason would find out, and, ultimately, so would Brock. That time would come, but it certainly was not *now*, not yet! They couldn't keep Marie hidden forever, though; meaning they couldn't keep the truth hidden—truth that went beyond who Marie was, to who Brock was, and who he would be. Collier needed to take some serious action, and he knew he had better do so quickly, or lose everything.

In all reality, Collier knew he might not live long enough to see any negative results against him, but he couldn't stand the thought of dying and leaving Marie to handle the fallout on her own. Collier had no business even being alive still. He had battled so many illnesses up to now that every doctor who saw him was amazed. Only one doctor, his own personal physician, had an idea of what might be keeping the old man alive. There was no scientific proof, of course—there was no way to gain such proof. But both men, men of faith as well as reason, believed they knew. It had been Dr. Jackson's idea, but Collier had quickly gone along with it, especially after Jackson assured him there should be no side effects. Plus, he had an idea on how to make it happen, without causing suspicion from Brock. He had Dr. Jackson approach the young man after his physical—mandatory for the work he did at headquarters—with what he felt was a magnanimous suggestion.

"Brock, you have certain markers in your blood that give me an idea. I'd like to have you come down here each month and give me some blood. Yours is a type that I believe could help other people. Just mark it on your calendar and be here each month."

So Brock faithfully gave a full pint each time. As soon as Brock left, Collier came to the infirmary and received that very blood. There was no proof, but they both believed that blood had kept Collier alive for the past ten years. It was, after all, the blood of the Healer himself. Whether it was because of that blood, or simply a blind faith that gave him an endorphin-driven boost, Collier would at least make sure he stayed alive long enough to protect the woman who had given him new life over thirty years before, and life to that healer shortly after that.

Daniel Winters wasn't watching the press conference on television. He was actually there and had been sitting only a few feet from Marie Auzman when Brock had pointed her way. Surprised he hadn't paid any attention to the striking woman before now, he realized who she was the instant his attention, along with all the press, was drawn to her. Only he didn't have to turn and focus a camera. He saw her before she covered her face and ran, and he had followed her out. Though he'd been paid to follow Brock and get as much dirt on him as he could, Winters had been at this long enough to recognize where the real story was. He could catch up to the candidate later. Right now he needed to know where this beautiful but obviously scared-to-death lady was heading, and why.

One positive thing about following someone who was scared was that they usually drove right to the first place they needed to be to regain confidence. The other thing that could be negative was that they feared being followed to that place. This lady apparently had no such fear, for she drove straight to her destination.

Winters followed from a safe distance and watched as she turned into the parking lot of a large building located in a business park he was unfamiliar with. The building was far too ornate for its surroundings, with several fountains, an awful lot of glass, and amazingly beautiful landscaping. Even now several young men worked diligently trimming hedges and pouring fresh new mulch. Assuming it must be headquarters for a very successful business corporation, Winters was surprised when he drove by the sign, identifying the building as the International Headquarters for The Brothers. He didn't have to wonder too long who these brothers were, as he saw, in smaller letters, *The Haemaelien Brothers*. He had never heard of the place or The Brothers, but at least he had the answer to the first part of his question: where.

That left only the second question: why was she there? That answer would take considerable more time—and money. If he was going to find it, he was going to have to contact Jason Collier and demand more payment.

Thirty-four

"I think you did a fantastic job handling all those questions! I certainly don't know how you can think on your feet like that, and come up with all those answers. I was in love with you before, but now I'm impressed!"

Mary had no idea that the majority of questions had been "planted"—given ahead of time to certain reporters who were already supportive of Brock and his campaign. Many of them were simply tired of Newman and therefore ready for any change; they would probably have been supportive of Brock even if he had walked in to the press conference with an axe.

But there were more than a few who truly wanted change of the kind that they felt Brock would bring. He was refreshing—not tainted with Potomac muck, and not a *prima donna* like Newman. Reporters were nearly as bad as average Joes—or, in most cases, Josephines—on the street. They goggled over him like he was a celebrity, and they ate it up every time he stopped to chat. More than once Mary had been forced to sit alone at a restaurant or even at the movies, waiting for Brock to finish shaking hands, listening to advice, or giving impromptu position talks to would-be supporters, including the press. He was kissed by more women than she cared to know, and even a few of the more ebullient men.

She took most of it in stride, but she knew that it was only going to get worse, and often questioned whether she was going to be able to endure this for what could potentially be the rest of her life. She was well aware that Brock was not going to stop with an election to Congress. His plan was to run for Senator Russell's vacant position after his term expired, then to investigate the possibility of a run for the presidency. Any way she looked at it, she knew that she was in for at least the next three years, if not many, many more of this life.

Right now, though, she had Brock alone, even though she knew better than to think that his whole attention was focused on her. He was always thinking about so many other things.

"Did you hear me, Brock? I said I was impressed. As in, I was there, I listened, I paid attention, and I responded with an emotion. Do you know what all those things are?"

"Hey, Mary, I get it, and I don't want you going there. You know I'm just getting started with this thing and there's an awful lot on my mind. Listen, I'm sorry that I wasn't paying attention to you just now. But it's gonna happen, and you're gonna have to get used to it. You can't be so selfish, Mary."

With that, he went back to his reading, and she began silently weeping. Once again, she couldn't believe it had been turned on her. Once again, it was her fault that she had needs, that she wanted to simply be noticed, let alone cared for. Well, far be it from her to let him be bothered with her tears right now. She got up to leave the room, leaving him to the material in front of him that had been delivered earlier in the evening by Mack Owens, the kid who had volunteered to do research for Brock's position papers. Like so many others, Mack was simply honored to be able to work in the campaign, and looked at Brock like some sort of god every time he was around. Honestly, Mary was getting a bit sick of it all.

"Where are you going?" Brock asked.

She couldn't believe it. He'd actually noticed her getting up from the couch and heading toward the kitchen of his small apartment. She had been sitting beside him for nearly two hours, and he hadn't noticed her at all. Maybe she should have left sooner.

"I'm leaving, Brock. I'm going home. I thought we were going out, or at least doing something together. But you're too busy, and I'm just in the way. I'll see you tomorrow, or whenever you can find time to actually notice me."

Brock set the papers down and crossed the room, taking Mary in his arms. "I really am sorry, Mary. I don't mean to hurt you. I certainly don't mean to make you cry, and I really don't want you to leave. It does me good just having you here. But I've got to learn this stuff before I debate Newman, or he's gonna wipe the floor with me. You gotta understand, and give me room."

"I do understand, Brock. I guess I just wish you understood me, my needs. But I know you need your space right now. I'm not mad, and I'm not even leaving because I'm hurt—though I am. I'm leaving because I need to. I need to be alone right now, and find my resolve. If we're going to get through this, I've got to get to where I can take many, many nights just like this one. So, yes, I do hope you get to where you understand what I'm going to need to get through this. But for now, I've got to go find that out for myself. Good night, Brock. Go back to work. I'll call you tomorrow."

Though he held her for a moment longer, she could tell he felt it was his duty more than his desire. She kissed him good night, then walked out the door. She knew she'd never leave him. She needed him too much, even if he didn't need her. Taking the elevator down to the street level, she decided to walk for a few minutes before hailing a cab. It was a cool evening, but she needed some cooling off.

Distracted, she nearly ran into two young men coming out of a coffee shop. They politely offered their apologies, even though it had been her fault, and one of them had even sloshed coffee over his hand. As they continued down the street, she couldn't help but wish Brock demonstrated even half that kindness to her. She decided to go into the coffee shop and grab a quick mocha. It would help warm her up as she walked.

She was surprised to see so many people at this late hour—and surprised that they all seemed to be together. Placing her order, she took a seat by the window and waited for her drink to be made. She was looking out the window so saw the reflection of a young man about her age approaching her. *Great,* she thought, *here comes a pickup line.* She couldn't believe her thoughts went immediately to that corny line of Brock's, so many years ago. That was why she had fallen in love with him then...but he was so different now. She turned to face the young man, who, to her utter amazement, was sliding into the table across from her. Some nerve!

"Excuse me, I don't mean to pry, but—are you okay?"

"Excuse *me.* What business is it of yours?"

"None whatsoever, ma'am. But I couldn't help but notice that you've been crying—sorry—and I just want to make sure you're okay. That you haven't been hurt, or are in some kind of trouble. None of my business, but still my concern. Okay?"

Mary was touched. She hadn't had anyone ask her anything like that, or talk to her that way, for as long as she could remember. Such kindness! Such genuine compassion. She could see it in his eyes, and it was certainly in his voice. She had been all set to just blow him off, but she couldn't turn away. And she couldn't believe what she did next. She actually talked with him.

"No, I'm not okay. I have been hurt—only not in the way you're probably thinking. Nothing physical. Just that old pain called emptiness. I'm afraid there's nothing you can do about that, but thanks for asking. I'm just waiting on my coffee."

"Why don't you come sit with us while you wait? We're all just sitting here getting to know each other—you might as well join us."

"What do you mean 'getting to know each other'? Aren't you friends with all those people? You all look like you know each other pretty well." Mary looked over his shoulder at the small group.

"Actually, no—this is the first night we've been together. We're trying to start a study group and decided this was the best place, not to mention the best time, for all of us. We've kind of finished our study time, and now we're just getting to know each other. Why not join us?"

"Study time. Are you all students or something?"

"Well, yeah, but probably not like you're thinking. We've been studying about a man who cared for people like us—like you. And we've been looking at some of what he had to say about life. Ah, heck, I might as well say it out loud. If you're going to join us, there's no sense in beating around the bush. We've been studying the Bible, and looking at what Jesus said about relationships and how to make them better. Some of us have had some rough experiences in that field and we just sort of found each other, and now we're working together on learning how not to mess things up so bad."

Bible study! Mary started to say, "No thank you," but something happened when the words actually came out of her mouth. Somehow the "no" got left out! And she found herself being led to the collected group of tables and the people sitting all around them.

"I'm James, by the way. James Larkin. Mind if I ask your name?"

"Mary Roller. Nice to meet you, James."

"Everyone! This is Mary. She's going to join us for a few minutes. Can we find a seat for her?"

And just like that, Mary found herself with a group of people who were, in so many ways, vastly different than her; but in one way, just like her. They were searching for truth, for hope, for real life, and real love. And they were finding answers. She felt deep in her heart, for the first time ever, that she could, too.

Thirty-five

Their meeting was scheduled for late that evening, in a small Korean restaurant that was almost impossible to locate in a rundown strip mall just off of Lake Cook Road. Jason drove by the place twice before he spotted the sign, largely due to the fact that half of the lights in the sign were burned out. He wasn't sure why the meeting with Winters had to be so secretive, but he figured this was simply how the man worked.

There were only a handful of people in the tiny restaurant, and none of them were Winters. He made his way to the back booth and suppressed the feeling of needing to wipe the seat and the red-and-white checkered table cloth off before sitting. He waved the waitress off, telling her he was waiting for someone. Fortunately, he didn't have to wait very long. The little bell on the door announced the entrance of Daniel Winters.

"Nice place. Eat here often?" Jason showed his disgust openly.

"Actually, I do. I love this place. You've gotta try their teriyaki chicken."

The waitress was, again, johnny-on-the-spot. Winters ordered his favorite. Jason declined any food, asking only for some hot tea.

"So, what's with the secrecy? Why this place? What did you find out?"

"Whoa, slow down, son. Too many questions. There's no secrecy—at least not on my part. I told you, I like eating here. Now there is some secrecy when it comes to you, or at least when it comes to that lady I followed, and your dad."

"That lady you followed was Marie Auzman. I saw the press conference and knew it was her, and saw you running after her. I figure that's who you followed."

"You figure correctly. Of course, I did the DMV thing—it's what you pay me for. Car's registered to Michael Auzman, husband. And, yes, their son, or at least her son, is Brock Auzman, candidate for Congress, running against you-know-who."

"Okay, I'm not paying you for information that I could read in the newspapers. You said there was something secretive about her, and you also said there was something secretive about my dad. Why don't you start with her?"

"No, you heard me wrong. I didn't separate the two. I said there's something secretive about her *and* your dad. Turns out that Brock Auzman is not the only baby boy she's ever had. Her maiden name is Foster, and she grew up in some little town in Kansas, pretty much on her own. She lived there for nearly all of her growing-up days, then made her way up here to Chicago, spending a summer working at a place you're familiar with, I believe. I'd never heard of the place, or the religion, until I followed her there after her flight from the press conference, but I've done a little research since then. Seems you know the big cheese himself, Duncan Collier."

Jason simply shook his head in affirmation. He wasn't about to give this slimy jerk any more information than he had to.

"Well, it turns out someone else mighta knew him, only I mean in the biblical sense of the word."

Jason shot straight up in his seat, eyes burning holes through the private investigator, jaw clenched. As much as he hated his dad, he couldn't stand the way this sleaze ball referred to him, nor how he was smirking. He wanted to reach across the greasy table and grab the man by his throat but restrained himself enough to simply ask, through clenched teeth, exactly what the man meant.

"Marie Foster worked for your dad, Duncan Collier, at the International Headquarters for The Brothers a little more than thirty years ago. Then, rather abruptly, she heads back to Kansas, all alone. 'Cept she wasn't all alone, it seems. She had a baby growing inside her. I know that because I found out that nine months after leaving here, she gives up a baby boy for adoption. Baby boy is adopted by a couple, name of Jack and Rita Parcells, from Tinley Park, Illinois."

"Okay, so what? That doesn't seem so earth-shattering. What's that got to do with my dad, unless he helped Marie Foster by finding a couple to adopt her son?"

"Gettin' there, son. That's exactly what I thought mighta happened. So I try to track down Jack Parcells. There isn't such a person in Tinley Park, or anywhere in the Cook County register. So I dig deeper and can't find a Jack, Jackson, John, or a Rita, or any other similar name anywhere close to Chicago. I found a Jack Parcells down south in Carbondale, but he had no idea what I was talking about. And his wife, though not named Rita, sure wanted to know who this Rita gal was, and why Jack was having her baby. No sir, there ain't no Jack and Rita Parcells."

Winters' teriyaki arrived, a slab of sliced-up chicken breast with an overage of pungent teriyaki sauce ladled heavily over a bed of white rice, all sitting on a large, wilted piece of lettuce. Between the smells, the sight, and the news, Jason was nauseous. He hated how the sniveling man whom he was paying handsomely for this very information dragged the story out, as though juicy news delighted him as much as his sickening meal.

"So, it's some couple who wanted to keep the adoption private. I don't know how it's done, or that it can be done, but they must have used false names on the adoption papers. So what?"

"Yeah, that's what I figured too. So I did a bit more diggin', only this time from a different angle. That's what I'm good at, son. That's why I earn those big bucks you're paying me. And you are going to be paying me. I looked to see who might have headed down to Kansas around that time from Chicago. Cost me quite a bit, son. Gonna buy me lots of this here teriyaki chicken and then some. I had to grease lots of palms to get this info, but it turned out to be worth it...."

Winters nodded. "I found out exactly who flew out of here on the very day that baby boy was released from the hospital and adopted. And there wasn't no Jack and Rita Parcells on any flights outta O'Hare or Midway, or even Rockford. But there was someone of interest—a couple—that did fly down to that little podunk town, just the two of them. Then they came back that very same day, only this time they had with them a baby boy. That couple was none other than Dr. and Mrs. Duncan Collier. I believe you know them as Mom and Dad."

Thirty-six

The kid was blubbering. Again. How could a kid that seemingly had everything—better than average looks, a tremendous education, and money—always be boo-hooing about everything in his life, like he always had it worse than anybody else? Newman himself had grown up in much worse conditions than Jason Collier could have ever imagined, but he had learned to pull himself up by his own bootstraps. Hard work and, of course, the right amount of charm, and you could go just about anywhere. Look at him! A Congressman, on his way to becoming a United States Senator. So what did this kid have to cry about now?

"Settle down, Jason. I can't understand a word you're saying right now. Get that ridiculous crying voice outta here and just talk."

Jason worked hard on the other end of the line to control himself. He knew how much Lawrence hated it when he wasn't in control of himself. Ever since the day he had first confided in him what he had discovered in the research library of the International Headquarters of The Brothers, Newman had kept him close by, but never too close. Not as close as Jason wanted to be. Having been rejected by his dad, he had turned to the distinguished president of Newman College as his surrogate dad. Ironically, Newman was as cold and distant as his own father, yet Jason could not bring himself to ever go back to him. And it must not have mattered to Duncan Collier that much, since he had never bothered to seek reconciliation with Jason.

Jason had stayed with Newman through all these years and had become his top assistant. He felt he had been a tremendous asset in helping Lawrence win his first election, and each subsequent re-election. Lawrence had even sent him back to Illinois to begin work on the next election, which was why he was here now—separated from the man he admired. Loved. Needed. So he needed now to collect himself so Lawrence wouldn't be angry with him. He needed his strong, smooth voice to comfort him, so he would have to get his act together quickly.

"I just finished meeting with Daniel Winters, that private investigator I told you about. He found out some very disturbing information about me, my dad, and Marie Auzman."

Newman, who had barely been paying attention to the whining of the kid, suddenly sat up with renewed interest. "What did you say about Marie Auzman? What information are you talking about? Why would Winters be digging up anything on her?"

"He followed her when she went running out of that press conference—the one where her *son* was announcing his candidacy against you."

"Get to the point, Jason. I know what the press conference was about. Why did he follow her?"

"Because I told him I wanted information about Brock, and he figured the real story was with her, the way she went bolting out of that place. Turns out, he may be right. But I'm not sure how it will affect Brock or his candidacy as much as it does me."

"What are you talking about? How does Marie Auzman affect you?"

"I think she's my mother. In fact, Winters is pretty sure she is, but I'm not sure just yet. And I'm not sure of the other bombshell he dropped. Winters didn't have any proof of it, but he sure made it sound like Duncan Collier may be my real dad, courtesy of an affair with the candidate's mother—*my* mother—Marie Foster Auzman."

Newman was uncharacteristically speechless. His mind was whirling a hundred miles an hour as he thought about all the implications of what Jason was saying...not only how it affected what he knew of Collier, and Marie Auzman, but also Michael. And, perhaps most importantly, at least for what he needed to know right now, *right now,* was how it affected what he knew, and what he would do with that knowledge, of Brock Auzman. There had to be some sort of political advantage in this. All he had to do was think.

But Jason was still rambling, whining. "What am I going to do? How can I look anybody in the face anymore? I'm not only illegitimate, I'm the bastard son of a man who seduced..."

"Jason, shut up for one minute! I need to think, and I can't think with you whining. I need to figure out how we can use this information."

"Use? You want to *use* this? Lawrence, I want to keep this quiet! There is no way you're going to use this for *your* advantage, knowing that it will kill me. How dare you!"

Finally the kid hung up. Now Newman could think. And that's what he was going to do. Pouring a drink from the cabinet in his inner office, he wandered to the window. Normally he didn't have much of a view from his side of the Rayburn House Office Building, but at this time of the year, and this late at night, he could see the Capital dome. He loved his job. He loved politics. And he wasn't about to let that pipsqueak Brock Auzman take it away from him. He had never been above the usual dirty tricks before, and he sure wasn't going to get a case of integrity now. He just had to think the whole thing through; he could not afford to have his actions backfire.

The worst thing in the world would be to make voters sympathetic to his opponent, and he knew how easy that was to do. Especially with someone already as popular as Auzman. He didn't know what it was about that kid, but people flocked to him like he was some sort of savior. It seemed that no matter where he went, crowds followed. And no matter what he said, or did, they just loved him all the more. Especially those college kids. Didn't they ever go to class? It seemed that no matter where Newman went when he was back home to candidate, there were hundreds of them, waving those stupid *Back Brock* and *We Want The Wiz* signs. He wasn't as bothered by those, though, as he was the *Nothing New In Newman* and the *Lose Larry* ones. He felt like ripping them right out of those lazy, liberal hands and hitting enough of them over the heads with them that the mob would disperse.

He had gone so far as to roll the window down on his limo and yell, "Get a job" at a crowd of long-hairs. Unfortunately it had been captured on camera and shown on newscasts for several days, not to

160

mention being panned on late-night talk shows. His record on employment and outsourcing was not very popular with organized labor, so his comments were blown out of proportion. And he knew Brock Auzman was behind most, if not all, of that. That little punk. He could say something similar, and people would have taken it as some sort of cheerleading encouragement!

Yes, Newman thought to himself, *I've got to figure out how to use this information in the most damaging way possible.* He had to take some shine off the idol that was Brock Auzman.

But he would need Jason to do so. He had let the kid stew long enough—time to give him a call to let him know he was still necessary.

After a few of the most sincere words he could muster up, he gave his reason for calling. "Jason, call your dad. Tell him you need to talk."

Thirty-seven

"Jason, you have no idea what you're talking about. Your mother and I simply helped a young woman who was in trouble. We had tried for so long to have children; you have no idea how hard it was on your mother. Then a supporter called, telling us of this poor girl he knew who had gotten herself into trouble. We simply did what any loving, honorable couple would have done. We helped her. We helped *you*, giving you a chance at life that you would never have had growing up in those conditions."

"How do you know that? People do come out of 'those' conditions, Dad, and they come out better for them. How can you know that what you gave was better? Do you think it was better for me to go through the humiliation of these last few years, being estranged from you? Do you think it was better for me to grovel at the feet of Lawrence Newman, just to be accepted by someone? Do you honestly think that any part of my life for the past ten years has been better than whatever might have happened to me if I'd simply been the son of Marie Foster? It sure seems Brock Auzman had done all right as her son! Maybe it would have been me being a candidate for Congress instead of him—or instead of me being some flunky for the man who is the congressman!"

Duncan Collier sat in amazement as he looked at this young man who was his son. His real son. Yet he realized that, though he had not had a real conversation with him in many years, he was already bored with this one. There was nothing about this young man that was in any way remarkable, or in any way attractive. Oh, he had good looks. His mother's beauty and even many of Collier's own distinctive features were evident, giving him an outward appeal. But that was quickly overwhelmed by a personality and presence that was disappointing. How could such strong genes have been so completely washed out, resulting in a complete personality vacuum? There really was no sense in trying to encourage him. What good would it do?

"Jason, you are not a flunky. But honestly, you would never have been a candidate for Congress or even close to being what you are today, an aide *to* a congressman. Son, count your blessings. You've not had that bad of a life. I regret that we have not had a relationship these past few years, but you left me, remember?"

"How dare you call me *son*. Or am I right, that I really am your son? Yours and Marie's. The illegitimate son from a sick, sordid affair. Is that what I am, *Dad?* Is that what happened, or do you have another one of your stories to tell? Those sad, heart-wrenching stories you tell to raise all your money? Well, I'm sure your supporters would love to hear this story. So start with me, your holiness! Tell me all about it."

"I did tell you, Jason. And I resent your tone of voice. There is no story to tell. Your mother, Marie Foster, now Mrs. Michael Auzman, *did* have an affair, or some sort of fling, and got herself pregnant. She had no family, and no job, but she knew a member of The Brothers. She was advised to give up her baby for adoption. And that's where your mother and I came into the story. We adopted you. We gave you a life. We gave you a chance that Marie Foster could never have given you. Yes, she got a chance of her own when she met Michael Auzman, and she had another baby boy. But the rest of your wild imagination? Forget about it, Jason. It didn't happen."

"Dad, do you think I'm blind? Or just stupid? So stupid that I would think we look alike because I grew up with you? C'mon, Dad. Give it up, confess this thing. What's the matter—you think I'm gonna run to the papers, tell 'em that you're my real dad, spread that fact all over the place? I just want to know. And I want to know just how I'm related to Brock Auzman. Is he also your son?"

"*Jason!* Would you drop it? I am not going to continue to give audience to what must be your emotional need of knowing who your father is. I understand it must be frustrating, even depressing. I'm sure it drives you. But right now I want you to know it is driving me crazy. And I want you to stop. Now."

"I'll bet you do. I'll bet you do. And so I will, for now. But, *Dad*, there are ways to find out the truth. And I will. And when I do, I will not ever talk to you again."

Once again, Collier was amazed at his reaction to what his son was saying. He couldn't believe that he was actually weighing the options of revealing a secret that he had kept for all these years, and wanted to continue to keep, versus losing his son. He knew his son was right—there were ways he could, and would, find out the truth. And if he didn't tell him himself, then he wouldn't be able to control the truth. As he thought through all of these things, he apparently stayed silent a bit too long.

"Never mind, Dad. You just gave me your answer. And I know why. You want what you want. That's your problem, Dad. You want things, so you go out and get them. You pride yourself on being someone who makes things happen. So, Mom wants a baby? You make it happen. She can't get pregnant. No bother, you'll make it happen in another way. You're a doer. And everyone knows you want this religion to be known as something more than a cult. You want it to be recognized as *the* church. So you make it happen. You did that, too, didn't you, Dad? You make it acceptable, or at least far more than it ever has been before. You did it. And I'm sitting here wondering exactly what else you've done. What else you have done to make something happen, Dad? What else have you taken into your own hands, and who's going to suffer for it this time?"

Thirty-eight

It was a call that she had been expecting for years, and especially since the press conference, yet she was very surprised when it actually came. Jason Collier asked if he could meet with her, and she knew that he must know. They scheduled a meeting for later that week, alone.

"Mrs. Auzman, thank you for meeting with me. I'm sure you wonder why I want to meet, but I know your son. We went to school together at Batterson."

"Oh Jason, I know who you are. And I'm guessing that since you wanted to meet, you know that, and that you know something else, also."

Reaching across the table to take Jason's hand—an action she had longed to do for over thirty years—she told him she was his mother. They talked, and Marie confessed...to a point. She refused to let Jason know who his father was. She had promised Duncan Collier, and she would keep that promise no matter what. She would not allow Jason to blame him, though she apologized profusely for what he had to interpret as abandonment from her.

"There was simply no way for me to provide for you, Jason. Your father and mother, the Colliers, offered a life to you that I simply could not give. Please do not think that I did not want you, then, or ever since then. I have wanted to call you so many times, to hug you, to tell you I love you. Every time I came to see Brock at Batterson, I also sought you out. I couldn't talk to you, or I would have spilled it all out. But I watched you. I saw you graduate—did you know that?"

Marie felt her eyes mist. "We came to see Brock purposefully that weekend, even though he was two years away from graduating himself. I knew you were speaking, and I wanted to hear you. And I came to see you when you presented at the Turners' hearing. You probably thought I was only there to watch Brock as he defended them, which, of course, I did. But I was also there to watch you. I was proud of you, and I hurt with you when you walked out. I wanted to come after you. You have no idea how difficult it was to watch the two of you stand on opposite sides of that room—opposite sides of the argument. My two boys!"

"Boys, but not sons. Not brothers. I can't help but notice that you are very careful in your choice of words. You don't refer to either of us as your sons—and I'm wondering why that is."

Had Marie been that obvious? For over thirty years she had been that exact, that careful. She could never refer to Jason as her son, for she knew what that would do to Duncan, to Michael, and ultimately to her. Nor could she truly refer to Brock as her son. Though she had carried him inside her for nine months, and had raised him through his early childhood, there was never a time that she felt he was truly hers. From the moment of his birth until even now, she continually looked for some sign of recognition, some sign of herself in him. And, of course, she never saw it, nor would she. For no matter how much she wanted him to be, Brock Auzman was not really her son. But that, too, she had promised to keep secret. Even from Brock himself.

"I'm sorry, Jason. Force of habit, you know? I have kept this secret in my heart for all these years and have learned to be very careful, no matter how much it broke my heart. But you are my son. And, yes, that makes Brock your brother. And I am so sorry for all the pain that it has caused both of you to not know the truth—truth that might have made things different for both of you. Truth that might have caused some pain, but might have kept you both from the emotional pain that I know Brock faced, and I'm quite sure you did as well."

Jason nearly choked. If there was anyone who showed no signs of emotional pain, it was Brock Auzman. He of the silver tongue and the instant popularity, wherever he went, whatever he did? Where was his pain? He couldn't let that one go without comment.

"Brock? Pain? I'm sorry, what I knew of Brock in school, and certainly what I've known of him since then, I haven't seen a whole lot of pain."

166

"Brock hid his feelings well, and kept them to himself for the most part. But he went through a lot of tough times that I'm sure were very similar to yours—wondering who his father was, what his background truly was. He was angry with me, as you are now, so much of the time. Our relationship had that constant strain to it, for I would not tell him. He closed Michael out completely, almost from the beginning. And he closed me out for the most part as well, especially the older he got. We knew he was drinking, sneaking liquor out of Michael's liquor cabinet, and we knew he was getting into drugs—marijuana, and, we found out later, even much stronger. That's why we finally made the decision to send him to Batterson, as part of a deal with the juvenile court. It nearly killed me, but Michael convinced me that it would be better to have him alive, even if so far away from us, than to have him in prison or dead."

This was news to Jason. Beyond that, he saw it for what he knew Newman would see it. This was ammunition. They talked quite a bit longer, but all Jason could think of were those few words. He couldn't wait to get to a phone and call Newman.

Thirty-nine

John had only been on the job for a few weeks and was already regretting it. He didn't think he was going to be very good at being Brock's campaign manager if it was going to involve many more meetings like this. Sitting in a small, sparsely decorated and windowless conference room off the main lobby of the small chain motel, he didn't think he could take another minute of Russell's advice. He knew the Senator was making a sacrifice of his own time to be here, and he should be more appreciative of that. But he still had a hard time respecting him, and, though he knew the relationship could be a big help toward Brock being elected, he was thinking at this moment that there simply had to be a better way.

He had been taking notes, as well as doing an awful lot of doodling on the notepad provided by the motel. He noticed a pattern with the doodles...or at least with his scribbled notes. At least five times on each of the last five pages he had written, in various forms, *Just kill me now.* And if Russell laughed that grating laugh of his one more time, or said "my years of experience tell me" just once more, John was *going* to either kill himself, or Russell. Or maybe Brock for talking him back into this.

"Brock, my years of experience tell me something you need to know right now. You will never get elected to anything just because you believe in something, no matter how convincingly you present it. For every belief you have, no matter how opposite it might be from your opponent—there are an equal number of people who don't believe like you do and will vote against you. It isn't just about beliefs. It's about the money. You've got to get people who believe like you to listen, then empty their wallets. And you've got to get more of those people than your opponent does. Whoever gets their name into the most minds—minds that will determine which lever to pull on election day—wins. Get your name out there, and get it out there at the right time, and that's you. Let your opponent win in the money game, and you go home poor."

"But Senator, we don't have much money. My stepfather isn't even a partner in his law firm, my mom doesn't work outside of the home, and I don't think there's any rich uncle living his last days ready to leave everything to me. I just don't have money."

"Ah, but you have something besides money. You have appeal— I'm gonna call it 'sex appeal.' You can make speeches in the right place, flash that grin of yours to the right people, and raise cash hand over fist. You've got that, and it's something that no one else running has, even if they start with more money than you. We've got six months to raise thousands and thousands of dollars, so let's get started."

John had heard enough. "Senator Russell, excuse me. I'm not sure I agree with you. How can you say that beliefs don't matter? You've got to be kidding me—a speech and a smile mean more than what you believe in? For that matter, *money* means more?" Turning to Brock, he showed his disgust. "Brock, I'm sorry man. You can't possibly believe that just getting elected is what you're after?"

"Son, you're not hearing me. You gotta have the money to *get* elected, and if you don't get elected, your beliefs don't matter. I know I told you that you've got to stand up for convictions—to make sure Brock stands up. And I still mean that. But there comes a point where getting elected *is* the most critical component, so that you can make a difference down the road. I've made a difference serving the people of my district; I've made life better for many, many of them. I've done things that my opponents over the years would not have done, had they been elected instead of me. And they would have been elected if I hadn't done whatever it took to beat them. Once you get elected you might have that influence, but until then, money is the name of the game."

Brock looked at his friend to hear his reaction. He wasn't disappointed. The look of distaste and disgust on John's face said it all, but he knew that John wouldn't be satisfied until he, the candidate, said it for himself. But this time, unlike just a few days ago, he felt he understood what Russell was saying.

"I'm sorry, Senator Russell. John makes a valid point, that I'm not interested in just getting elected. But I also hear what you're saying, and I want you to know that I'm more than willing to give as many speeches in as many places as it takes, and smile at people until my face freezes. But I told you before, I will be myself. I will say what *I* believe in those speeches—without compromise. I don't think that will cost me the election. I think there are enough people out there who are ready to hear what I have to say that they will support that."

"I hope you're right. And I know you can be pretty convincing. But Brock, are you sure you know what you believe? It's not enough to just be opposite or different than your opponent; you can't merely stand there and say, 'He's wrong, I'm right.' People want to know, need to know, and will demand to know what *you* believe. And Brock, they deserve to know. Too many people have been elected to office simply because they had more money, more fame, or even more charisma than the other guy—and once elected, they've been nothing but the pawns of those who put them there, or the ones who offer enough to literally buy them, their vote, or their influence on committees."

As though noticing his water glass for the first time, Russell took a long drink. He wiped his mouth with the linen napkin, then held the mostly clean napkin up to Brock, pointing out one obvious smudge on the otherwise pristine cloth. "This is a dirty business, son, and too many get down in the dirt and never come out clean. Too many have been willing to dance with the devil to get here, then find out that the devil owns them. The only ones who don't—and they are few and far between—are the ones who come in knowing, absolutely knowing, what they believe, and knowing that nothing, and no one, can move them away from that belief. Do you have that, Brock? Because if you don't, and you can't make it very, very clear, you'll get eaten alive. And, quite honestly, I won't back you for this office or any other, even if it's the county dog catcher." He ended his warning by wadding the napkin into a ball, letting it drop to the table.

Brock looked deep into the eyes of this confusing man. Had he not just said two opposite things? On the one hand, saying you had to do whatever it took to get elected, then on the other saying you had better stand on your beliefs, never wavering? Which one was it? Was he simply being the consummate politician, speaking out of both sides of his mouth? Or could you do both without being contradictory? And what of Russell himself? Had he followed his own advice, or was he giving a warning that he should have paid heed to during his own years of service? Brock wished he had studied the old man's voting record a bit more closely.

"Senator Russell, I appreciate your challenge. I appreciate what you are saying, that I need to know and clearly communicate what I stand for, stand on. So I'm not sure why you say that I must be willing to do whatever it takes to get elected—to earn the money to get there. I know what *I* think—that people will follow me, support me, because they do know what I believe and believe it with me, and I won't have to compromise what I do believe to get them to support me. Again, I believe they'll support because they, too, believe."

Russell was impressed. But he, of all people, certainly knew the difference between bragging and producing. He pressed further. "O.K., we've beat around this bush enough—and played the game of politics quite well. We've talked *about* your beliefs, we've talked about how *important* your beliefs are, and we've even talked about how other people will believe what you believe. That's great debate, son. That's politics. But it doesn't answer the question, which is exactly what most politics do: talk about things without actually saying anything. What do you believe, Brock? What do you believe about social issues, about moral issues, about taxes, about the poor? What do you believe about life, as well as death? People are going to want to know, son. Who are you, and why are you here?"

Brock was confident that he could have answered most of those questions, and would have right then and there, not only for Senator Russell's sake but for his own. He knew that he needed to be able to clearly express his views on any number of relevant topics. It was that last sentence that threw him off, leaving him speechless. When it came to who he was, and why he existed, he simply had no idea.

Forty

The drive from Springfield to Oak Brook Terrace usually took about four hours, but an accident on I-55 had brought traffic to a standstill just outside of Joliet. They had crossed the Des Plaines River and were stuck, as they had been for over half-an-hour, behind a tractor trailer—leaving absolutely no view in an area where there wasn't much to look at anyway. It was still too cold to call it spring, but it had been a beautiful sunny day, giving the sense that spring couldn't be too far away. If they hadn't been behind the truck or stuck in traffic, John would have rolled down the window just to enjoy the fresh air. As it was, both the air outside the car and the tension inside it were nearly unbearable.

Brock hadn't said much since leaving the motel, and John knew better than to bother with small talk, even though he knew what was weighing on his friend's mind. They had known each other for many years now, and John knew he was as close as anyone to Brock—and vice versa. Since his parents' accident he really didn't have anyone else he even talked to, and he had pulled away from Brock for quite some time, partly because of the changes in himself, partly because of the changes he now saw so clearly in Brock, and partly due to Brock's continued involvement with Collier.

Not only did John have lingering bitterness over how his parents had been banished by the man, then the near ex-communication; he was still haunted by the nagging feeling that Collier was somehow involved in, if not directly responsible for, their death. Even though it was Brock who had spared them the shame, John still felt somewhat estranged from his friend since he had chosen to stay under the tutelage of the "cult leader," as John had taken to calling him.

Some of their distance was for that exact reason. John had been doing quite a bit of studying since his parents' death—studying some of the very things that he had at first fought over, then simply discussed with his father. And some of those things involved the very discussion that John had just witnessed with Brock in front of Senator Russell. His dad had challenged him that he needed to search for answers to some very similar questions: where did you come from, why are you here, and where are you going from here?

John had not given thought to those questions prior to his dad asking him so many years ago, but he'd hardly thought of anything else since then. He didn't have too much trouble with the first one, simply because he didn't care so much about all the arguments and discussions that he heard the skeptics have. There was too much of a divine order to not realize there must be a divine plan, meaning, logically, there was a divine planner: God. Beyond that, he didn't get involved. Let the skeptics and the people much smarter than him debate all they wanted about that one. He could accept that by faith, since he felt there was clearly an object to and a reason for that faith. He knew that was the one that bothered Brock the most, and they had discussed it many times, but he simply couldn't relate to Brock's struggle.

But the other two questions? Those were more difficult. Like Brock, he struggled over his purpose, at least most of the time. Right now, however, he felt he knew what his purpose was. He was here, quite simply, for Brock. Not just to get him elected, but to be a voice for him. He didn't know all that would be involved in that, but he knew that much. Knowing that, he knew he couldn't stay quiet much longer, or stay out of the way. It was time to find some answers for Brock, if not for himself.

Perhaps he should be finding the answer to that third question very, very soon. His friend just might kill him once he found out what he was going to do. Seeing an exit just a few hundred feet up the road, he determined his plan of action quickly.

"Why are you getting off here? Do you know some shortcut?"

"Not a shortcut, Brock. We're turning around. We need to go see your stepdad."

"Michael? What on earth for? Haven't you had enough hot air advice on how to do this campaign stuff for one day? Do you have any idea what you're asking for when you open a conversation with him, especially when it comes to me and my future?"

"I don't want to talk with him about your future, Brock. I want us both to talk with him about your past. We keep hitting this same roadblock, and I honestly don't think you're going to go anywhere until you know where you've come from. And I don't mean a test tube, or whatever bunk you've heard or imagined. I mean straight out—who you are, who they are, the whole thing. I know you've asked and I've asked, but this time *we* are going to ask, together, and we're not leaving without the answer. I'm sick and tired of this game; I can't imagine how you must feel."

"You're right, John. You can't imagine. You know your past, your parents, your life. I'm not sure how Michael can help, but I like the idea of trying. Go for it."

Perhaps it was providence that Michael was not home, but Marie was. Brock had not had a chance to really talk with her since she had left his press conference, other than a quick phone call to make sure she was all right. She explained that she'd had a sudden upset stomach, and that she didn't want to make a scene. He laughed it off on the phone, letting her know that throwing up might have been less difficult to explain to the press than her sudden disappearing act.

"Oh Brock, I'm so sorry about the other day. I don't know what happened, but I just couldn't stay in there. I was so proud of you, I guess I just got overwhelmed with emotions." She gave John a hug, then held him away from her. "John, you're looking good. Now, you boys sit down and I'll get some dinner started. I was going to just have some soup, but I've got some steaks in the freezer. It will only take a minute to thaw them in the microwave. So sit. Sit."

"Mom, we're really not here to eat. We need to talk, and since Michael's not here, you win the prize. Let's go into the family room and talk."

Marie knew exactly why they were there. She knew they had gone to Springfield to meet with Senator Russell, and she could imagine what he might have told them. She also knew that Brock had hit another one of his snags lately. She could see it on his face, hear it in his voice. At a time when he should be pumped up and excited about this opportunity to get into politics, she heard something that was of concern. Never known for having thick skin, he was unusually touchy, almost angry, over some of the questions asked at the press conference. She looked at his eyes and saw the pain—a pain that she could in some ways relate to, yet could not begin to understand. She knew what it was to feel used. She knew what it was to lose your own identity. But she had no idea what it was to feel as though you have no identity whatsoever.

"Okay, I think I know where this is going. You're right. It's time to talk. In fact, Brock, I'll be honest with you here and now. I don't know how you're going to take this, or what the outcome is going to be, but I think it's time you learned the truth. I'm way out of my role here. I'm supposed to keep quiet and simply be your sweet ol' mom. That was my role from the beginning, but I can't play it any longer. I can't stand living a lie one more day. I'll tell you boys again, sit. I've got to go get my journal. I don't want to miss any details."

Forty-one

Once again, the slimy but effective Winters had done his job. He had copies of the arrest report, the juvenile court hearing, even the letter from Batterson stating that they would hold the young Auzman on probation for the court system. It was a gold mine of documents that were supposed to be sealed by the court since Brock had been a minor, but, again, Winters had his ways. Neither Jason nor Newman wanted to know the how. They were simply overjoyed with the what. Jason had earned huge brownie points with this, and he knew it. Newman was going to hold a press conference and had asked Jason to stand at his side as he did so.

Things like this had a certain protocol, however. No matter how beneficial the news was going to be for one, thus devastating to the opponent, common courtesy directed that a warning be given to the opponent's camp. Though it could be quite bloody, politics did have its manners. Newman himself would make the call. Again, protocol said he should talk directly to Brock, but he really didn't care who he spoke to. Due mostly to the lateness of the hour, he had expected to get an answering machine at their campaign headquarters, where he could leave a message instructing Brock to call him in the morning. The fact that Brock himself answered rattled his thoughts for a moment.

"Oh, hello, Brock. I'm a bit surprised that you are there, but even more that you're answering the phones. All your volunteers gone for the night already?"

"I was expecting a call from someone and, yes, sent everyone home. It *is* late. I'm sorry, who are you?"

"This is Lawrence Newman, Brock. I know I'm calling late, but I'm afraid I have some bad news for you, and I wanted to give you the courtesy of hearing it first, before I'm forced to go public with it."

Brock did a quick analysis in his mind, wondering what bad news Newman could be talking about. In milliseconds he went from the discussion that he now knew about between his mother and Jason Collier, to the possibility that Newman had tracked down his real father and was going to reveal that he was an axe murderer or something. Since those were his thoughts, he was unprepared for, and therefore laughed at, what Newman actually "had" on him.

"I have become aware, Brock, and feel it is my duty to make the voting public aware, of your usage of illegal drugs."

For the second time in this short phone call, Newman was rattled. Expecting silence, or argument, or even begging, he was unsettled by the outburst of laughter that came from Brock.

"I'm not sure what you see as being so humorous about this, young man. I assure you, I don't believe voters will see the same humor, hearing that a candidate for the United States Congress took the laws of the land, laws passed by that Congress, so cavalierly. People consider the usage of illegal drugs and violation of the laws of this land a bit more seriously than you apparently do."

"I apologize, Mr. Newman. I'm not laughing at our laws, or at voters. And I do appreciate the heads'-up. I will make a statement tomorrow."

Brock hung up the phone and, still chuckling, walked over to the office where John, also working late, was poring over some recent poll numbers.

"What are you smiling about?" John asked. "I take it that phone call was some good news? Better than these poll numbers, I hope? Newman's pretty popular, my friend. I can't believe it, 'cause I wouldn't vote for him if he was the only candidate running, but apparently I'm in the minority. At least, if we figure the plus or minus four factor in."

"Forget the numbers, pal. You'll never guess who that phone call was from, so I'm just gonna tell you. It was Newman."

"*What?* What in the heck was he calling for? We're weeks from the election. He's not gloating over these numbers this early, is he?"

"No, he wasn't gloating over numbers, but he was gloating. Oh, he tried to hide his cockiness with some sort of feigned deep sorrow, but it was there. I wish you could have heard the seriousness of his voice—that rich golden voice, trying to act so sympathetic: 'I'm afraid I've got some bad news for you, Brock.' It was classic Newman. So smug and so fake that it makes you choke, but..."

"Hold it, good humor man. I don't want a play by play of how the man sounded. I've already heard more than enough of him, without hearing poorly done impersonations. Get to the point: what was the bad news?"

"He thinks he's got me over a barrel—probably thinks that I'm going to announce that I'm getting out of the race tomorrow. I did tell him that I'd be making a statement, but it won't be what he thinks."

"*Brock!* It's late, I'm tired, I'm hungry, I want to get home some time tonight, so get to the point! What was the bad news?"

"Hey, settle down, John. I came in here to give you the same laugh that I'm getting out of this. You don't have to get so hot. All right, you want the "bad news"? Here it is. Apparently Newman's camp has been very hard at work digging up dirt on yours truly, and they think they've bagged the big kahuna, the hangman's noose, if you will. Newman is set to hold a press conference tomorrow telling all about my—how did he put it?—'illegal drug usage.'"

"What? Why on earth would he say you used illegal drugs? Is he nuts? Doesn't he know that making such blatantly outrageous allegations can only backfire on him? I don't get it. Why would he do such a thing? Why would he *say* such a thing?"

"Maybe because it's true. Yep, I did illegal drugs. Smoked 'em, snorted 'em. Got in trouble for them, and ended up at Batterson over them. You asked me once why I chose Batterson. I've never forgotten that. But you weren't really listening to hear my answer. I didn't *choose* the place. I was sent there. Punishment. Probation, actually. I think that what I told you was something about being a minor. Well, it was more like I was a juvenile delinquent, complete with what was *supposed* to be a private record."

John sat back in his chair, the wind completely knocked out of him. He had known Brock for nearly fifteen years, had considered him his best friend, and vice versa, yet with sudden realization it hit him that he really did not know this guy. He wasn't as concerned that he didn't know about the drug usage as much as he was concerned that Brock had never told him. They had confided so much in each other that to hear this, now, was a bit much for John to take.

"Brock, I'm stunned. And *angry!* You couldn't tell me this before now? I have to hear it because the whole nation is about to? I'm supposed to be your best friend, remember? I'm supposed to be your campaign manager, too. And things like this—that *might* have been told to a friend, most certainly should have been told to your campaign manager. Ever heard of the little thing called disclosure?"

"Heard of it, and about to do it, my *friend.* Gee, I'm glad to know I've got your full support on this thing. I would have thought you, of all people, would be a bit more understanding of youthful indiscretions. This thing is so small in the whole scheme of things. Nothing but a blip."

"*Youthful indiscretions?* Listen buddy, you can stand before the public and talk about youthful indiscretions when you tee-peed somebody's house. You can talk about youthful indiscretions when you knocked over a mailbox or two—which, even that, I might remind you, is illegal vandalism. But you broke the law! And you broke laws that matter to voters, and *should* matter to you. Yet you act like this is a big bother, instead of what it is. And what it is, Brock, is wrong. Yeah, you're right. It's a little thing—a blip. But you know what? It's like that old saying 'death by a thousand papercuts.' You allow, or overlook, even indulge in enough of those little things, determining by yourself or by popular opinion whether something is big or little, right or wrong, and all of a sudden you've got one huge problem. I don't know why you're smiling, unless it's because you're going to join with those who laugh you out of this campaign."

Brock's answer reflected his still-flippant attitude. "No, I'm not joining them. And I'm not fighting Newman either, which is exactly what he thinks I'll do. But I'll tell you what I am going to do. I'm going to have my own press conference, and beat Newman to the punch. I'll just do a little 'so what, big deal' song and dance, and the people will melt. You forget, John, they love me. By the time I'm done, most of those listening to me will support me for being like them. You think I'm the only kid who toked and snorted? They'll all think I'm the best thing to happen to stodgy old politics since J Frickin K."

John leaned forward, elbows on the table in front of him, eyes focused on the young man in front of him—his friend that he admired with everything in him. Or had admired, until this moment. He had watched Brock struggle with so many things, and overcome them. He knew that many, many of Brock's characteristics danced along a very fine line. His persistence was only a few ticks to the right of being stubbornness. His wit often strayed over the line to become caustic sarcasm. He was short with the many volunteers who were working at the campaign headquarters, and he snapped at the press when they asked questions that he didn't like. Yet people still loved him, so he got away with it all.

But now he observed something else that bothered him about as much as anything else he'd observed. He saw an attitude of demanding pride in Brock. It was like he expected people to do what he wanted, which had always been a part of his natural leadership abilities; now, however, it didn't come across like leading as much as driving. People who had started serving in their volunteer positions out of respect and a desire to simply be with him now either deserted, or stayed more out of fear than respect. Right now, that was how John himself felt, only he knew he couldn't do either one. For him, deserting his friend was not an option, but neither was serving a man that he was rapidly losing respect for.

Forty-two

Brock was right. People loved him, and his announcement did exactly what he said it would: it only enhanced his image in the public eye. Papers and reporters that had previously sent candidates to an early withdrawal for offenses far less damning than his were praising his openness and forthrightness, calling his honesty a breath of fresh air. He had managed to beat Newman's press conference and completely stole any advantage his opponent might have had by stating that he had chosen to come out with the truth now, before it became a campaign issue. He did explain it as a youthful indiscretion, something he had done during a stressful time of his life—a time of confusion over family issues. And he used it to encourage young people to not repeat his bad behavior. Rather, learn from his mistakes. Find a better way, a proper way, to get help for your emotions. He was a pure hit.

And it all made John sick.

"I'm taking a break, Brock. That's all. I'll be back, but I need a couple of weeks at least. I've got to get my head together, and I can't do it in this grind. I love you, Brock. You are the most important person in the world to me right now, and this election is the most important thing. But I can't be this way right now. I can't compromise like this. And apparently that's the way this game has to be played. So I gotta decide whether I can play it, or not."

"Now? Now you want to get a conscience? Now you want to think? Could you have picked any worse time to be taking a break, John? We're closing in on Newman! How can you even think of leaving *now!*"

"First of all, Brock, I'm not just now getting a conscience. I've told you all along whenever I've not liked things—little things you've said in speeches, or little things you've done along the way. My conscience has been loud and clear all along; you've just chosen to ignore me. And I've ignored it a bit too much lately also. But not anymore. Hey, Buddy, do I need to remind you why I took that scholarship to Dartmouth? It was because I liked their motto: 'A voice crying in the wilderness.' That's me, dude. I just need to get back out to the wilderness for a while. I said I'd be back, Brock. And I will—even if it's just to tell you I quit. For right now, put Dorman in charge of things. He can keep things going for a couple of weeks, and you'll do fine. I'll be back."

And with that, John walked out of the office. He had no idea where he was going to go to get away, and he didn't know what exactly he was hoping for, but he did know that he wanted to come back. Not for himself, but to see Brock succeed. But not at any price, and especially not at the cost of whatever values he still had left.

Mary had returned to the coffee shop study several more times. She was strangely drawn to the place but was equally afraid of telling Brock, or having him find out about it. Yet when she heard that John had taken a leave of absence from the campaign, she called him—and invited him to join her that evening. She wasn't disappointed. He simply asked for the address and said he'd meet her there.

"James, this is John Turner, a friend of mine. I hope you don't mind, but I invited him to join with us this evening. He's a friend of my fiancé as well, and he's been asking a lot of the same questions that I've been asking, looking for the same things."

"John, James Larkin. Great to meet you, and of course you're welcome to join us. I hope, though, that Mary hasn't given you too much of an anticipation of what we do. No real answer men here, but a lot of other people searching. Don't be afraid of asking any questions, and don't be too bashful about speaking out. We hope we can all learn something from each other, but the main thing we want to do is learn from this."

He held up a Bible, only it wasn't what John was used to. No big black cover, no gold edged pages. It looked more like a college text book. Either way, John didn't have one, though he noticed, for the first time, that Mary was carrying something very similar. They went to place their coffee order, talking as they stood in line.

"Don't worry, John, we can share. I'm still learning how to use this thing. Did you know it's not just *a* book, but a compilation of sixty-six books? But what a read!"

"Mary, I grew up with this 'thing' as you call it. But I never really paid much attention, unless my mom was teaching me. She could tell the stories and make me feel like I was there. Oh, my dad could teach, too. But he taught in such a way that I just tuned him out. And he wasn't just teaching the Bible; in fact, he usually only used it to reinforce The Brother's teaching manuals. Even then it was like he didn't really believe that stuff. Now that I think about it, he did get a bit more excited when he got away from those books and opened that old Bible of his. And I'd see the two of them reading from it quite often. I'll bet I've got their Bible in my storage unit, along with all their other stuff. Maybe I should dig it out?"

"John, that would be great! Maybe they have some of their notes in there, and you can learn from them still. That could really help in this study. Who knows? You might end up teaching the rest of us!"

Forty-three

A United States Congressman has basically three distinct roles. He, or she, is elected to represent their home district, legislate, and serve on committees. There have been over one hundred committees since the first was organized in 1789 that are now defunct, and the Legislative Reorganization Act of 1946 reduced the number of House committees from forty-eight to nineteen, most with any number of subcommittees. A congressman's day is filled with attending committee meetings, hearings that relate to those committee meetings, and the occasional vote relating, usually, to those committees and subcommittees. President Woodrow Wilson once said that Congress in session is Congress on display, but in its committee rooms it is Congress at work.

One such subcommittee is the House Agriculture Committee's Subcommittee on Livestock, Dairy and Poultry, responsible for the jurisdiction over water conservation, forestation, and all agriculture, including the health and welfare of animals. It is not a particularly powerful committee unless the member was from a rural state, but recent scientific breakthroughs were making it more powerful. And today that power was being exerted.

The Subcommittee On Livestock, Dairy, and Poultry had been given the responsibility to hold hearings on cloning, and the overarching ramifications of it. It was, Newman thought to himself, the epitome of irony that he should be sitting on that committee this day as it discussed the issue of cloning of cows, and the ethics of such. It had been many, many years since he had debated the very issue as a young man, under far more private conditions, and about far more serious matters than cows. He had lost that debate, and the loss had changed his life. Now, with new information, new reasoning, and new purposes, what did he feel?

The President was calling for a ban on federal funding for human cloning experiments in the United States and was urging a voluntary moratorium on privately funded experiments as well, but his suggestions were falling on many deaf ears. Several coalitions and political action committees believed that cloning was the answer for their various causes: infertility, spinal injury research, diseases of various sorts, and just plain technological advancement. People believed that there should be human cloning simply because there *could* be. Hollywood had gotten involved, sending various stars and such to testify before the various hearings throughout Capitol Hill, as well as the multiple gatherings out on the Mall. Religious spokesmen were lining up on the other side of the issue, and there wasn't a member of this subcommittee that had not been personally visited by Dr. Jay Dodge, one of the most listened to radio preachers in America. They all knew that their political careers would no doubt be affected by whatever decision they made.

In all reality, every member of the committee, and probably every voice outside of the hearing room, knew that the best they could do was postpone the inevitable, especially Lawrence Newman. He had already argued that fact, so many years before, so knew it firsthand. "Human cloning will occur," he had said, "even if the government is against it, even if the scientists are against it, even if ethicists are against it, if there are people who want it bad enough, and are willing to pay enough money."

The first argument presented set the tone for the rest of the hearing. As several scientists stated that cloning of animals was not a natural step toward cloning humans, one congressman asked if the scientists believed that it should be okay to clone humans or not. A scientist from Harvard argued that no one would want to proceed with human cloning unless they were absolutely convinced that the procedure was not going to cause harm to the baby that would come out of that procedure. His argument continued that if the child could be born healthy and happy and loved by its parents, then it really shouldn't matter how that child began its development.

"In other words," countered Congressman Lee Harwood from Arkansas, "as long as we can promise favorable results in the long term, you think it is perfectly okay to do this procedure, even if should be at the expense of, say, a 46 percent failure rate? Are you aware of that, sir? That in Scotland, in the effort to produce that one cloned lamb, 46 percent of the cloned lambs died in the perinatal period—either late in the pregnancy or shortly after birth? That, sir, is a horrendous rate. How can you think that we should take *that* risk with sheep, let alone that kind of risk with a human baby?"

"Excuse me, Congressman." It was the scientist from Harvard again. He had written a book on ethics and cloning, and apparently had several infertile couples who were willing to pay big money to his private lab to be human guinea pigs for his cloning experimentation. "We have long known that virtually every cell of the body contains a person's complete genetic code. The exception is sperm or egg cells, which contain half the genetic material until the sperm fertilizes the egg and a new human being with a complete genetic code begins growing. We have now learned that the partial genetic material in a female's unfertilized egg cell may be removed and replaced by the complete genetic material from a cell taken from an adult. With a full genetic code, the egg cell behaves as if it has been fertilized and begins to grow. The research necessary to develop human cloning will likely cause the necessary termination of several, if not many, of those fertilized eggs. That may seem like a high price to pay, but the technological and medical advances made would, in my opinion, far outweigh those losses. We've been anticipating this possibility in humans for decades and have been playing around with its possibilities. It's now time to take this step with the full backing of our government."

Harwood's response was equally terse. "The experiments of Nazi Germany and the resulting Nuremberg Trials and Code taught us long ago that there is some knowledge that we must not pursue if it requires the use of immoral means to get it. To the extent that the research necessary to develop human cloning will likely cause the deaths of human beings, the cost is unacceptably high. In the case of the sheep cloning process, it would seem likely that many human embryos would be lost as the technique is improved. Those, sir, are *human* embryos; human beings."

It was Newman's turn to enter into the debate. "My understanding is that cloning typically involves genetically copying some living thing for a particular purpose: a wheat plant that yields much grain, a cow that provides excellent milk. The problem with such a utilitarian approach to human beings, however, is that they are made in the image of God. They have a God-given dignity that will not allow us to use them merely as a means to fulfill our human desires. We must not, for instance, produce clones with low intelligence to serve society's needs for menial labor, or produce clones to provide transplantable organs, in that the identical genetic code would minimize the threat of organ rejection. We should not even produce a clone of a child who dies tragically in order to remove the parents' grief, as if the clone could actually be the child who died.

"All people are special creations of God who should be loved and respected as such. We must not demean them by fundamentally subordinating their interests to those of others, forcing upon them conditions that they might not have had consented to had it been possible to consult them. We need to at least investigate those kinds of questions, ask what values people think are being promoted by creation of children by cloning, and ask whether those are the values we as a people want to endorse."

The Harvard scientist leaned into the microphone to answer Newman. "I don't think the ethical issues will ever be settled. I don't think we will ever reach a consensus in the same way we've never reached a consensus on the abortion issue. There are going to be people who don't like cloning for what I consider to be religious reasons mostly, and then there are going to be people who do want to use this technology. Human beings have a very powerful drive to want to have biological children, and there are certain people who are unable to do so and will spend large amounts of money on in vitro fertilization, for example. Cloning will be just one more technology that will allow certain kinds of infertile people to have their own children. They don't want to have anybody else's children; they want their own, and I think it is their right. I don't see this as being bad. Yes, there is a certain cost. But, I repeat, I believe the good realized will far outweigh the price of a few non-birthed embryos."

A freshman congressman from Ohio, known to be quite liberal, and known to be very much in support of human cloning, asked a question that had been on the minds of many. His youthful enthusiasm resulted in a lack of the mental brakes that most of the rest of the committee had been applying thus far. "What excites me about cloning is the possibilities it presents. Could we not clone some of the world's greatest people? Could we not make another Michael Jordan? A Mother Theresa? A John F. Kennedy?"

Newman blanched and swallowed hard, thinking to himself, *What about Jesus Christ?* He was at first pleased, then terrified with the thoughts of what might be the opposite, when the Harvard scientist responded.

"I'm sorry, Congressman. Were clones of any of our heroes to begin growing today, these clones would not turn out to be our heroes, for our heroes are not who they are simply because of their genetics. They, like us, are shaped by genetics and environment alike, with the spiritual capacity to evaluate, disregard, and at times alter either or both. It would be someone with presumably similar physical abilities but might completely lack, for instance, the competitive drive that Michael Jordan has. Clones could end up being the exact, polar opposite of the hero we hoped for. Clone Jesus, for example, and you might not end up with the Christ as much as the antichrist."

Excusing himself, Newman nearly ran from the hearing room.

Forty-four

"Listen, Auzman, I know what Collier wanted to do. I fought with everything I had to stop it, because I felt then, and I still feel now, that it is just plain wrong. I thought it was trying to play God, and I still do. It was wrong. I know you won the argument to *do* what he wanted to do, though I still don't know why you did that, because I don't think you actually thought it was the right thing to do either—not just violating the integrity of the cloak, but the whole scientific experiment. You, however, seemed more afraid of Collier than his idea. I know all that, but I just want to know if he did it. Did they actually carry out the project? Did it succeed?"

"What difference does it make to you, Newman? It was nothing to you once you lost the debate, so why does it matter now all of a sudden?"

"I'm sitting on a subcommittee right now that is discussing this very thing. We're looking at the ethics of cloning, and I gotta tell you, Michael, this whole argument scares me the same way it did three decades ago. I've heard a lot of argument today that the chances of being able to clone a human being are very unlikely, but I also know Collier wouldn't have given up easily. He was bound and determined, and I want to know if he succeeded. I know you left Headquarters sometime after I did, but were you there long enough to see the project you argued for to fruition?"

Michael Auzman was stymied. He couldn't tell Newman the truth, but he knew he couldn't tell him a lie either. That would only make Newman go somewhere else—probably Marie—and though she didn't know everything, she did know that she had carried a baby to full term that had been, as she put it, "planted inside her." That would lead Newman to go further, and, all too soon, he *would* eventually get to the bottom of it. Somehow Michael had to get him off the track right now, and the best way that came to him was to tell him something else—something that would distract him from this all-too-damaging hunt.

"Lawrence, I know you want answers regarding Collier's project, but those are answers I'm not able to give you. But I think I do have something to give you that you might be very interested in. But not over the phone. We need to meet in person, and we need to meet soon. I have some information on Brock."

"I'll be in Chicago this weekend. Let's meet."

There are 435 United States Representatives, nineteen from the state of Illinois. The 9th District covers much of greater Chicago and a good portion of Cook County. It is a prestigious district due to its size and the fact that Chicago is the third largest city in the United States. The Congressman from Illinois' 9th District normally carries a fair amount of power and prestige in many insider circles in Washington D.C., simply because many people want the ear of the voice that influences so many people.

But Congressman Lawrence Newman, now running for his fourth term, could still walk into many high-end restaurants in downtown Chicago and not even be noticed. He was handsome, strikingly so, which resulted in more than a few second glances from patrons, and some might look with a quizzical glance as though they realized that they should know him, but couldn't quite place him. But there would be little or no actual recognition. Usually that fact bothered him to no end and made him itch all that much more to become a Senator. *Then* they would recognize him! He certainly wouldn't be able to walk into a place like Joe's and be left alone then.

But tonight he was thankful for the anonymity. His purpose called for a quiet location, a quiet conversation. He didn't want Auzman scared off, and he knew the man didn't like any kind of crowd. He directed the *maitre d'* to find him a booth in the back.

True to form, Auzman walked in like a cat expecting to find a dog just around the corner. He kept his head down and slid his eyes back and forth to look for the Congressman, refusing the help of the *maitre d'*.

Newman stood and waved him over to the booth, then shook his head in amazement to watch what had to be the most antisocial man he'd ever known make his way through the crowd, working so hard at not being noticed that nearly everyone looked up to watch him. Fortunately, he did not notice.

"Michael, you haven't changed. Take your seat, please. I know you want to keep your back to everyone, so I gave you that side of the booth."

They went through the formalities of getting reacquainted, which was largely Newman talking and Auzman listening. He did draw some facts about Marie out but didn't approach the topic of Brock until they had ordered.

"I do want to thank you for meeting me, Michael. I do want to know what happened with the Messiah Project, but you mentioned on the phone that you have some information. Let's get to it."

Michael had practiced his presentation nearly as much as he used to back in their days before The Council. But it wasn't working. He was more nervous than he had ever been, not so much because of what he had to say, but what could happen to the entire project if he couldn't get Newman off track.

"Lawrence, I know you have concerns about Brock gaining on you in the polls, and you might even be afraid he could possibly beat you. But I want you to know, that's not going to happen. Not only because you have a stellar record and there is no reason for the voters to oust you, but because Brock is simply not ready for national office. He needs more seasoning. I wish there was some way he could actually work with you, under you, to learn at your side."

As much as Newman agreed, and liked what Michael was saying, he knew there was absolutely no conviction in the man's voice for what he was saying. It was all a crock. "C'mon, Michael. Give me more credit than that. I know you've worked hard on this campaign, and you haven't done so with the expectation that Brock would lose, and certainly not that he would become my student. That's laughable, and we both know it. I couldn't agree more that he's not ready, not tested. There's no way he should win, but this is a funny business. He doesn't *have* to be seasoned, or even knowledgeable, to be voted for. Your son is very charismatic...downright charming. And as long as he doesn't trip all over himself and do something downright stupid, he'll get an awful lot of votes. In fact, he just might beat me. He's young, appealing to the first-time voters, and the fact he is untested in Washington waters can be a plus in some of those voters' minds. It makes no sense, but how many elections have you seen where it wasn't the sensible vote that won? Maybe that's why it's called the 'popular' vote."

"You're right, Lawrence. I have worked hard on this campaign, because I started out believing, and I guess still believe, Brock could win. But I have never been convinced that he *should* win. I've had some problems with Brock for a very long time, and I can't say that I've seen a vast change in his attitude or his behavior during these past few years, and I'm worried what such an attitude would do in the national spotlight, not to mention what it might do to Congress! Brock is simply too much of a lit fuse, and no one knows when he's going to blow up."

"Fine, Michael. That's all just fine, and I'm in agreement. I've had dealings in the past with Brock and his campaign manager, as you well know. But we both know that a bit of a temper or even attitude will not keep people from voting for him. In fact, for every person who won't vote for him because of those things, there are probably two or three that will. You surely didn't have me fly all the way here and have this meeting because you're worried about his bad attitude. I thought you said you had some information for me. Sorry, Michael, you'd better have more than this."

Michael swallowed hard. He could feel the sweat beads popping out on his balding forehead, and picked up a napkin to dab at the drips. His hands were even worse, and his throat was suddenly dry. Setting the napkin down, he grabbed his water glass. Taking a long drink, he finally set the glass down and cleared his throat. There would be no bluffing of Lawrence Newman, and if he couldn't get him to bite on what he was about to tell him, he'd watch the congressman go after the other story, the real story, like a rabid dog. He also knew that if Newman did bite, and went after the information he was going to give, Brock's campaign was over.

"Lawrence, Brock's attitude of arrogance led to more than just some youthful rebellion. I know that you know about his drug usage, which, as you probably also know, is why he was sent to Batterson. That was part of the deal worked out in the juvenile court. He wasn't just using, Lawrence. He was dealing. Not much, but enough to get him in a lot more trouble than he did. Collier helped, you know. He pulled some strings and called in some favors, and got a judge that belongs to The Brothers. So that, alone, would probably keep him from beating you in the election. Get that word out, and most voters are going to think twice about putting him in office."

"Most. But certainly not all. Sorry again, Michael. I've gone that route with his drug usage and I've watched people treat his 'confession' like he's a hero. At the rate he's going right now, admitting that he dealt will only cause people to think he's just a great guy who only wanted to help people feel better. They'll give him even more support! Your son apparently has a very unique medical condition: his feces aren't odorous. Tell you what, Michael. Why don't you just tell Brock to drop out, wait until next time? Why are you so anxious to bring him down, or to have my campaign do so?"

"I already told you, Newman! I don't think he *should* be elected. I think he needs to be knocked down a notch or two. I couldn't agree with you more—he can do no wrong in too many people's eyes, and they'll put him in this office, and whatever else he decides to run for, and I just don't think he's going to do this country any good. He's out for this thing for himself. You don't know him, but I do. And there's no way he's going to listen to me, especially regarding him running for office. *Your* office, Lawrence. He never has listened to me. He's not about to start now. No, he won't drop out. But you can stop him. At least for now. Maybe he'll get some humility through a loss, and become more willing to listen to sound advice. He just needs to be stopped now."

Lawrence Newman looked at his former opponent for a long moment. That argument sounded reasonable, and maybe it was his true motivation. But he somehow still doubted. He was hiding something, and trying to pull an end-around to keep him from pursuing it. And he was pretty sure he knew what it was. But he also knew he didn't have much time, as Brock was gaining on him in the polls. He might eventually get to the bottom of the real issue, but it would probably be too late; the election could already be lost by then. If Auzman was offering him something right now that could derail the young man's steamroller, he was willing to grab it. He could always dig deeper later.

"All right, Michael. Enough of the potholes. What do you have that will really stop him?"

"Have you ever wondered why neither he nor John, his very best friend, his campaign manager, has ever gotten married?"

Forty-five

Brock slammed the paper down in disgust and literally stomped into John's office. John was on the phone, but Brock wasn't going to wait. His phone hadn't stopped ringing all morning with the news, asking for comment, but this was his first opportunity to read for himself the newspaper with its damning accusations.

"Hang up."

"I'm on the phone, Brock. I'll come over to your office when I'm done."

"You're done now. Tell whoever you're talking to you'll call 'em back. Hang up."

John had seen his friend angry, and knew what he could do when he blew up. And he could see he was about to do just that. No small wonder! Indeed, it was rather amazing that it had taken this long for Brock to lose his temper. John knew he had been reading the report in the morning paper, but normally one could even hear Brock doing that, as he made loud comments about any and all things with which he disagreed. Surprisingly, John hadn't heard such outbursts this morning, which he could only interpret as meaning the anger was more deep-seated than usual. He excused himself from the caller and obeyed his angry boss, hanging up the phone.

"Did you see what Newman said? Did you know he was going to say that stuff? I'm heading over to his campaign office and demanding a retraction, an apology, a denial! And if he doesn't do it, I'm filing suit for defamation of character today. And you'd better be doing the same thing. He cannot get away with this. He knows with just days to go until the election he can use this thing to cause voters to think twice about voting for me. We gotta make this thing backfire on him. *Now!*"

"Had you listened to the phone conversation you just made me drop," John said in a determined tone, "instead of busting in here with your angry demands, you'd have heard that I've already started damage control—which you should be doing instead of going out filing lawsuits. Yeah, we're probably gonna sue his pants off, but the first thing we're going to do is call a press conference, with Mary at your side, and you and she are going to profess your undying love for each other. And you are going to find every girl you've ever gone out with and have them start singing your amorous abilities. We're going to make that geezer regret he ever tried to pull this stunt. And I don't know who the heck his 'anonymous tipster' is, but I intend to find him and hang him by his thumbs as well. Someone from inside our campaign? Are you kidding me? What a crock! There's no one here that would say anything like that, man. You know it, and I know it. So this is just one more part of his lie. Don't worry, Brock. We're going to nail him, but we're going to do it my way. Heads *are* gonna roll!"

"I want to make them roll right now! What you're talking about is going to take time, and he's already getting a full head of steam. We'll be rolled over before we even get the press together to hear my side. I think I need to go confront him, and make him deny this whole thing right now, publicly—no matter what it takes."

"I'm not so sure you should get your hands dirty in this thing, Brock. Let me do it, and let me do it *my* way. If I go down, so what? You simply claim I acted on my own, you distance yourself from me, and you still have a chance to win. But if you go down, you take this whole ship with you. Yes, you hold a press conference alongside Mary, and you deny, deny, deny. That part ought to be very, very easy, seeing how it's the truth!"

Brock was not surprised how the conversation went. In fact, it was just as easy as he figured it would be. John, who was usually pretty easy to play, was doing exactly what Brock had figured, as he had learned he could get things done through masterful manipulation. It was simply a matter of finding out the area of greatest weakness in a person, which Brock was able to do in very subtle ways. He worked very closely with each of his staff aides, meeting with them in informal settings. He was able to ask them what they felt their strengths were—what they added to the team. Then he would ask them, oh so compassionately, what areas they felt they needed most to work on, and how he could help them. He had done that, of course, with John, and knew John felt he needed to work on his own humility, recognizing that his was not always the most important voice to be heard. Brock knew he could use that recognition now to force the very action John was now taking.

Of course, he truly felt the same way John was stating; anyone else was expendable, but not him. He was the candidate. He was the campaign. And, he thought to himself, he was the hope for any real change in this country, and anyone could tell change was needed. As much as he loved John, and felt he was needed in this campaign and all future ones—well, better him than Brock. And they certainly couldn't let Newman's camp get away with the slanderous comments, even if he claimed they came from within Brock's campaign. The man would pay. But let John be the collection agent and, if necessary, the payment, too.

Mary hated this with a passion. She had known all along that Brock's campaign would lead to a release of the press hounds, and that they would not be satiated until they had sunk their teeth into a juicy story—the juicier the better. Since Brock's announcement she had figured the story would be her and her abortion. But for someone to slander Brock—and by inference, John—went too far. The accusations were so far off base that they would have been hilarious, if they weren't so potentially damaging. She was worried about what this would do to the campaign, but more worried about what it would do to her and Brock.

Watching him now, fuming, she knew he would be very distant until this issue was settled. That was just how he was. It was one of the reasons she didn't know if she could take this life; she knew the issues, whether personal or political, were only going to get worse. Which meant the distance would only get wider. But she also realized that now, especially now, was certainly not the time to leave him! It would be absolutely devastating to his chances, considering the accusations leveled in the press. So, as much as she hated this, she would have to stand by him at the press conference, smiling, loving...faking. For now she didn't think she actually loved him anymore.

She wasn't sure when it had happened. Certainly not how. She had so loved Brock, and had loved being in love with him. She had always looked forward to being with him, spending any time at all. There were times she had given up going somewhere with other friends just so she could have a cup of coffee with him for five minutes in between appointments. He was more important than anything or anyone else.

Or had been, until something happened. She had felt a distance growing between them, but blamed it on the campaigning. After all, he was gone so much, it would only be natural they would grow apart somewhat. But she had to be truthful—it wasn't Brock's fault, nor the campaign. And how could she blame James? It wasn't his fault she had wandered into the study that night, and had heard—and seen—things that, without realizing it, she had been searching for all of her life. The more she studied, and the more she understood what she needed to do—to believe—the further away she felt from Brock.

Sadly, he didn't seem to care. That hurt, but it also made what she knew she had to do that much easier...until Brock had called this morning and told her she *had* to be with him at the press conference. She had expected something like this after reading the newspaper story, but expectation did not mean anticipation. There was nothing to anticipate about any of this. If there was any way to do so without absolutely pulling the plug on Brock's hopes, she would run out of this place right now. Instead, to her somewhat surprised frustration, she would stand by her man, smiling, but definitely faking.

Brock stood confident and poised before the press gathered in the hotel ballroom. He waited patiently at the podium as a few last-minute attendees strapped their microphones or micro-recorders to the various appendages already filled with the network-identifying microphones. Though it was noisy—even a bit raucous—due to the anticipation of what Brock was about to say, there was still a modicum of decorum, almost like a crowd might be at a public execution. That, in fact, was exactly what most of those gathered thought they were about to witness. Odds were running highest that Brock was simply going to withdraw from the race. Such news didn't make the majority of them happy, as they had come to appreciate the humorous, unflappable demeanor of the candidate, not to mention what they considered the freshest thing to hit politics in many years. It was a shame, most agreed, that he would no longer be around. Others argued, albeit quietly, that he wasn't about to run from this, but that the effect would be the same; there was absolutely no way he was going to win the election now, so, they all agreed, he probably would be better off to simply quit.

All sides quieted down as Brock stepped forward, grabbed both sides of the podium, and scanned the assembled crowd. Behind him, just off his right side, stood his fiancé and his campaign manager, and a few other staff personnel. All of them stood in stark contrast to the candidate himself. They looked like they were attending a funeral, while Brock stood with that sly but determined grin of his, arms folded, nodding to a few of the press he knew better than others, and simply waited for everyone to get quiet. Finally, he held up both hands to bring the crowd to complete quiet, cleared his throat, and began.

"Ladies and gentlemen, I have a brief announcement, after which I will not be taking any questions. I believe you all know two of the people standing on the platform with me today, but let me introduce them. The big guy standing here sweating, hoping I won't say the wrong thing, yet looking, might I say, very, very manly, is my campaign manager, John Turner. John has been my best friend since we met in prep school, and has stood with me through some difficult times in my life. I love the big guy, and am not ashamed to say so."

Then, with a sly smile, he added, "But I assure you, he has never, will never, and cannot ever compete with the other person standing here: my fiancée, Mary Roller. My fiancée, folks, because I love her, this woman, in a far different way than I love him, that man, my friend. One, I will marry. The other, I will golf with. Got it? You better get it, because that's the last you'll hear me say about it. The only other thing I have to say is this: I am going to beat Lawrence Newman, no matter what kind of dirty politics he plays."

To the instant clamor of the assembled press trying to outshout each other with their questions, Brock walked over to Mary, kissed her deeply, hugged John, and arm-in-arm the three of them walked out of the room.

Forty-six

Whatever advantage Newman might have hoped for quickly disappeared immediately after the press conference. Brock's brief statement, and the passionate kiss that lasted nearly as long, was the lead story on every Chicago channel, and even some of the national networks. With that kiss, Brock went from being the underdog candidate of a congressional race to being spoken of for a presidential bid in the near future. His poll numbers shot past Newman's in hours, and stayed there. People loved him, and loved his flair for the dramatic. He quickly rebounded as the comeback kid, and his numbers went from the low thirties to the high forties in nearly every poll.

But Collier knew polls could be deceiving. And he knew, as much as he wanted Brock to someday be a presidential candidate, such things were a long way off. Right now he needed to focus on this campaign, and beating Newman. There was still time for people to change their minds, or to simply not vote. A low turnout was usually bad for the challenger, so they needed to continue to work at getting all those people who spoke highly of Brock actually out to vote. "The kiss" was certainly a great picture, and it caused a lot of fervor, but it, alone, wouldn't win the election.

Brock had a plan, but he needed to continue the pursuit of legal action against Newman, and John was dropping those plans. He said there was no sense in pursuing the legal battle since they had taken such a large lead, and needed to spend their time, effort, and, of course, money on the last days of the campaign. Brock knew it wouldn't do any good to argue with his friend, so he had come to Collier for advice.

"I know you can get him to stay at this, Brock. He does anything you ask him, so simply ask him. And if that doesn't work, then tell him. He can't ignore an order, so give him one. Your campaign *needs* to keep

201

the pressure on Newman's, while at the same time you keep moving forward. Yes, pursuing a lawsuit will cost you money, but it will cost him more. Besides, you need to keep him in a negative light as much as possible. Let the voters see the difference in the two of you, and keep pounding on your theme that you represent change. Action, not words. This is not the time to let up."

"I couldn't agree more. That's my plan. But how do I get John to continue to sue? I could turn it over to someone else, but he's my best bet to actually go after Newman. He's relentless once he gets the smell of a kill, but he just doesn't have the killer instinct on this one. I have asked, and I have ordered. He said no to the request, and he outright laughed when I gave him the order. We don't work that way—never have—and he knows it. I can usually persuade John to do about anything; it's simply a matter of knowing what he really wants to do anyway and just encouraging him to do it. But this time? I don't know why, but he just doesn't want to."

Collier wasn't upset that Turner wouldn't be the bulldog on this. He didn't like the kid and knew the kid didn't like him. Collier hadn't had any say-so on the campaign unless it was directly with Brock, who would then tell John what needed to be done; and he knew he would be shut out of the legal route as well if Turner was in charge. He had an idea but didn't think there was any way in the world that Brock would go for it. He knew a man who could tackle this case, and be every bit as relentless as the Turner kid; he had seen him in action many, many times. Collier was going to put Michael Auzman on the lawsuit.

There was a reason that John had lost the will to fight. He did want to see Newman defeated, but he wasn't so sure that he wanted to see Brock elected. This wasn't the first time he had felt this way; not even the first time since returning from his leave of absence. He was normally rock solid in his convictions, not only knowing what should be done but willing to do whatever it took to do it. But when it came to Brock being elected, he found himself driving hard for it one minute, losing all interest the next. He could not continue working this way. He knew that he needed some answers, specifically about his very purpose, and had come to this very strange place to find them.

He was sitting in a storage unit on a cardboard box full of books, having just removed a dusty, black-leather bound Bible from it. He truly had no idea where to even begin searching for those answers he needed, but he was amazed at how many notes his dad had written in the margins of nearly every page. Then, on a whim, he turned to the book that had his name, the gospel of John. There, above the title, was a note, written in his father's strong handwriting, addressed to him, and dated on the day of his birth.

Dear John, my son.

Though your mother and I specifically had John the Baptist in mind when we gave you your name, this gospel bears that same name, which means "beloved." You are loved, my son. We have waited so long for your arrival, and now that you are here, we cannot wait to see what God has in store for you. May you find answers for your life in the pages of this book, and may you know His love for you as well as ours.

With tears welling in his eyes, John began reading. He read the story of a leader who sought Jesus by night, with the Teacher telling him he had to be born again. John had heard those words, but now, reading them, they finally made sense. Then he read the story of a woman who had been married several times and was a social outcast, meeting Jesus at a well. One phrase especially jumped out at John, when Jesus told her that her people worshiped something that they knew nothing about. John read the note written by his dad in the margin:

Oh, my Lord and my God! This is what I have done and have led so many others to do for all these years! Forgive me, Lord, and help me tell The Truth in the years I have left.

John continued reading, both the text and the handwritten notes

203

of his father. He read of the bread of life, and how receiving Jesus was the only way to life—life eternal, and life abundant. His dad's notes leapt out at him as though he were sitting next to him, urging him to grasp the truth of these words and know the true Jesus. It was very easy to tell the notes written prior to his genuine conversion and experience, and those written since. There was an obvious tone of reality and joy in the more recent notes. His notes reflected a genuine faith, as opposed to an academic pursuit. It was easy for John to recognize the difference in the two, as he realized that he did not have what his father, and mother, had found. He didn't even have the academic pursuit! And he certainly had not found the joy, the peace, or the purpose that literally jumped off the pages at him as he read.

As the sun was setting and it was getting dark inside the small, dusty storage area, John realized he had not stopped reading for nearly two hours. He had been crying and realized it was because he'd been reading of the crucifixion of Jesus Christ. Of course he had heard the story, but he now realized how little he knew about it. Though he had heard the phrase "washing your hands of" something, he had never known that it came from Pilate's efforts to wash away all blame for Jesus' death.

He continued to read and came to the verses that told of the actual death of Jesus, as well as the two thieves on either side of him. The Roman soldiers broke their legs, but when they came to Jesus, they found that he was already dead. So they didn't break his legs, but stuck a spear through his side, causing blood and water to gush out. In the margin, next to that verse, his father had written:

The beginning and foundation of the Haemaliaen Brothers faith.

Then, below that, in a shakier hand, obviously written after finding genuine faith, John's father had written:

A false faith—built on the wrong belief that it was the blood on the cloak, rather than the willing sacrifice of the Savior, that provides for our salvation.

John remembered his father telling him those exact same words so many years ago on that hot day on the mission field, when he told him of finding a real faith. John had refused to listen then. How he longed for his father's presence now, sitting next to him in this darkening storage room, explaining these words to him once again. He read through the verses, and the accompanying notes, over and over. And, finally, it hit him. When Jesus said, "It is finished," he was saying that salvation was paid for. Yes, his blood had to be shed, which it was. But there was nothing that needed to be added to that. Not a cloak, not a stone, not a cup, or a basin of water. Not even a drop of blood. The blood had covered the sin, but salvation came by faith that what Jesus did by shedding his blood finished the requirement of salvation.

John closed the book. Looking out the garage door of the storage unit, he saw that the sun was now completely down. The sky had turned a beautiful deep azure blue with one last streak of red, the entrails of a high jet plane streaking somewhere—a certain destination that had been preplanned and was now being realized. He realized that was an apt description of his life. He saw the hand of God in so many things, leading him to this moment. Turning back to the unit, now mostly dark except for what could only be described as a holy glow, he knelt down by the box he had been sitting on, and prayed.

Forty-seven

Michael had not sat in Collier's office for many years, but realized immediately almost nothing had changed. It seemed that the same stack of file folders were stacked in the same places they had been the last time he had been there. The office was clean, and could even be called neat, but not tidy. Hundreds of books filled the numerous book shelves that lined three of the four walls, with books stacked on top of books on many of the shelves. Though there were no open shelves, there were a few gaps on some shelves filled with a variety of knick-knacks—things that had been collected by Collier himself or given to him by various followers and supporters. The fourth wall was mostly window, but below the window was a large, low credenza, the top of which was covered with even more piles of file folders as well as more knick-knacks, and a few pictures. The desk was huge, and it, too, had very little open space. The stacks were neat and orderly, and Auzman was sure that Collier knew exactly what was in each stack, though he probably had not touched half the stacks in several weeks.

Everyone knew that the old man had a mind like a steel trap, but because he read and studied so many various issues and topics, he was always starting new methods to attempt better organization, none of which worked. His best method was his oldest method: just keep the active folders out in the open and rifle through the various stacks occasionally, reshuffling the piles until the next time. Each time he did that, he learned more, reorganized more, and threw out more. But the information just kept piling higher.

Collier was looking out his window when Michael tapped on the door and let himself in. Collier rarely closed his door these days. He didn't have the usual receptionist or scheduler out in the front office anymore, mainly because he didn't have the energy to see many visitors anymore. His sickness, though somehow still in check, was obviously draining him slowly of life, so there weren't as many visitors allowed. Brock had once sat in that outer office, ushering in the wide-eyed pilgrims who came to see their leader for encouragement, hope, or a simple word of advice. Gone, now, were the days of up to ten hours of meeting with followers, touching the sick, praying for their needs, accepting their checks. Oh, the check writers were still seen, at least the big checks, but the biggest givers were seen outside the office in better settings than these. Michael knew Collier saw no more than two people a day now, and those were very short meetings. His, however, would be a bit longer.

"Come in, Michael. And close the door behind you. I doubt anyone is going to come up here at this time of night, but I can't take any chances. We've got something to talk about that can't be overheard."

"I gathered that from the phone call, Duncan. Is this about Brock, or about Marie? They both seem to be on your call lists, even if I haven't heard from you for years." Michael knew that Brock, of course, sought Collier's advice for the campaign. But he also knew that Marie had both called and visited him lately, and though he wasn't sure why, he didn't like where his thoughts had taken him. Apparently, neither did Collier.

"Shut up, Michael. You know full well why I've been talking to Brock, and will continue to do so. And the only reason I've talked with Marie is because she called me, needing some advice, after she ran from Brock's press conference. So get over yourself, again. This isn't about you, Michael. It's about Brock and his campaign. I need you to do something that will help him, and I know you want to do that. So here's what I need you to do."

"Wait a minute, Collier. You only *think* I want to help Brock. I argued for this whole project, and I wanted to be an integral part of it by raising the kid, shaping him, developing him into what we knew he could be. I've done my part, and though he might not think it or ever admit it, I did a pretty good job of it. I did all I was supposed to do in the project, including keeping it completely secret, especially from him. Now that he is what he is, and will soon find that out for himself, he's on his own. If he's going to go somewhere, it has to be because he is who he is, not because we continue to manipulate circumstances for him, or even because he thinks that who he is deserves some sort of special treatment. So I won't be put on some new phase of this thing with you thinking that I'm going to simply jump and ask how high later like before. I'm done."

"No, Michael, you are not. You'll be done when I'm done with you. Now close the door, and sit down."

It had been forty years. Michael had only been fourteen years old when his parents were killed in an accident, leaving him an orphan. His mother's sister, an aunt that lived on the west coast, was given custody. She had driven across the country to get him, but he was not at all what she had expected. She had hoped for a nice young man who would become her own son. What she found was a sullen, moody, and geeky pimple-faced kid. He couldn't stop crying, which would seem normal given the circumstances of his parents' death, but she had no idea what to do about it, or him. She wasn't very loving, and possessed no natural maternal instincts, and was coming to the conclusion that she had made a very bad mistake coming here to get him.

Having been a follower and supporter of Dr. Duncan Collier and The Brothers for years, and knowing that she was not that far from the International Headquarters, she called for advice, and help. She was counseled to bring the boy to the office, where someone could give her help. What she couldn't possibly know was that there was an office-wide awareness of the Collier's desire to have children, so there was always a look out for adoption opportunities, regardless of how remote the possibility might be.

When she arrived with the tall but gangly boy, most everyone knew that, indeed, the possibility was very, very remote. Mrs. Collier wanted a baby, and he was a far cry from that. One of the staff counselors took the aunt into a side office on the executive suite level, leaving young Michael to sit in the reception area. And that was where he was spotted by Duncan Collier, on his way to his own office. In what appeared to be a moment of rare genuine compassion, Collier sat by the boy and struck up a conversation. He had placed his arm around him, offered him his own handkerchief to wipe the tears and even blow his nose, and even wept with him. He eventually took him into his own office, leaving instructions for the aunt to be brought there when she was finished with the counselor. By the time she entered, Michael asked her to allow him to stay in Chicago, living at the International Headquarters, and serving under the tutelage of Dr. Collier himself. Though somewhat surprised if not shocked at the request, the aunt was more than happy to do her part for the cause of The Brothers, releasing herself from the undesirable responsibility of raising Michael. And Collier had a young man that he could have as a pupil, and, perhaps, more.

Michael sat down. He had never had the resolve to stand up to Collier, and still didn't. He had no idea what Collier wanted, but it really didn't matter. It never had. It never would. Forty years later, and Collier still controlled him, and, like always, he would do the bidding of his mentor. Since that first meeting, when Collier had told him what he needed to tell his aunt, he had done exactly what the older man asked. He had honed his debating and presenting skills under the man, learning how to win just about any argument. But he could never argue against Collier. It simply wasn't allowed.

Collier, as usual, moved quickly from anger to his smooth, almost hypnotic, voice. He was smiling—almost exuberant, as though he had a secret he couldn't wait to tell. Leaning forward, placing his forearms on his desk and making a tent with his hands, pointing them toward Michael, he waited to start until Michael sat down.

"Michael, I want you to sharpen your legal skills. We're taking Newman to court for slander, and you're going to do it. You need to get all the information you can from John Turner, and file the necessary papers. Turner's wimped out on us, but we need to proceed with this. This is where you shine—so go shine."

Whatever resolve Michael might have pretended to work up as he drove to the International Headquarters and parked his car completely disappeared with Collier's challenge. Bad enough that he was even asking, but asking with such ebullience only made what Michael had to say that much more difficult. In fact, downright impossible. He knew he was about to burst Collier's balloon, but the result would be more like a land mine, with the shrapnel heading completely in his direction.

Ready to bleed, Michael took a deep breath, blew it out, and faced what he knew would be the end of any future relationship with this man. He had admired him, hated him, feared him, and loved him. He would now do the one thing that he had always recoiled from doing the most, because it always had resulted in the most pain—emotional and physical. He was about to disappoint him. Disappointment, from Collier's viewpoint, meant disobedience. And disobedience usually resulted in banishment. It had been mostly his choice to have not seen Collier for the past few years. It would not be so now, not after this.

"I'm not so sure I'm the man you want to do this, Duncan. I've had a recent meeting with Newman, and I don't think I have the leverage against him that this case is going to require. I respectfully decline."

Collier's eyes burned through the balding, gangly lawyer. He had tried so hard to give the kid some backbone, but it just wasn't there. How dare he try to act like he had one now. He needed Newman destroyed, and he knew that Auzman could do it. He was a wimp in every other arena, though he covered it well with his false bravado, but when he was given the opportunity to present facts in order to destroy an opponent, there was none better. With the exception of the argument over the Messiah Project, he had never been a dynamic presenter. But his clear presentation of facts put opponents away hands down. Now, however, he was bored by the man.

Feeling absolutely exhausted by Michael's continued spinelessness, he held his head in his hands, elbows on the desk. Sighing deeply, he finally looked once again into the dark, hooded eyes of this man whom he had grown so tired of so often, so early.

"Okay, Michael. I'll bite. Exactly why do you think you've lost leverage with Newman—whatever that means?"

Taking another deep breath, Michael told about his meeting with Newman just a few weeks prior. He told how he had been forced to do something drastic to keep his former nemesis from pursuing the truth about Brock. Stammering, stuttering, and sweating profusely—his usual demeanor in front of Collier—Michael knew there was no sense in stalling. Collier was going to blow his top anyway, so he might as well get it over with. He finally let him know that he was the one who had started Newman on the path of slander that Collier now wanted to sue him over, planting the thought that had become a full-blown scandal in Newman's all-too-ready mind.

"I thought I was doing the best thing, Duncan. He was putting two-and-two together and was getting way too close to blowing this whole thing up, long before we're ready. He wants to win this election badly, and he will do *anything* to win. We know that he knows the importance of this project, if not the actual details of it. But I honestly think his drive to win is greater than his willingness to see this thing through to the end. I had to divert him, Duncan; I had to. And what I did worked!"

"Temporarily, Michael. Only temporarily. Since Brock's press conference and the slam Newman took on that, you know he has to be even more determined to do something. I had hoped to stall him with this lawsuit, and use you to do so. That's obviously out, so now I've got to come up with something else. Thanks to you, Michael."

Michael was back to whining. "I thought I was helping. Honestly. You know I've worked hard on this whole thing, from the beginning. I certainly wouldn't purposefully do something to ruin it now. You've got to believe me, Duncan. I thought I was helping."

Collier honestly didn't know whether to kill Michael now, or wait until after the election. But he would kill him. That was now a given. All that remained was the method, and the timing, and he would have to think about both of those later. Right now, he had to think about Newman.

Forty-eight

"I don't know what to think of it, Brock. It isn't anything I planned, but I have to say, I'm sure glad it happened. I've been playing around with beliefs of any kind for too many years, and I needed to find answers. And there they were. Yeah, the notes from my dad helped, but only because they gave me guidance to the proper passages that I needed to go to."

"I'm still not buying it, Clops. You are simply not the religious type—just like me. People like us? We don't need that crutch, man. You were going through a tough time, needed a bit of slapping around, and found the slap you needed from your dad's notes. End of story. I'm sure it all felt pretty good; why wouldn't it? You reconnected even if it was only from some writing of his. That's natural, John. Why do you think so many people try to communicate with their dead loved ones? Some people need that touch. Well, you got yours. No big deal. And I think you'd be making a big mistake if you tried to make it a bigger deal than that."

"Brock, you don't get it. I'm not talking about finding religion. I'm talking about finding a genuine relationship that is unlike anything you or I have ever known in our lives. And that relationship isn't about what you can or can't do, but what you either have or...don't have. You're absolutely right—I'm not the religious type, because, like you, I see too much of religion as a sham. You know I've never had a problem pointing that very fact out to Collier, and most of his cronies. But this isn't religion, dude. Religion is nothing but a bunch of rules and regulations, telling you what you can do, or can't do, and when you can or can't do it. Nothing but a bunch of negatives mixed with a lot of sour people telling you no."

"Are you telling me this is any different? Are you saying that Bible you walked in here with doesn't have a bunch of rules—not to mention a ton of negatives? C'mon, John; I've read enough of that thing to know you're wrong."

"Rules? Yeah, there are rules, and I guess a lot of them come across as negatives. But is that always so bad? For instance, isn't it a good thing that there are rules against things like killing, or stealing? Don't you think God might have our best interest in mind with many of those so-called rules? Don't they protect us as much as restrict us?"

"Don't give me that. I'm talking about all the fun-killing rules, and you know it."

"Yeah, and I also know that a lot of what we call fun has a lot of high price tags to it. I'll never forget that story my dad told me about changing the price tags. And I'm afraid that a lot of what I've always called fun—cheap fun—has a lot of high-priced consequences. I guess I'm tired of paying that price for the few fleeting moments of pleasure that many of those things claim to bring. And I'm worried that you are paying too high of a price for what you're looking for as well."

Brock sat across the booth from John, staring at him whimsically. He had seen others go through this same *conversion,* but they were the weak ones. John wasn't like them.

He looked beyond John to the several other patrons gathered in the restaurant at this hour. Many of them were much more the type to seek after religion, or some sort of meaning. Brock could see right through them. In a matter of moments he had sized up the couple in the corner booth. It was obvious that they didn't know each other all that well. Apparently they were on a first date, both trying to impress the other with their charms, each hoping that tonight might lead to something else—though it didn't take much to see that the something else was entirely different for the two of them. She was obviously hoping beyond hope that this could lead to some sort of long-term relationship, and he was just hoping for a good time—and was willing to drop a few compliments, laugh at and tell a few jokes, even pay for the meal and whatever else might be necessary, all to accomplish his goal.

Next to their booth were two men sitting on opposite sides of a table, both with work piled up on the empty spaces between them. They, too, were working out some sort of deal, and Brock could easily tell which one of them had lost the upper hand on the negotiation. He was a bit more urgent in finding a file and opening it for the other man to read, but he also had a way of leaning forward and mouthing the words written on the pages as the man read, hoping the other man would be convinced by those words. Having lit at least three cigarettes during their conversation, he put each one out long before it was smoked so that he could focus on presenting his next argument. The waiter had re-filled his water glass at least four times in the past few minutes, only to have it drained as soon as he walked away. The older man simply sat and listened, taking each new file and reading the presented paper calmly, but apparently not too thoroughly, before handing it back to his younger colleague. Brock couldn't hear their hushed conversation, and didn't need to. He could tell that the younger man, too, would be willing to sell his soul to strike the deal he was after.

Four other tables were occupied by single diners: two women, two men. All four stole occasional glances at the others, but it was obvious that they were all too shy to take any steps toward any kind of conversation that could lead to some new experience or relationship. They might have come in here looking for more than a simple meal, but it was apparent that each would either return to their home, apartment, or motel still empty, or would take their search to another spot. There would be no filling of what they might have sought as their true hunger—not here, not tonight.

It all led Brock back to John's assessment of cheap thrills with expensive price tags. How much had he himself paid in manifold efforts at finding something that would fulfill. His drug of choice, his high, was prestige. His constant search, his longing to be somebody, came from the obvious frustration of feeling like a nobody. It seemed that no matter what position he had held up to now, or what possessions he had gained, or even what people he had used, he still felt empty. He was quite certain, however, that it wasn't an emptiness that any religion was going to fill. He knew what it would take, and he was on the verge of reaching the first step toward it. As much as he valued his friendship with John, there was no way the big guy could divert him from his pursuit of national office at this point. Taking a deep breath and exhaling, he leaned forward on his elbows and folded his hands together as though he, himself, were praying. He looked straight into the caramel eyes of his friend to show him his sincerity as well as his intensity.

"John, I'm glad you've found something that makes you feel better about yourself, about life. I agree with you that a lot of things in this life cost a lot more than just money. But I've got to believe some of them are worth it. And what you are preaching to me would require me to give up some of those things that I do believe are worth pursuing. Contrary to what you believe, I am not simply pursuing an office so that my name will be in some headline or on some office door. I have a purpose—a calling! I intend to change things, John. I intend to make things better. Things I haven't seen religion do much of anything about, like peace, and poverty."

"Give me a break. You have no idea what actions people are taking about those things, so you, like so many other people, throw them around like weapons. But have you done anything about world peace? Have you done anything about poverty? And do you know, or have *any* idea, what *is* being done about these things by people of faith? Do you have a clue about what efforts churches or Christians are taking to change things?"

"Oh, I don't know, I suppose they are *praying.* Right?" Raising his hand over his hand and shaking it in imitation of an Elmer Gantry type evangelist, he continued, "They're hittin' the knees, man. Oh, and probably passing the collection plates, using all those poor people's hard-earned money to do all sorts of good things around the country, right? Of course, that's *after* they collect their take off the top. Can they help it if their needs end up taking most of it? It's expensive running all those fancy ministries and paying all those family members to sit around and do nothing. Except pray, of course!"

"Brock, you're disgusting. I thought you might be willing to hear me out on this, and give me a few minutes to tell you what's happened in my life. I wasn't expecting you to jump up and shout hallelujah, and certainly not to fall on your own knees and repent. But I figured you, of all people, would at least listen. And I figured you to be the kind of guy who wouldn't prejudge something without any facts. You talk big about changing things, Brock, but you're afraid of looking at yourself and seeing if you, yourself, might need to change."

"Things need changing, John, and you know it. And you know that I can do something about those things while your religious friends just keep sitting in their fancy buildings praying about them. Those prayers haven't done much, my friend. But I will."

Forty-nine

"Politics makes strange bedfellows." Though the phrase has been used often during most campaign seasons, it is, in reality, a misquote—or at least a paraphrase. Probably first used by Charles Dudley Warner, editor of the Hartford Connecticut Courant in 1850, it is an adaptation of the line from Act II, scene 2 of Shakespeare's *The Tempest*, which says, "Misery acquaints a man with strange bedfellows." In the play, it is spoken by a man who has been shipwrecked and finds himself seeking shelter beside a sleeping monster. Mostly it is used to represent the obvious reality that political interests can bring together people who otherwise might have very little in common.

The phrase certainly fit the scene taking place in the vestibule of St. Rita's Church and the two people now facing each other. Marie had not seen Lawrence Newman in many years, and had called him now only because Duncan Collier was using her, again. She was willing this time because he had convinced her it would help Brock's election chances. She had also convinced herself that Newman might know too much, and use it against her and her son.

The vestibule was empty at this hour, including the priest, who had drifted off before Newman had arrived, accepting Marie's wave and smiling explanation that she was meeting someone who wanted to talk to her in private. The vestibule had a sterile feel: white brick, white marble floor, white ceiling, and even white doors leading into the sanctuary, as though there was hope of purity simply by entering. The exterior wall was all glass, floor to ceiling, even though there wasn't much of a view. There was a fountain in the middle of the patio and sidewalk that led out to the parking lot beyond, but there was very little to inspire the soul. Not that Marie was lacking inspiration at this point. She was on a mission.

217

"You need to back off, Lawrence, and fight fair, or this is going to come back to haunt you. You know that Duncan will do whatever it takes to stop you, and you know he will get his way."

"C'mon, Marie. We're not teenagers anymore. Collier is just an old man with delusions of grandeur. His little band of followers may think he's capable of ruling the world, but you can't honestly think he still exerts the power he claims. You don't, do you?"

Marie knew Lawrence could see right through her. She didn't believe that Collier could control such things as an election, but she knew for sure that he did control her, and always had. That control had led her to do things that now defined her life as a wife and a mother, and now a behind-the-scenes advocate of Collier's wishes. As much as his control, however, was her fear of seeing her son hurt, should Newman continue to pursue digging up dirt on Brock in order to win the election.

"You can't use what you know, Lawrence. Or what you think you know. You will ruin innocent lives, and it won't help you anyway."

"Innocent, Marie? Who's innocent in this matter? Collier? Michael? I'm sorry, Marie, but not even you can claim innocence. You knew what you were doing, and you were willing to do it, regardless of whether it was right or wrong."

"It wasn't wrong, Lawrence. It wasn't immoral, or even blasphemous, or any of the other arguments you used before The Council. It was a desire to move our faith into popular acceptance in the culture, and the culture toward a new way of thinking, of believing. It was an effort to bring people hope. Real hope, Lawrence. Far beyond the empty promises of politics, or even religion."

"Interesting you should talk about the empty hope of religion, Marie. Or that you should be the one to determine if your actions were immoral or blasphemous. You've learned well from your mentor. Collier has never had a problem using religion when he wants to gain from it, and making his own rules. Considering our present surroundings, you, apparently, don't either."

"Duncan Collier is a great man, and what he is doing is a great thing. You can't stand in the way of it, Lawrence, at least not forever. You might win this election, but there will come a time that Brock will win, and when he does, the world will be a better place. In reality, Brock does not need this office nearly as much as this office, this country, needs him. But if you try to stop what is inevitable by revealing something you don't even know for sure, you could ruin all of that. So I'm here to stop you."

Newman wasn't all that surprised by Marie's bravado. He knew that she loved Collier and, of course, her own son. Both of her sons. He also knew Collier had brainwashed the woman since she began working at The Brothers' International Headquarters so long ago. There was no telling what she truly knew, or what she believed, especially when it came to Collier or, for that matter, her son Brock. Collier could have convinced her of anything.

"Marie, I'm not sure what you're talking about, or what you think I'm about to do. I admire Brock, and think he could someday be a great congressman, serving his district honorably. But he's not ready. I've been saying it, and I will continue to do so. Beyond that, I think I've learned I'd better simply tell the voters who I am, not who I think Brock is. I listened to someone else in a private conversation try to get me to attack your son, and it backfired. I won't make that mistake again, letting someone tell me what to do."

"I'm not *telling* you anything. But I am asking you to stay away from spreading rumors about my son. You were part of the presentation that led to some crucial experiments, but you left before knowing if they worked or not. You seem to be making some assumptions about what might have been the outcome, however, and I'm asking you to please stop before you ruin Duncan's reputation, not to mention my son's."

"Now we're getting to the real reason you're here, Marie. It isn't about this election, or what's best for the country. You're defending Collier again, like always. The man is an egomaniac who wants what he wants and doesn't care what it takes to get it. I argued that fact thirty years ago, and I'll continue to fight him. He may have you believing he has done some great thing, but I'll never believe it. He played God, Marie, and he's still trying to do so with people's lives. He did it to you, with Jason as the result. He did it to Michael. And now he wants to do it to the whole country through his man-made puppet."

Marie slapped him. She wasn't sure whether it was because of what he was saying about Duncan Collier, Jason, or what he had just called Brock. Probably all, as she loved each with all her heart. Newman simply stood where he was, staring her down, his cheek showing the clear imprint of her hand.

"Listen to me, Marie. You need to be honest with yourself. You were used, and you are allowing yourself as well as your son to continue being used. Collier is an evil man, no matter what pretense he gives publicly. At the heart of all those charitable things he puts forth, and all those outward acts of benevolence he performs, there's nothing but selfishness. *Performs* is actually the right word. The man deserves an Oscar for all the performances he puts on for his followers. Sadly, I'm afraid that someday he's going to drop the curtain and, too late, people are going to realize their mistake for giving their lives to him. And you know what, Marie? That especially includes you, Michael, and your son Brock. You've all sold your soul for a mess of pottage, my dear. But do you want to know my greatest fear? It's that Brock has swallowed the whole thing so completely that he has, in fact, become the second coming of Duncan Collier: underhanded, cutthroat, and just plain evil, with a nice sugar coating on top to make it all seem so good."

This time Marie didn't slap him. She didn't have the opportunity. Newman had already grabbed his coat and was out of the church before she could even respond to his soliloquy. She sat on the bench at the end of the empty vestibule and, with every emotion at full boil, broke down crying. She had never felt so empty in all of her life. As she wiped her eyes, she looked at the only splash of color in the vestibule, a painting of the crucifixion. She took a closer look. The blood flowing from the spear wound in the side of Jesus brought her to a sudden clarity. She involuntarily let out a small but audible gasp, causing the priest to come running from somewhere in the back of the foyer. Apologizing, she let him know that she still didn't need to talk to him.

She needed to talk to Duncan Collier.

Fifty

Marie didn't wait for the receptionist to buzz Collier. She stormed into his office and walked straight to his desk. Even to her it felt a bit like a scene out of some movie, but she didn't care. She was furious, and determined.

"I want to know the truth, Duncan. As much as I have given to you, I think I at least deserve that much from you."

Collier was quite surprised at Marie's boldness. In all the years he'd known her, he had never seen such emotion and passion. True, she had come close when he had first approached her with the Messiah Project, when she realized that it was her opportunity to have another chance at motherhood. She had been depressed from the time he and his wife had come to Kansas and had taken Jason to be their son, but that depression lifted a few months later when he told her that she could carry another child. He didn't give her all the details and she didn't care to ask at that first meeting, as she was simply thrilled to *be* a mother. Details came later, and with them tears. Marie was upset that she would be mother to some *science experiment,* as she put it, but it didn't take long to convince her, once she was assured everything was as normal as any regular birth, except for how she would conceive. And she would then raise the baby as her own. She had been emotional and passionate then, though with an entirely different emotion.

"Sit down, Marie. I'll be glad to discuss whatever it is you barged in here over, but not with you standing there like a rabid dog about to attack."

"I'll sit when I'm ready to sit, Duncan. You may call me a rabid dog, but I won't be told when to sit, beg, or fetch by you anymore. I'm tired of taking orders from you, and tired of the results of doing so. I don't know my sons, and neither of them know who they are. And

221

now, before Brock goes off to Washington and I lose him all together, I want to know the truth, and then I want him to hear it from me."

"The truth about what, dear? Truth about your willingness to sell yourself? Isn't that what you've done, Marie? Twice, no less? Two sons, both out of your willingness to do just about anything to be a mother. Now sit down, and settle down. I don't appreciate being talked down to."

Stunned, Marie sat. She was somewhat surprised at herself, but even more shocked that this man who had always shown nothing but love and care toward her, had basically called her a prostitute. She started crying again as Collier came from behind his desk to sit in the chair next to her and handed her his handkerchief.

"I'm sorry, Marie, but you took me by surprise when you came barging in like that. Obviously something has shaken you up, and you need to talk. Now what is it that has caused you to be this way? What 'truth' do you want to know?"

Marie was ashamed of herself. She had come in to his office with determination and resolve not to fall prey to Collier's hypnotic power, yet here she sat, once again bawling her eyes out in his handkerchief. It took her a few minutes to get her tears under control, but she was finally able to talk.

"I need to know who Brock is. I need to know, Duncan, if he is who I think he is—who you've allowed me to think he is all these years. And he needs to know too. He has lived his life with so many unanswered questions, and I haven't been able to tell him what he needs to know. I've kept quiet and been the good little girl you wanted me to be, but no more. I will find out, and you know it. So you can save us both a lot of trouble by telling me the truth now."

What on earth, thought Collier, had caused this? Had someone involved in the project leaked information? Or had someone spoken directly with Marie? She had never been like this before, and he wasn't sure what to say.

"Marie, he is your son. You carried him and gave birth. He's about to become a congressman, giving you a lot to be proud of. Be proud.

And be content with that."

"He may be my son, but who is his father? Or does he have one? I know what you were trying to do, Duncan. I know you were trying to get blood from the cloak and do something with it. What were you doing, Duncan? What were you trying to do? Were you trying to clone Jesus? And did you succeed? Is my son Jesus?"

There it was: the question that had been avoided for over thirty years. Duncan took a deep breath before answering, knowing that Marie would take whatever he said straight to Brock. He had hoped to continue to avoid this discussion for at least a few more years, until Brock had more influence, more power, knowing that he didn't need the extra pressure of his unique background being an issue. *The* issue. Suddenly he felt very tired, and very old. He took her hand and looked into the eyes that had haunted him so many lonely nights. In spite of her anxiety and the difficulties of her unhappy marriage, they were still the most beautiful eyes he'd known.

"Marie, Marie, Marie. You are right. I wanted to do exactly what you just said—to clone Jesus. We have the blood, and the technology is constantly developing. Michael was the one who came up with the idea."

"Michael? My Michael?" Marie was stunned. She had never looked upon Michael as anything but a diminutive, soft-spoken lawyer, and a weak husband—not to mention an even weaker father.

"Michael had studied what was, at the time, the very new science of genetic engineering. He argued that we could do a blood wash on the cloak and extract the DNA of Jesus Christ from it, which could then be implanted into an egg. The egg would be stripped of its own DNA, allowing the DNA of Jesus to be injected. The new DNA would cause the egg to react as though it had been fertilized, and a baby would be conceived. Your egg, Marie. Your baby."

"Did it work? That's what I want to know, Duncan. Is Brock—how can I even ask this? Is Brock actually Jesus?"

He wasn't. The experiment had failed. But only Duncan knew. Scientists had tried but could never extract usable DNA. But no one knew that, at least not now. Only two of the actual team had ever known it. And only the doctor who had performed the procedure that did lead to Marie's pregnancy knew that it was not an embryo from the project. All three of them were dead. As a result, Duncan had been able to keep the truth of the failure to himself. He had also been able to allow the falsehood, the lie that Brock *was* a clone of Jesus, to go unchecked. He had played along with the assumptions made by those who knew of the Messiah Project, allowing The Council members to think whatever they wanted to, simply by not denying whatever they assumed.

He had also allowed Michael to jump to those same conclusions, even to the point of his desire to marry whomever would carry the embryo to term, deliver, and ultimately raise the Messiah as her own. It had always made Collier sick to his stomach to think that Michael would therefore be married to his Marie, but he knew there was no way he could have her. Why not let her have someone he knew she would be sick of in due time, never truly loving? She had only acquiesced to the arranged marriage when she understood "no Michael, no baby." Collier had explained the importance of a father figure, and that Michael Auzman would provide her son not only a stable environment, but a highly intelligent one as well. In addition to the young man's natural intelligence, Michael had been, after all, Collier's very personal disciple.

"My sweet Marie. You gave birth to a brilliant child, and have raised him to be a scholar, a leader, and a tremendously capable young man. He will bring life, joy, and healing to many, including this nation. He owes you so very much. And the world also owes you for giving him to us. You sacrificed much, Marie. Now you should be given much honor. Brock will win this election, and others after this, all the way to the top. He has what it takes. And you, Marie, will be honored and highly esteemed."

"Very flattering, Duncan. Just like always. You say so much, while not saying anything at all. You still have not answered my question. Is Brock Jesus?"

"But I did answer your question. I just told you things that the angel told the Virgin Mary about her son, and herself. Those things that were said of Jesus can now be said of your son. Can I say it any more clearly, while purposefully not saying too much? I cannot tell you more at this time, and you must understand."

Marie did understand. Only hours before she had felt devastated and hopeless. Now her whole demeanor changed. She felt her life truly had been one of purpose. Smiling, she released Collier's hand and stood up, as did he. She gave him a hug, and even a kiss on his cheek. He wanted more, attempting to hold her a bit tighter even as she was pulling away.

Without another word, she left his office, believing exactly what he had wanted her to believe about Brock.

It was merely a matter of letting her assume what she wanted to believe, Collier thought. He had discovered years before that he could make people do just about anything, once you found their need and met it. It pleased him to see that his young disciple had that same ability. It helped to make "the lie" all that more believable.

Collier went to his window, hoping to see her walk to her car. As usual, his heart was broken and empty as he felt the same amazing loss he always felt when she left him. But this time, he had to sit down. He felt flushed. The pain was actually physical. Suddenly he realized he was having a heart attack—an extremely forceful one. Turning from the window, he reached for the phone, but it was too late. Clutching his chest, he collapsed to the floor, grabbing the phone cord as he fell. The phone was too far away, but several papers and, mercifully, a pen fell within his reach. It took all he had, but with his last bit of strength he scrawled three simple words: "Brock not Jesus."

With his death, the truth about Brock would live.

Fifty-one

Though he would never know it, Collier was absolutely correct about Marie. She did exactly as he thought she would. She headed straight to Brock with her assumed belief about who he was.

In her haste to leave the parking lot she paid no attention to what should have been a very familiar car parked just down the street.

Michael watched in anger, not even caring if Marie saw him watching her. She didn't, which only served to further his anger. He had followed her from St. Rita's to the International Headquarters, knowing all along it was where she was heading as soon as she had left the church. He had no idea why she had met Newman, nor why she had followed up that meeting with Collier. What he did know was that, whatever her reason, he was, once again, left out of her life, her problems, and her sought-for solutions. That fact pushed him to do now what he should have done years ago: to confront Duncan Collier. Though he couldn't figure out why, he knew Marie had always been more attracted to Collier, but he was going to put a stop to it, no matter what it took.

Fishing through his glove box, he found his old key card, got out of the car, and walked as quickly as he could to a side door of the International Headquarters, marked *Staff Only*. He had spent so much of his life in this building, presenting various cases and studying their impact, but it had been several years since he had last entered. Would his key card still be valid? He had his plan in mind, and he certainly didn't want to have to stand and wait for a security guard to grill him or, worse yet, call up to Collier's office and alert him. He wanted the element of surprise.

The card worked. As he opened the door he had to laugh that the cheapness of the old man had probably led to keeping the same system from years before. Michael himself had convinced the board back then that the system would bring needed security during the critical experiments, and all he had to do to get it past Collier was to tell him it would make The Brothers cutting-edge. Collier had always been an easy mark for the newest and best—"bright and shiny" was how most of the staff referred to it. At the same time, Collier hated spending money, so would have convinced himself that his now antiquated system was still the best, like a classic car that never loses value.

Michael chose the stairs over the elevator, remembering that the tone would ring in the office suite, announcing the arrival of the elevator. For some reason, he felt the element of surprise was more important than the ease of the elevator ride. The extra time to think of what he was going to say couldn't hurt either.

As Michael expected, the only light on in the entire executive suite was Collier's. What he didn't expect was the mess of papers on the floor in front of and beside the desk. As he entered the office, the reason was clear. Collier had obviously pulled them down as he fell, and even now lay on the floor in the midst of those papers. Though Collier's back was to him, it was obvious the man was dead. Michael didn't know how he knew that, but he could tell. Perhaps it was from the way he had obviously fallen, or simply from the fact that even if he had one breath left, Collier would have never allowed a mess like this in his office.

Not knowing what else he might find, Michael cautiously entered the office. His first thought, which nearly caused him to turn and run, was that Marie had killed him. Looking closer, he saw no evidence of blood, and he knew Marie would never have used a gun or a knife. No, Collier must have had a heart attack.

Stepping closer to the body Michael saw the pen, held in Collier's stiffened hand like a two-year-old would clutch a crayon. He realized that Collier had attempted to write a message, even as he gave in to his death. Kneeling next to the outstretched hand, he saw the three scribbled words. He could barely make out the writing. Parts of words were barely there, while other parts the pen had scratched through the paper, tearing the words into the paper. The first word, Brock's name, was easy, and it led Michael to extract the page from under Collier's bony hand, revealing the last two words: not Jesus. As the full reality of the statement hit Michael, he was shocked. He, along with everyone else involved in the Messiah Project, had been told by Collier that the project had been a complete success. He had given his life to raising the young man that he believed was Jesus Christ; or at least, the clone of the Savior. There was no way this news could get out to anyone else, or Michael's life—and all that he had worked for—was a waste.

Michael stood over the lifeless body of the man who had controlled him, as well as the project that had shaped him for so many years, and made his decision. Collier could no longer control him, and he would not allow him to control what he now knew was the truth about Brock. Wadding the scrawled note into a tiny ball, he stuck it in his pocket and walked out the door, not bothering to call anyone to inform them of the dead man in his office. Let someone else find him in the morning. They would realize instantly what Michael had seen himself—that Collier had died of natural causes.

Michael had things to do.

Marie knew that this wasn't going to be easy. How does one inform their son that he is the Messiah?

Fifty-two

The Council was the unofficial name of the group of men who had rubber-stamped Duncan Collier's decisions and directions for the past few decades. The official name was The Council of Twenty-four, though there had not been twenty-four men on the council since the first general session. Six men had attempted to stand up to Collier and found their authority wasn't as strong as they had been led to believe. For any number of reasons most of their positions were never refilled. In fact, over the years, the number varied from as high as twenty to as low as nine. There was little explanation given by Collier over how many were needed, or who was chosen, or why. It was his call, and he had always made that fact very clear without having to say a word.

But now he was gone and the seventeen men currently on The Council were responsible for some major decisions, not the least of which were the funeral arrangements. Collier had left specific instructions regarding the details of where he should be buried, what songs should be sung at the funeral, and even who should speak. The sealed envelope with the carefully planned instructions had been delivered to the acting chairman, Jefferson Strong, by the corporate lawyer within hours of Collier's death. Strong had opened the envelope in the company of The Council and had read the instructions to them.

Most surprising was the fact that Michael Auzman was selected to give the eulogy. Few of the men currently on the council had been in their position when Auzman and Lawrence Newman had presented arguments regarding the Messiah Project so knew little of his presentation skills, but those who did remember knew that he was anything but eloquent. Factual, yes. Even passionate when he had presented the Messiah Project. But not eloquent. They were also surprised when Auzman, upon being told of Collier's instructions, asked for a special meeting to discuss those arrangements. He told them he had a very special request, and they were willing to hear him out. Thus, all seventeen men were present in the specially called meeting just two days before the funeral was to be held.

"I'm honored that Dr. Collier would ever have considered me for the privilege of giving his eulogy, but I'm quite confident he must have written those instructions many, many years ago. We were close at one time, as some of you know. At that time I'm sure he considered me an adequate speaker and knew that I would have remembered to mention all of his accomplishments. I could still do so, but there are many, many others who are far more capable of presenting facts and anecdotes in a far more interesting way. In fact, I know just the one who should take my place."

It was Norm Baker, one of the newest members of The Council, who challenged Michael first. "Though I admire your humility in offering to have someone else take this tremendous honor, I have to state that to do so, to reject the specific instructions of Dr. Collier himself, would be tantamount to blasphemy. He asked for you, sir, and I, for one, must insist that you honor his request."

"Get over it, Baker," Ken Stallings said. "Collier's dead, so no need in continuing to suck up to him. His ghost isn't going to be all that flattered, and I highly doubt that wherever he is now he cares one whit about who gives his eulogy, as long as whatever is said is as filled with as much hot air as you're blowing right now."

Though the rest of The Council might have felt somewhat the same as Ken Stallings, even before Collier's death, none would have been bold as he had just been. Stallings, however, wasn't through.

"As for you, Auzman, I have no idea why Collier chose you to even show up at his funeral, after the way you deserted him. But he did. I could care less if you follow his instructions, or even if you 'blaspheme'"—Stallings gave a contemptuous look at Norm Baker—"but I do care that whoever speaks does not embarrass The Brothers any further. We need a voice that is worthy of being quoted on national TV. The man might not have been liked by many, but his death has made national news, and so will his funeral. So, Auzman, I'm interested in knowing just whom you have in mind, if not you."

"Mr. Stallings, I couldn't agree more. This is news, and the networks will be there. So I say we take absolute and full advantage of this opportunity to finally present what we have worked and prepared for the past three decades. Gentlemen, I propose to you that we use the funeral of Duncan Collier as the world stage upon which we introduce the culmination of The Messiah Project. I want to introduce to the world the Messiah Himself, Jesus Christ—my son, Brock Auzman."

There was an audible collective gasp from the members of The Council. Most were absolutely shocked that Auzman had ever been the one who had been chosen to raise the boy in the first place. For him to refer to Brock as *his* son truly did border on the blasphemy that Norm Baker had referred to. They had suspected all along that Auzman's involvement had been much more remote and distant way than what the man was now implying. Little did they know.

The rest were stunned by Michael's proposal. Having been told by Collier himself that the Messiah Project needed to be kept absolutely secret, as recently as days before his death, they had a hard time believing that Auzman was proposing the exact opposite. Some who had been around for the past thirty years had nearly overthrown Collier over his reticence to move forward. The project had driven everything, and the high price tag had nearly bankrupted The Brothers. These men had put up with much public humiliation, and they were ready for some return on their investment, not to mention revenge on the unbelievers. The newer members of The Council knew few details of the Messiah Project, but they, too, longed to see their faith vindicated, recognized, perhaps even accepted.

Stallings was the first to react. "I don't know what you take us for, Auzman, but we are not fools. You'd better have some powerful reasons why you think now is the time, when Collier himself preferred to wait."

"Duncan—Dr. Collier—had *his* reasons. He was concerned that Brock wasn't ready, for good cause. Brock still has some rough edges, to be sure. He sometimes speaks without a full knowledge of what he's talking about, yet he speaks with such eloquence and conviction that people give him latitude. His opponents won't, though, so he must learn to curb his tongue. Dr. Collier knew that, and wanted to work with

Brock. As you know, I may not have the eloquence of our beloved leader, but I do have the ability to work with Brock on facts. I intend to take on much more of an active role in this campaign, and that includes promoting the reality of just who Brock Auzman is."

"I think it's too early." It was Norm Baker again. He was still smarting from the putdown by Stallings a few moments earlier, but was not about to let that stop him from speaking out. He had admired Duncan Collier and would not stand for this group or any other demeaning the man, or his wishes. "Not only because Dr. Collier thought it too early, but for several other reasons. You certainly hit one reason, Michael. Brock has made many comments that are simply out of line, and he has to learn much more than simply curbing his tongue. He might not get too many second chances, so we can't afford to have him blow this. But of even more concern to me is the simple fact of his age. It isn't just that he is too young—which I believe he is. It is the pure, simple fact, gentlemen, that he is not thirty years old."

"Oh, come on, Norm. You've got to be kidding me. I get it—he's Jesus Christ. Are you also expecting him to die on a cross three years later?"

"Once again, Mr. Stallings, you border on blasphemy!" Norm Baker retorted. "Listen to me, all of you. I don't know how the rest of you feel about this whole project, especially those of you who were around when this whole thing was presented so many years ago. But I do know this. Had I been on The Council at that time, there is absolutely no way I would have stood for this—this sham. We have no idea what we have done. We have no idea what we actually have in this young man. Do we have Jesus?"

Several of the men were shaking their heads yes to the question.

"Do we?" Baker pressed. "Do we know, for certain, that the young man being pushed on us right now is actually, in reality, the Son of God? Come on, gentlemen. We will be far more than some little recognized and largely ignored 'cult' if we go through with this. We will be the laughingstock of the nation. Of the world! Our names, and the name of our very faith, will be plastered across every tabloid, right next to the alien babies and UFO sightings. We'll never have the chance of being taken seriously again."

"We're not taken seriously now!" cried Michael. "This will give us the credibility and the recognition that we have fought so hard for. This *is* what we have fought so hard for. And if we don't do this *now*, everything that our leader, Duncan Collier, lived for will be wasted. Lost on a generation of skeptics and slanderers. Now is our time, gentlemen, and we must not let it go."

They all sat in silence, until Stallings, again, turned to Michael.

"Mr. Baker brings up a valid question, Michael. What is our proof? How do we know that Brock is actually Jesus? Collier kept all the information and research very secret—close to his vest. No one has seen all of the information all together. We have only been shown various components of the experimentation. Collier always said we needed to keep faith, and that seeing everything all together would lead us to place our faith in the wrong thing—in the science of the whole experiment. So I ask you again, sir: what proof do you have that Brock is truly Jesus?"

"Oh, how similar you all sound to the Pharisees and Sadducees!" Michael said. "Did Jesus Himself have *proof?* No, he pointed them to the crowds, to those who followed because He had the words of life."

"What's your point, Auzman? What are you getting at?" asked Baker.

"Have you listened to Brock speak, gentlemen? Have you seen the crowds that gather whenever he does speak? Have you watched the faces of those disenfranchised by politics as usual? Have you looked into their eyes as they recognize something different about Brock, about his words, about his very actions? The young and the old alike are willing to follow him anywhere. They are willing to open their checkbooks and their calendars to give and to do anything to get him elected. They would follow him to hell!"

Once more, Baker broke the contemplative silence. "That's what I'm afraid of, Mr. Auzman. That he just might be leading them there."

Fifty-three

Brock had heard enough. Tipped off about the meeting, he had snuck in the back chamber where Duncan Collier used to wait as he prepared for his inevitable grand entrance into the council presentation room. Brock had sat with him several times during his internship, waiting to be sent on the various errands that Collier always seemed to need done before he would enter. At first Brock had relished every opportunity to wait on the great man, but it hadn't taken long to realize that most of the errands had no other purpose than to show that he could boss people around. Brock had never been bold enough to disobey but had learned that he could take a bit longer than what was expected, leaving Collier no choice but to head into the presentation room before Brock returned with whatever meaningless thing he had been sent for.

At any rate, Brock had been sitting in the anteroom, listening to the proceedings taking place. At first he had been amused, listening to the pontificating of the various men who acted so authoritative now that Collier's domineering presence was palpably absent. These same men had cowered in silent fear for years, but now ranted and raved as though they actually had some authority.

Amusement turned to anger, however, as he heard what they were saying about who he was, or at least who he could be. Why had this been kept from him? Why had so many—including his own parents, as well as Collier—lied to him for so long?

And what did it all mean? Was he, in form if not fact, the second coming of Jesus Christ? Did that mean that his influence over people— the influence that he had always assumed was as much from a gregarious personality as anything—was far more? In fact, was anything he had ever done truly him, or the fact that he was a clone of Jesus?

One thing he did know for sure: there was no way he was going to let The Council reveal this. Not now, for sure. Maybe not ever. If it was ever revealed, it would be in his time, in his way. He needed to stop the fiasco.

As he was about to barge through the anteroom door and shout for them to stop, a sudden thought hit him. He had to stop and laugh at the thought—a statement he'd heard John make a few times during some critical discussions over policy and campaign direction. He had scoffed at his big friend, though mostly to himself. Their relationship had become quite strained and he hadn't wanted to make things worse by laughing at what John obviously did not consider humorous.

The thought was certainly humorous now, though. He had actually stopped himself with the question, "What would Jesus do?"

Humor quickly changed to renewed anger, however. How dare that thought hit him now, or ever? He *was not Jesus!* He was Brock Auzman. He himself might not always know exactly who he was—who the "real" Brock Auzman was. But he knew he was not some ancient prophet, or king, or whatever Jesus had been.

He reached for the doorknob again, but was stopped with another thought that rushed into his mind like a bolt. He realized he knew practically nothing about Jesus. He knew that the man had supposedly lived two thousand years ago, professed to be the son of God, and was killed for it. But why? Why was he killed for being delusional? And why were there still people who followed him two thousand years later if he was nothing but a lunatic? Brock realized he knew nothing of the man's teachings, yet he had rejected him anyway. Why? Was he afraid of knowing the truth? Was he so set in his own ways, his own beliefs—whatever they were—that he unwittingly refused to know if he just might have been wrong all these years? Had he allowed his own plans and pursuits to so rule his life, there was simply no time left over to give thought that a higher power might have some say in those plans?

Then, as quickly as those thoughts hit him, he dismissed them. No, he thought to himself, he didn't need or want to know much more than he already knew about Jesus or the man's teachings. With the exception of John, every person he had ever known who had professed to be a follower of Jesus had not been anyone he wanted to associate with. If they weren't fruitcakes, they were hypocrites—at least in his opinion.

Why know their leader if they were like him? He had to admit that he had made these judgments without really knowing them, but he felt strongly that what he did know was enough. In fact, he was convinced of it.

But again, what if he were Jesus? Or the clone of the man? Shouldn't he, at the very least, familiarize himself with some basic facts?

Backing away from the council chambers door, he made a mental list. The first thing was to leave The Council alone. From what he had heard, he realized that the one person he most needed to stop was Michael. And he knew just how to do that.

First, though, he wanted to talk to John.

Fifty-four

They had known each other for nearly half their lives, and try as he might, Brock could not think of one single time that he had needed John. It had always been the other way around, from that first time when Brock had defended John in front of the disciplinary meeting at Batterson, all the way to now. That wasn't to say that he didn't think of the big lug as his best friend—in fact, the most important person in his life. He had benefited from John's gentle giant demeanor in many situations, and had always been thankful that John took whatever he threw at him and just came back for more. But *need* him? No—at least not that he could think of.

But he needed him now. He needed answers, he needed support, and he needed...what? Faith? He didn't think so, but right now he wasn't sure what to think. To say the props had been kicked out from under him would be a huge understatement. But was it faith in God that was lacking, or just a renewed faith in himself, his own abilities, and his own self-confidence? Those had served him well before. Surely he only needed the encouragement of his best friend, his best supporter, to restore what had been shaken.

Unfortunately, John was not alone when he finally tracked him down. When he hadn't been at his apartment or at work, Brock knew the next logical place was the coffee shop. He had hoped to find John sitting at his usual table in the back of the dark room. Instead, John was right up front, sitting at the window seat, with two other men. He recognized one of them as the man who had talked with Mary, then John, about religion matters—the last thing Brock had wanted to talk about when they pointed the man out to him a few weeks earlier. Now he and another guy sat with John, probably still talking religion, since that seemed to be about all John wanted to talk about anymore.

To make matters worse, John had seen Brock walking up to the coffee shop door, so there was no escaping and hoping for a better time to talk. John was already up and waving him over to their table.

"Brock! What are you doing slumming in this place?"

"Hey, John. I've been looking for you, hoping you might have a few minutes to talk. But you're busy. I can catch you later…"

"No way, man. You're here, we're just about finished, and we haven't really talked to each other in days. Why don't you go order a coffee while we finish up?"

The two young men had sat silently during the interchange, but the older of the two finally interrupted. "Uh, John, don't you think you ought to introduce us to your friend?"

"Oh man, where are my manners? Like I ever had any! Brock Auzman, I'd like you to meet a couple of guys who have really had an impact on me lately: James Larkin, whom you might have heard Mary talking about, and Rob Carpenter. Guys, this is the guy I've been telling you about—my boss, my best friend, and your future congressman!"

James was already standing as he extended his hand to shake Brock's. "Besides all that John has said about you, Brock, I've heard so much. Mostly good!"

One of the things that Brock had found he hated the most about campaigning was having to respond to empty chatter—and empty chatterboxes like this guy. But he put on his best face and shook the extended hand. "If you heard it from John, I hope you considered the source. He has trouble putting too many words together at one time, so you might not have gotten too much from him, good or bad."

They all had a good laugh before James hit Brock with a completely unexpected challenge. "Brock, I obviously have no idea why you came searching for John, but part of what John has said about you is that you are struggling with some things, especially since your mentor's death. My guess is that you have a lot of questions, but haven't really found answers—or even someone who can give you some answers. Am I right?"

"Thanks, James. But no thanks. I just want to catch John up on some of what's happening with the campaign, as well as…"

"Brock, dude. Sit down and talk to this guy. He can help you. Swallow that pride of yours for a few minutes and get some help—help that I can't possibly give you and you know it."

Brock wasn't sure he wanted to discuss his questions with James—a total stranger. But he did want some answers, and he didn't really know if John would have what he was looking for. What could it hurt? He pulled up a chair.

"All right, James—you're right. I do have some questions. But they have nothing to do with Collier. I'm actually more interested in knowing more about what *you* believe. More specifically, what you believe about Jesus. Who was He? Why did people follow Him with such reckless abandon? And what did He teach that made them do so?"

Brock almost laughed out loud when he saw the response of the three around the table, especially that of John, whose mouth was literally hanging open. He had obviously hoped that the conversation would eventually lead to an opportunity to tell Brock more about his faith, but for Brock to be the catalyst for the conversation was too good to be true.

James, too, was momentarily speechless, but recovered quickly. "Whoa, Brock—that's a pretty broad subject. I'd be happy to try to answer, but might I ask what specifically you want to know? Or, perhaps, why you're asking?"

"Let's just say I'm curious. I'm curious about the man himself. I know he was a teacher, but how did he get started? Did he just walk out one day and start talking? And, if so, why would people listen? And, yes, I would like to know what he taught. Why would people follow him? Why him, as opposed to any other teacher of his time, or even today? Why him, and not, say, someone like me?"

"The last one is easy, Brock. Why not you? Because you're not the Son of God!"

I'm not so sure, James, thought Brock. *There might be more to me than you know. And maybe you won't be so sure of yourself after that.*

Brock's thoughts were interrupted by the younger man at the table, Rob Carpenter. The young man had been observing him quite closely, though he hadn't said anything until now. Brock was none too happy with what he did say.

"I read a story recently, Mr. Auzman. It was a story of a man who had survived the Holocaust and lived long enough to see one of those who had tortured him, a deputy of Hitler himself, brought to trial. He was sitting at the witness stand when the prisoner was brought into the courtroom, and he broke down in uncontrollable weeping. Most thought he was weeping because seeing the man brought back too many painful memories. He would share later that he wept for an entirely different reason. 'I wept because I realized he was not a monster—he was just an ordinary man. And I realized that I could be just as evil as he.' You are capable of evil, Mr. Auzman. So am I. The only one who never sinned was Jesus. Only He could pay the price for sin, so he did. Yours. Mine. Everyone's. And that is what you need to know."

Brock was momentarily silence. *You see, Clops,* he thought, *I recognize* that *in me. Which makes me question all the more: can I ever be what Jesus was?*

Fifty-five

Brock wasn't sure why he hated Michael. He knew it wasn't just because the man had pretended to be his dad all those years—he had only found out that fact a few years ago. His hatred had developed long before. In fact, he couldn't remember a time when he'd ever looked up to him, or even liked him. Even when he was young, before the man had sent him off to Batterson, the seeds of hatred had been sown. Brock figured he had been sent to The Academy because Michael saw those seeds and simply wanted him out of the picture. Certainly the hatred had come to fruition during those long, lonely years.

It was funny, he mused, how easy it had been to allow that hatred to simply degenerate into apathy. There had been a time when he couldn't stand to be in the man's presence. There had been times when he felt like fighting him. He hated to think about it, but he had even entertained thoughts of wishing Michael was dead. Recently, however, he found that he simply didn't care. He had come to the realization that the true opposite of love was not hate; it was what he felt—or rather, didn't feel—now. He didn't care if Michael did or did not show up at a campaign rally. He didn't care if he spoke to the press, gave interviews, or stood naked screaming obscenities in front of any one of the numerous billboards sporting Brock's handsome face. Though such action would certainly cause a stir in many, Brock, though amused at the thought, found that even that would not matter. He did not care.

Until now. Now he felt something, and he was shocked to recognize it was the old, familiar hatred that had driven him years ago. For most of his adult years he had been able to simply ignore Michael, even when Michael had forced his way into the campaign, volunteering himself to be the Chicago-area campaign manager. The position was mostly titular. Brock had made sure it stayed that way by keeping any major decisions out of Michael's scope, especially his speaking schedule.

In the beginning of the campaign Michael had scheduled him to speak at a Senior Center. He knew he needed to meet with all people, but he had been completely unprepared for the questions they had asked after his speech. He felt that Michael should have done a better job of letting him know what they would be asking, or have planted the questions. He had blown up at Michael afterward, shouting that he never again wanted to speak to people who probably wouldn't even be alive by election day. Someone had overheard him, and it had hit the news that night. As a result, he had been forced to spend far more time than he would have ever wanted in other senior centers to prove that he was not ignoring the retiree voters. The other result was to take the speaking schedule away from Michael.

But now Michael could no longer be ignored. Before he had the chance to stop him, Michael had overstepped the ban on scheduling in a big way. He had done more than schedule some inconsequential speaking engagement—he had agreed to a televised mini-debate with Newman! Though it would only be thirty minutes, Brock knew it was a set up by Michael, and he vowed to get even. Considering what Brock had overheard taking place in The Council Chambers, he feared that Michael might have agreed to the appearance in an attempt to go public with the information he had. He certainly wasn't afraid of Newman. As talented a speaker as the man was, he didn't have the charisma that Brock had in front of a camera. But he was afraid of what Michael had planned, or what he might have told Newman.

There was no time to find out. The cameras were rolling, the moderator was introducing both candidates, and he would be on in seconds. Brock realized it wasn't the heat of the lights that was making him sweat. Sitting across from his opponent in the small studio he could hardly breathe. What did Newman know? What had Michael told him, or one of his handlers? And what would he say if Newman, who wasn't past trying anything to win this election, actually tried to challenge his birth, or his background? Brock himself had no idea what to think of it all. How would voters react? How would anyone? He would forever be known as the freak that he had so often felt himself to be. He had never known why he felt that way—why he felt so empty. But they would!

Then it hit him. He knew how to avoid the inevitable attack. He knew how to take the questioning and the challenges off of him. Just before the moderator asked him the first question of the night, he cleared his throat and, with the fear suppressed, flashed his most charismatic smile and asked if he might ask a question first. Though somewhat taken back, the moderator agreed.

"Thank you, Mr. Walters. I know this is highly unusual, but this has been an unusual campaign. I simply wanted to ask my opponent a question before we officially begin."

Turning to Newman, who was clearly confused by the tack the moment had taken, Brock leaned forward on his elbows and clasped his hands together, giving the appearance that what he had to ask was painful, yet imploring his opponent to be truthful. "Mr. Newman, I know that you have a long history of campaigning for scientific progress and I applaud you for that." He went so far as to lean back and give a very methodical clap of his hands a time or two. Newman looked even more confused. He started to answer, but Brock continued before he could be interrupted. "However, Congressman Newman, is it not true that as a younger man you were deeply involved in a most unscientific experiment of attempting to clone human embryos? Is it not true that you spent several years as part of an organization that made every effort to clone not just a human embryo, but to clone none other than Jesus Christ?"

It worked. What happened next was even more than Brock could have hoped for. Newman turned beet red, stood up from his chair and, with obvious rage in his voice, attempted to speak. No words came out. Instead, clutching his chest, he collapsed. The moderator, along with nearly everyone else in the studio, sat stunned, but Brock moved quickly. As someone called 911, Brock loosened Newman's tie, peeled back his suit jacket, and began CPR. The studio fell silent, with the only sound being Brock counting as he pumped the older man's chest. In their shocked state no one thought to go to commercial or turn off any cameras. As a result, on live television, Brock Auzman brought his opponent back to life. It was a miracle.

Epilogue

Newman never fully recovered. What was thought to have been a heart attack turned out to be a massive stroke, and ten days later, three days after the election, he died. Brock was the master of civility in apologizing profusely for being any part of the man's death, and promised to do all he could to provide for his family. Newman's involvement in the failed human cloning experiments that had taken place in a cultish laboratory years before was denied, and soon forgotten, not even mentioned in the numerous news reports covering his state funeral.

Brock was elected in a landslide, and most pundits stated that he would have been even if the events of the previous week had not taken place. He was simply too much a force to be reckoned with. He was, they all agreed, destined for something far greater. No one doubted that he would someday run for, and probably win, the White House. There was just something about him. No one could quite put their finger on it, so they simply compared him to so many great leaders before him. Whatever "it" was, he had it. Everyone agreed, he would go far—and take many with him.

Mary knew it too. She watched as he was sworn in. She listened to the accolades and forecasts of greatness, and knew they were all correct in their assessment that the man she had loved was destined for something far beyond what anyone could imagine. What she didn't know was why she felt so afraid of what that might be. She felt a small shiver as she turned off the television.

John stood proudly by with Mr. and Mrs. Auzman as Brock was sworn in. He, too, felt something was out of place and, like Mary, couldn't clearly identify what was wrong. He certainly had not liked what Brock had done at the televised debate with Newman, calling his friend out on the obvious cheap trick. But he knew he had to forgive him, and felt he was needed now more than ever by his friend. Wherever he was going, he was going to need a voice of conscience to keep him on the right track. John was committed to be just that.

Brock finished the swearing-in ceremony, strode confidently toward them, and accepted his hug and his mother's kiss. But when Michael extended his hand to offer congratulations, Brock drew back his clenched fist and punched Michael sharply in the nose, sending him to the marble floor. Even more shocking, he reached down and, grasping the man's hand, helped him back up as though nothing had happened, then walked out.

John ran after him, catching up to him in the parking lot. He had no idea what to say—though he felt he knew why Brock had done it. Looking at the man he had called friend, whom he now called congressman, and whom he felt he would one day call Mr. President, he said the only thing that came to his mind.

"You've got blood on you."

About the Author

With a name like *Read*, it only seemed natural that RONN READ would love books. From early on Ronn liked to read stories of various athletes, especially baseball players—largely because of his love for sports. That love would reciprocate by giving Ronn the opportunity to get his education through baseball scholarships, including the chance to go to seminary while serving as the assistant baseball coach at Liberty University. It was there that Ronn discovered a different kind of book, and a different purpose for not only reading them, but writing as well. He has written several unpublished devotional books, as well as a guide for counseling those who have experienced the pain of losing a parent, whether through death or divorce.

Blood Reflection is Ronn's first attempt at writing a novel. His natural ability to tell a good story comes through in this intriguing account of a young man who can't quite seem to grasp his self-identity, and who struggles with making right decisions as a result. Much of Ronn's own similar struggles show in both of the main characters, including how one comes to know Jesus Christ in a very personal way.

Ronn and his wife, Janie, have raised five children and now have ten grandchildren. They live in the NW Suburbs of Chicago, where Ronn is Senior Pastor of Alpine Chapel.

You may email Ronn at docread45@hotmail.com.

For more information:
emptyreflection.com
www.oaktara.com

Breinigsville, PA USA
24 November 2009
228101BV00001B/30/P